BLOODLINES
INSURRECTION

LIFE DEATH BLOOD

Cedric R Curry

ISBN: 061598309X
ISBN 13: 9780615983097

ABOUT CEDRIC CURRY

Bloodlines Insurrection is Cedric Curry's first book. The book is set in southern California, early summer 20th century. Cedric is a college student currently reaching for his bachelor's degree in Science in Psychology, and is in his second year. Before that, he worked various odd jobs after retiring from the United States Navy having dedicated 20 years of service. He has three daughters who are doing exceptionally well in their own lives, and three grandchildren. He now resides in LaVerne California with his surviving sister, and is at work on the second book of the Bloodline series.

CHAPTER ONE

Ann Ct, Santa Maria California, 5 p.m. Inside a small suburban home, the alarm clock comes to life, and the relentless beeping noise drowns out the sound of heavy breathing. Exhausted, Eric buries his face against Robin's neck and reaches over blindly to turn off the annoying alarm.

"Jesus! I'm as healthy as a horse, and in my prime. I would think my stamina at least a match in our bedroom," Eric argues, rolling on to his back with a satisfied grin on his face. Robin giggles as she snuggles up next to him, pressing her head against his shoulder.

"Are you complaining?" she asks, lifting her head to study his expression while she waits for an answer.

"Not at all," he answers. "I would like to believe that our sex life is adding youth to this aging body of mine."

"Well rest assured that I am completely satisfied with your performance, Mr. Taylor, and as for stamina? I'm not exactly your ordinary everyday girl – you know that." She reclaims her earlier position; her head pressed against his shoulder, satisfied that she had a man who placed so much emphasis on pleasing her.

"True. I'm every bit a spring rooster at twenty-six as far as years go. You, however, give new meaning to the term cougar."

"That wasn't nice." She laughs in protest, elbowing him gently in the side. In return he wiggles his fingers in the area beneath her arm pit where he knows she's most ticklish, and she squirms for a second or two before breaking free.

Feeling pretty good about what he has come to accept concerning, his less-than-ordinary life Eric reached for Robin and pulled her to him. They began kissing one another, as passionately as they had the day they first kissed.

"Do you love this much older woman of yours?" she asks.

"With my whole heart," he answered, placing his right hand over his chest.

"Good because I love you too much, my younger man. I have to get ready for work now."

As Robin rolled over to climb out of the bed, he reached for her, but the only thing he managed to grab hold of was a hand full of molecules. "I hate it when you do that," he groans. Robin laughed, and then disappeared into the bathroom where she began running the water for her shower.

"I still have to get used to the idea of you working. We both know that it's not necessary." He raised his voice over the noise of the running water, and then reminded himself that Robin possessed a heightened sense of hearing and could probably hear him whisper if she set her ears to it. She doesn't respond, but he is almost certain that she has heard his every word. He lies there, staring up at the ceiling. Minutes go by before Robin exits the bathroom, wearing a towel tied above her breasts.

"I keep telling you. One of the reasons I left my covenant, was so that I could live again as close to normal as possible." Robin walked into the closet, and then exited with a white sundress in hand. *Pity I can never wear it for what it was intended for,* she thought. The sun remained her greatest danger to date. Robin allowed the towel to drop to her feet, and then leaned her head to one side. But my greatest reason without argument was to be with you." She smiled at Eric.

Exhausted as he was, the mere sight of her standing in the middle of the room with nothing on, held his eyes captive. He rolled out of bed and meandered over to where Robin stood.

"You have to forgive me, he asked. It's just that you're immortal. I'm fighting for shared time with you because I'm not."

"I get that babe, I really do. It's not fair to either of us – I know that. Still you have to understand that life will only give us but so much. We have to grab what we can if we are to be happy at all."

He felt guilty for having brought it up, so he stretched his arms out towards her as a form of truce. She accepted, and leaned into him, placing her head against his chest.

"I promise I won't bring it up again," he told her, though he knew such a promise would be hard to keep. He spun her around slightly and then taped her on the butt. "Finish getting ready for work. I'll make your breakfast," he said.

"Thank you, you're a sweetheart, another reason why I love you the way I do." That was good enough for him. He turned around and exited the bedroom heading towards the kitchen in the buff. *Never mind putting clothes on, only grownups within these walls. He understood why she defended those liberties so strongly. Having lived in the shadows for so long, it was brave of her to even attempt to live the life that she longed for. It goes without saying. Robin possesses the sheer desire to live like a normal human being. Her sisters on the other hand, as she describes them, have long since shed the shackles of their former lives, accepting what fate has chosen for them, and so they live within the parameters of their existence.*

Eric entered the kitchen, and then opened the refrigerator to remove a pint of blood.

"Ah....breakfast for champions, minus the human race." She had it pretty easy, was the thought that always came to mind whenever he prepared her meals. *One stop shop, that's what it is, no variety here, and yet variety is probably what's killing over seventy-five percent of the human race today, that, and a million other things.* Still, it was hard to imagine a life without the occasional cheeseburger.

He opened the door to the microwave and placed the blood inside. *Not much to it, about forty seconds and we're as close to room temperature as we're going to get. Robin will down it as though it were a glass of ice cold tea on a hot summer day.* He set the timer and pushed start. While he waited he thought about the relationship that he and Robin shared. He would never have thought in a million years, that such a thing could be possible. Forget the fact that vampires are real and not myth, that alone is enough to boggle the human mind, but he had gone one step further by taken one as a lover, as easily as if the details were the same as that of a human boyfriend, and girlfriend relationship. *That's as real as real can be. Robin is a credit to the female race vampire or not, with her exotic nature, and a beauty that goes beyond all understanding.* Those were just some of the reasons he loved her so much. Their lovemaking, he reasoned, fell somewhere close to the realm of dream and imagination. Taking him to heights he could have never thought possible, at least not in his previous reality.

What could be said of his acceptance of it all was? He had not been overly afraid of her after finding out that she was something other than human. From the moment that he had laid eyes on her, to be a part of her life was of such importance. He had discovered a gentleness in her that pushed away the fears that should have been a part of reason. Nevertheless their life together was normal except for the dangers that were but a stone's throw away. The greatest of course being the rays of the sun.

He removed the packaged blood from the microwave, and then grabbed a pair of scissors from a nearby drawer. He cut a slit large enough near the top, and then poured its contents into a tall glass. Raising the glass to eye level, he studied the red substance before setting it down near the counter's edge. Okay, the thought of missing out on something as minute as a bag of potato chips, let alone a cheeseburger jolted him back to reality. Having prepared her meal for the evening, he scampered back towards the bedroom where Robin should have been fully dressed by now. He entered the room just as she was putting the finishing touches on her hair.

"So what are you going to do with your night off?" Robin asked.

"Skins verses Cowboys of course," He grinned. She wasn't a hard-core sports fan, but she could sit and watch a game or two, and enjoy the time spent as long as she was spending it with him.

"Cool. You know I could just about eat a horse right now," she said as she was walking out of the bedroom towards the kitchen.

"Horse is on the counter," he yelled after her. *A horse,* he thought. Comments like that sounded funny coming from her. He reached for the pair of shorts that were draped across the arm of a chair and then quickly put them on. Then he scanned the room for the T-shirt that he had taken off before going to bed this morning.

"There you are," he said, placing it near the foot of the bed. When he returned to the kitchen, Robin was standing next to the refrigerator with her head tossed back, emptying the last of the remnants from the now red stained glass. He opened the refrigerator and began scanning it for something more desirable than what he had prepared for her.

"Hey, would it be asking too much, to ask you to walk me home tonight? It could be romantic," she said, trying to argue her point while wearing her best smile.

Eric removed a carton of eggs from the refrigerator and then turned around. Robin was standing there, butt pressed against the counter with a sultry look about her presence, like she really needed the extra to sway his decision her way.

"You know something, I would love to walk you home, because I am mister romantic, and that thing you got going on there, what is that?" he teased.

"I have no idea what you're referring to mister, Robin shrugged her shoulders. Oh you mean this," her expression changed again to a very impressive sexy and seductive look.

"Does that actually work on guys," he teased. Robin gave him a playful punch in the shoulder.

"It worked on you, didn't it?" she said, pouting and crossing her arms.

"If I remember correctly it wasn't needed with me," he said, setting the carton of eggs down on the counter next to her. He wrapped his arms around her waist and kissed her with a mild passion; mild, yet passionate enough to kindle their already ignited flame.

"I have to go," she said, pushing him away after having felt the growth beneath his shorts from their brief closeness. He laughed. He enjoyed moments like these when the pleasure could be derived from the teasing.

"Enjoy the game," she said to him, backing away to exit the kitchen.

"I'll see you later," he said, grinning after her. He took a moment to glance down at the noticeable erection beneath his shorts. *Go away,* he commanded his swollen member with a thought. "Stubborn," he says, shaking his head. "I forget that you have a mind of your own, and rarely take orders from the likes of me." The front door opened, and then slammed shut. *Time I put something in my stomach*, he thought as he reached down to remove a skillet from one of the lower cabinets. *An omelet sounds like a great idea right about now*, he thinks, turning back to the refrigerator to remove some of the necessary ingredients that it would take to create the masterpiece. All that would be left for him to do once he ate was enjoy the rest of the night.

Robin walked down her residential street at a moderate pace, taking in some of the structural designs of the other homes. Some of the yards were so pristine you would swear that they were kept by twenty four hour maintenance crews, with guards posted and waiting to issue ticket violations to the unfortunate individuals who wondered onto the grass.

Both she and Eric owned cars, but she rarely drove her own since her job was so close. Because he normally drove whenever they ventured out together, he was more comfortable driving his. As for her, she enjoyed walking. It allowed her to notice the things that might seem insignificant to most people. Hard to do when traveling at speeds over ten miles per hour. Of course it helped having a job that was within walking distance. It worked out perfectly.

Her mind wandered, and she found herself thinking about her sisters and what they might be doing at this precise moment. The comparison between her, and the women which she considered to be family was night and day. The analogy sparked a grin. Night and day, probably not the best analogy to use considering what she was, yet it was suitable enough to get the point. She was different than most of her sisters in many ways, and she was also the youngest at age ninety-seven, although she didn't look a day over twenty-five, and she never would for as long as she lived.

Her transformation from human to vampire had been an act of compassion, a fair assessment for sure. For as long as she lived, the events of that night would forever be ingrained in her memory. Near death, and baptized in mortal pain, the ingredients of her cocktail that night had been rape and a numerous number of stab wounds from which she was certain to die, but it was Raven who had found her and saved her life. It was a second chance that had come at a price, but a price that had been easy to accept, after having gone through such a traumatizing ordeal. In other words, dying at the hands of a low life scum of the earth worm was not the way that she had envisioned leaving this life. It wasn't until much later, after she had regained consciousness, that she would understand fully the circumstances of her recovery.

She had awakened in an unfamiliar room, staring up into one of the most beautiful faces that she had ever laid eyes on, with skin that reminded her of smooth milk chocolate. In all her life, be it television or magazine, she had never seen a more beautiful black woman than Raven. Perhaps it was that very thing that had played a role in making her transition so easy. Like how could something so beautiful, be so equitably bad. Her reasoning turned out to be in a matter words well founded. Unlike her sisters, she has never been a product of the old ways. She has never fed on or taken the life of a human being for the sake of nourishment, or had to for that matter.

The covenant, thank God, has long since abandoned those ways, utilizing blood bank industries as a source for food and a means for staying alive. This was, and has been for the longest time a world where both comfort and needs could be bought at almost any prize, and blood was no exception to the rule. The covenant, let's just say, is a sisterhood in possession of its own wealth. They have had centuries to lift themselves to a status were money is no long an issue. Robin realized that she was still using the word covenant in the singular since. Not really the correct word to describe her family of late because of the division that had weaved its way into their mist. Perhaps, she felt that despite the covenants divide, and the differences that have risen within their numbers, they still remain a single covenant as one might imagine a single race.

The eldest of the vampire family is Raven, thank God, with Ambrosha falling beneath her in age though not by much. It has never been a comforting thought to imaging a scenario where the roles and the level of respect were reversed when it came to those two. They are without doubt completely different in nature, reminiscent of two siblings, yet formed from different matter. Raven possessing all the qualities that make one endearing and bearable to be around, and Ambrosha possessing all the qualities that make up a troubled child. She has always been the live wire, that one. It is because they are so different that the house is now divided. Lines were drawn, sides were taken and all that remains is the bitter tree which continues to thrive among them.

There were those who were drawn to Ambrosha's rebellious personality, and there were those who took comfort in the fact that there would be no unpleasant surprises if they followed Raven. Loyalty divided, what was once one house is now two. *Even so, it is Raven who has and always will command the highest level of respect no matter the division, and although my allegiance is to the covenant as a whole, if a side must be taken, it goes without saying, I choose Raven, and yet here I am, removed from all of them, the reason? What else, love. Truth be told, my heart will forever remain unconverted. Sure, I'm full vampire, but my desires are almost equally human. For me, it has always been one foot in, and one foot out, a fact, that has never gone unnoticed by any of my sisters, and one that if not understood, it is at least accepted for the most part.*

My meeting and falling in love with Eric couldn't have come at a better time in my life. It seemed that I was constantly longing for the kind of companionship that could only be enjoyed from human experience. At least that's what I thought. Vampire and human relationships have never been encouraged by the covenant for a million reasons, but I became the exception, and Eric made that easy by keeping whatever fears he might have had at bay. It wasn't easy sharing my secret with him, but the fact is, I want what everybody wants in life, and that is to have a fulfilled life defined by what I deem to be fulfilling. I may never look upon the sun again, and God knows how much I miss its warmth, but I am not about to forfeit love, no matter my existence. It is my opinion, that love is what keeps us tethered to life, and it is just one of the reasons why I still envy mortality. Because male vampires do not exist, nor can the human male be turned to become one; there lies the imbalance.

Oddly enough, the virus is not as friendly to females either. The likely hood for a successful female change is somewhere around fifteen percent or less. For those of us who have managed to survive the change we inherit strength and speed far greater than that of any human being; equal to some of fastest and strongest land animals. We possess the ability to heal at a much faster rate than any of God's creatures, and one other neat trick that Eric has come to hate. We can shift from solid matter to a dense mist state, but the transformation only last for seconds at a time before we have no choice but to shift back, quite useful if you want to avoid the many things that are capable of causing you bodily harm.

When I was first shown the ability I wondered how could such a thing be possible. As with all my questions, Raven provided all the answers. She had explained how although our bodies molecular structure undergoes such a severe change, our conscience is still present in the less than solid state. Robin rounded the corner to find that Frank still hadn't fixed the pub's sign. In big red letters, the sign that ran along the roof's border which read, Franks Pub, still had the bulbs burnt out in the letter k. That one detail might be enough to persuade passerbyers that if the place wasn't kept on the outside, then what could be said about the inside. She'd have to bug him about it again, or else it would remain unrepaired for who knows how long. Robin opened the door to the establishment and stepped inside.

"Hi Frank, how's it going?" She addressed the obese man who sat on a bar stool next to the door, reading a section of the newspaper. Frank had to be somewhere around three hundred and fifty pounds easily at a height of about six feet four inches tall. How he managed to stay glued to that seat with out toppling over was a mystery to her. The big man acknowledged Robin with a grunt and continued to read his paper.

"Oh yeah Frank, when are you going to get that sign fixed? It's a real eyesore, you know."

"Got somebody coming to take a look at it tomorrow," Frank answered, eyes glued to the newspaper.

"Okay, just thought I would remind you, I believe you would have procrastinated into the New Year if I didn't." Robin gave him a quaint smile, and then headed towards the bar where Amanda wore an expression on her face that was all too recognizable to be mistaken for anything else. It was the one that said, *thank God you're here Robin, because I'm ready to blow this joint.*

"Has it been terribly busy tonight?" Robin asked as she approached.

"My feet seem to think **so,**" Amanda answered, "and it would do me little good to call them liars."

Robin stepped behind the bar and reached beneath the counter to grab an apron, while Amanda was serving one of the customers a draft beer. She donned the apron and tied the straps around her waist.

"I can take it from here, Amanda," she said.

"Music to my ears – my feet are killing me. I swear, I never hear you complain, I would shave my head to know how you keep your spirits up for these wages, and how can you bare to wear heals in this line of work and not feel the effects?"

"You're forgetting that I'm only part-time, Amanda."

"True, but again with the shoes – the ones I wear are like Cadillacs compared to yours, and yet I suffer something fierce while you don't."

"A nice long soak in the bath should do you some good," Robin told her, but Amanda's expression was that of disagreement as she removed her apron and tossed it on the shelf beneath the bar.

"It's all yours sweetie, I'm out of here," Amanda said.

"I'll see you tomorrow Amanda, remember, a nice hot bath."

"Yeah yeah," Amanda sighed. Robin shook her head and then turned to notice that a customer was hailing her with one hand raised at the far end of the bar. She smiled politely and then headed his way.

After a little over three hours had gone by, Robin noticed that the bar was beginning to thin out. Not unusual for a Monday night. She allowed herself a moment to reflect on her life decisions. Bartending is not the most sought out job in the world. The fact that she enjoyed it as much as she did only meant that she could appreciate what most people might consider a drag or mundane.

Her life at this point, as far as she was concerned, was pretty close to perfect, which made her wonder. At which turn would she and Eric come face to face with the next major challenge in their lives. The first one was obviously becoming an item to begin with. One might think, if they were given all the details, that she and Eric have gotten over what should be the greatest obstacle in their relationship. *Hardly the truth because of what I am. There will no doubt be greater challenges ahead for the both of us. I just hope that as a couple, as different as he and I are, that together we will be strong enough to get through whatever comes our way. I believe that we are, and I'm pretty close to certain that he feels the same way.*

CHAPTER TWO

Raven stepped out of the garden bath tub onto the thick floor rug, and then reached for the towel that was draped across the back of the toilet seat. She wasn't big on showers, feeling that they took much of the relaxation out of the entire bathing process. Who can argue the fact that they were designed for the hurried, and meant to be quick, although there are those who feel inclined to stand under the things for lengthy amounts of time to get what they are missing from a long hot bath. As revolutionary as the shower might be, it doesn't compare to the bath when it comes to relieving tension and stress.

She patted away the droplets of water and moisture that had settled on the surface of her creamy dark colored skin. With her hair dripping wet, she quickly wrapped it with the already dampened towel, leaving her body naked and exposed from the neck down. She rarely ever forgot her bathrobe. At the moment it was laying across her bed, where she had placed it only moments before walking into the bathroom to get in the bath. She turned to stare into the long length mirror on the wall to study her ancient but otherwise unchanged image. *The gift of immortality*, she thought.

Born of African descent, her blood, despite the infectious virus, which is the proprietor for her long life, is still probably the purest to date. As aged as it may be, it still maintains the purest properties that are of her heritage. With another birthday just around the corner, a major one at that, signaling a whopping five hundred, she could never have imagined in a million years a life eternal, and yet, what little she could remember of her life before this, did bear some signs of a special, or rather a marked destiny. But again, who could have imagined one such as this.

From the time she was a young girl, and barely old enough to piece together the simple puzzles of life, she could recall the stories told to her by her mother. How she, the child who moments after her birth was given the name Raven; had entered the world different from those of her tribe, with skin far richer than the fairest of her people, hair as long as a three year old toddler's, and black as the feathers on a Raven wing. *This is how you came from my womb her mother had told her, and so Raven was the name that I gave you.* Raven removed the towel from her head and allowed her hair to fall to its full length resting just above her firm round butt. She raised the lid on the dirty clothes hamper and dropped the towel inside.

Her bedroom was lavishly designed. The queen size canopy bed was probably the most cherished item that she owned, with the hand carved wood post, and the cherubic guardians staring down through the transparent veil towards the center of the bed. It was a beautiful sanctuary that she could retire to at the end of a long night. Raven donned the bathrobe, and then slid her feet into a pair of fluffy black slippers. Walking over to the vanity, she settled into the chair and gazed at her reflection in the mirror. *In all my four hundred plus years, I might have cut my hair a half a dozen times,* she thought picking up the brush. As she began to brush the cold black strains, she thought about her sisters that at the moment were in different parts of the house. *There are currently six other women living within the spacious mansion where there was once fifteen. It was the number totaling the last of their kind as far and as certain as she knew. Immortals, monsters, or demons we have been called, each name true depending on who you ask. For some we have been all three, but for most we still reside in the realm of make believe.*

As leader of a now divided covenant, I endure the responsibility for ensuring that the human race continues to see us in light of the later. There are laws that must be followed if we are to survive among the very creatures that we too were once like. I have failed in what might be considered the most important area of any leader; that being unification no thanks to Ambrosha, who has all but poisoned the minds of half the covenant. I am her elder by little more than a hundred years, and although removed from this house all be it of her own free will, she will always be subject to the regulations that stand as law for each us.

Raven set the hair brush down, and then picked up one of the body lotions that were aligned, to the left and right of her vanity. The vampire's skin is not governed by the same laws as humans. The virus as it is called provides for a no maintenance care. It is the fragrances that are of a bigger deal for her and her sisters than the moisturizing elements contained within the products. Raven let the robe slide down over her shoulders and began rubbing the lotion sparingly onto her skin and arms. Her feet were always the last to receive the otherwise pointless treatment that would in today's case provide her skin with the smell of lavender.

When she had finished applying the lotion to nearly every inch of her body, she set the bottle down and placed it neatly back. She glanced over her shoulder to check the time on the bedside clock. Ten minutes to nine. Normally she would have been up already, but she had stayed up a little later than planned this morning, watching the world news. Hunger was now dictating her next move, says the rumbling sound erupting from the depths of her tummy. Raven stood up and walked over to the queen size bed where she had also laid out a name brand T-shirt and matching sweat pants. She had no intentions of going out tonight, so the outfit made for comfortable wear around the house, and after donning the clothing she stepped out into the corridor, and headed for the kitchen where she was bound to find one or two of her sisters sitting around.

The lighting in the corridor was consistent. The lamps along the walls on each side were similar to the ones that could be found in elegant hotels, and then there were those along the ceiling that were never used because of their heightened vision. While the upstairs corridor remained dimly lit, rooms like the kitchen, living room, and din cast light like any other house once the sun went down.

Three rooms down to her left, a door opened. It was Gelsa. She was a petite Australian girl with short blond hair and a spitfire personality. She acknowledged Raven with the rooted accent that she had chosen to keep over the many years. It is not something that we as vampires are bound too since we possessed the innate ability to master any tongue.

"Sleep well, Raven?" Gelsa asked as they descended the stairs together.

"I did, and may I ask, for what occasion are you dressed for tonight?"

"We're going to Minks. It's a fairly new club that Guiliana, Thandie, and I have decided to check out. You should come with us," Gelsa suggested.

Raven laughed lightly. "I don't think so, but you guys go right ahead."

"Come on," Gelsa argued. "When was the last time you stepped out to grab some fun? I'm not suggesting that you paint the town, just hit a club or two and rein in some obviously long overdue good time."

Raven giggled. "Maybe next time."

"Seriously Raven. It wouldn't hurt you to get out a little more. There's gonna be men and lots of them."

"Believe me when I say that there has been no shortage of men in my life."

"If you say so, but you're gonna have to dust that thing off and use it again someday. A man is going to find it difficult to enter if the cobwebs have sealed off the entrance."

"Thank you for that rather disturbing image, Gelsa."

"Don't mention it," Gelsa giggled. The two women entered the kitchen. Its spaciousness allowed for all the necessary amenities needed to prepare large meals in half the time it would take for a kitchen of moderate size. It was a dream for someone who might have a passion for the culinary arts, but it had found its uselessness under the owner-ship of a house filled with vampires.

Raven opened the refrigerator door and removed a plastic bag. It contained a pint of 0 positive blood. Gelsa took a seat, facing Raven on one of the kitchens bar stools.

"I take it you've already eaten?" Raven asked, set to prepare her own meal.

Gelsa raised her arms above her head, arched her torso to one side and stretched as far as bones and muscle tissue would allow.

"You know what they say about the early bird, Raven," she said.

"Thankfully that saying carries little weight when it comes to our food supply," Raven countered. You guys must have risen pretty early then?"

"I rolled out of bed just after seven," Gelsa answered. "Guiliana was already up. It was Thandie who needed the shaking."

"I take it the other girls have passed on tonight's outing as I have?" Raven asked.

"Yes, but there is a big difference," Gelsa argued. "They are only passing on a night out of fun, you have given up altogether. Can you even remember the last time you were on a dance floor shaking it up?"

"I can remember," Raven answered, "and it really hasn't been that long."

"Whatever you say," Gelsa replied.

Thandie entered the kitchen with Guiliana in tow. "It's about time ladies," Gelsa barked. "I swear, you guys are worst than a couple of drag queens who spend an endless amount of time in the mirror trying to cover up the truth that they in fact have the face of a man."

"Gelsa, don't hate," Thandie shot back sticking her tongue out for good measure. It really isn't a good look for you sis." Thandie stood about a foot taller than her impatient sister. Thandie was a Caucasian girl with dark black hair and big round eyes. She stood at five foot six and had a painted personality that was one hundred percent Goth and gore, at least for the time being anyway. Such was the life of a vampire.

The extended life span tended to contribute much to the different phases that a vampire went through over the years or decades. Such has been the case for us, and such was the case with Thandie who began painting her fingernails black, and dressing predominantly in black clothing ten or more years ago. Before that, you wouldn't have been able to guess that the girl standing in the kitchen right now was one and the same. Guiliana equaled Raven in height. She stood at five foot seven, with chestnut colored hair. She reminded you of a school teacher, always serious and business like. Even now while Thandie and Gelsa carried on like a couple of school children, Guiliana remained calm and reserved.

"Are you two finished?" Guiliana asked. "If so, then I am ready to go." Gelsa and Thandie look at one another. "A truce for now," Thandie said, pointing a finger at Gelsa. They never really fought, but they often enjoyed disagreeing just to get on one another's nerves.

Raven made eye contact with Guiliana. They shared a look of mutual understanding; that being to keep her sisters out of trouble.

Once the three women had exited the kitchen, Raven was left as Gelsa had pointed out in so many words alone. No man, no lighted dance floor, and no fun. She raised the glass of blood, and drank nearly half of it in a single gulp. She welcomed the bloods revitalizing effects. It takes a great deal of money to swing human blood in the capacity for which they needed it. Finding crooks at the head of corporations such as these that were willing to sell the commodity for higher profits was no easy task.

Our suppliers know nothing of the true nature of things, neither do they care for what purpose the blood is used for. Money is their only concern.

Raven raised the glass and finished what remained. "Hm....now that hit the spot," she said, running her tongue across her lips. She picked up the bottle of dish washing liquid that was kept near the sink and squeezed a small amount into the glass. She then washed it until it was clean and then placed it in the drain rack.

When she was finished, she left the kitchen and headed for the den to see who, if anybody was occupying it. As she drew near, she could clearly hear the television running. *Looks like another night of movies and listening to the girls who had stayed behind share their latest experiences.* She really didn't mind spending her evenings relaxing and taking in a movie or two, and there was reading. She loved a good book, but what if Gelsa was right? *Maybe I have been in this state too long. Maybe I should get out more.* Raven entered the den where she found Natalia staring at the television, and Savana reading one of the latest fashion magazines. The two women acknowledged her, and she them as she walked over and took a seat next to Natalia.

"What are we watching?" Raven asked, suddenly recognizing the movie that she had seen somewhere around eight months ago. "Never mind," she said, remembering how much she had enjoyed it, and thought that it was a movie that she could stand to watch again, so she got comfortable on the sofa and focused in on it. It was the third installment of the movie underworld, and from what she could tell it was only about a quarter of the way through the beginning. Raven leaned back on the sofa and then settled in for the rest of the movie.

Eric grabbed his keys from one of the hooks that were fashioned into the wall, and then opened the front door to step out into the night air. His mood couldn't have been any better thanks to the 30-27 win favoring his team. *Not a bad night at all,* he thought as he started for Robin's place of employment. It was warm out, so he welcomed the light breeze that caused the leaves to flutter and sway on the trees around him. It was 1:30 a.m., and he was strolling through the neighborhood as though it were a sunny afternoon.

A group of loose leaves caught flight on a gust of wind that carried them across his path. *The wind held such magic,* he thought. *It was without shape or form, yet it made its existence known.* He smiled as he entertained a thought, one which has crossed his mind on more than a few occasions over the past few months.

There were absolute moments in time when he literally felt that he would give almost anything to be like Robin, but even if he was dead set on it, immortality was impossibility for him. His mind trailed back to where they had first met. He'd stopped in at a pharmacy to pick up something for the congestion in his chest. They first noticed one another in passing on one of the stores aisles, and he had wanted to say something to her right then and there, but who really has courage enough these days to stop a random stranger inside a pharmacy store, and strike up a conversation that they hope will lead to something much more. He had counted himself lucky afterwards of course, remembering how he had ended up behind her in the store's checkout line.

Needless to say, he still may not have had enough courage to talk to her, had she not uttered the first words which were, *I think you will find that whiskey, lemon, and honey work much better than the product you have in your hand. Call me old-fashioned,* he remembered her saying. She had laid a bridge for him to cross, and cross it he had done. They exchanged phone numbers outside in the pharmacy parking lot before parting ways, but further contact didn't happen until a week afterwards. Twice he had made what anyone would call a solid effort, but when she hadn't responded to any of his phones calls or text, disappointment weighed in so he just gave up. So it was really a surprise to hear her voice on the opposite end of the phone line when she finally decided to called. About a month after they met, she came clean and told him with great difficulty what she was.

Naturally he had needed some convincing; a rather easy task for her. Needless to say they didn't communicate for about a week after that, however in the end he just couldn't stay away.

Robin later confessed that it during that week she had been a nervous wreck. She had shared how it had been irresponsible of her to share with him something that could have easily placed her and her sisters in danger, but it was only from that view point did she feel regret. Apart from that, she was happy for them having met. *It's not like I would have killed you to keep you quiet,* she later teased.

When they had finally decided that being in a relationship was what they both wanted, despite the foreseeable and unforeseen challenges that they would obviously face, he had more than happily applied the slight alterations to his own life. He would have to sleep during the day as she was required to do, and work during the night. Not unheard of. A number of human couples functioned much the same way, because there has always been a demand for second and third shift employees depending on the type of employment involved. Whatever business he needed to conduct during the daylight hours, he would simply lose a few hours of sleep to see it done. Every alteration that he has made in his life to be with Robin has been well worth the adjustment.

Her sisters as he has come to know are not nearly as horrific as the stories books or cinemas make them out to be. They are vampires for certain, and they are capable of some amazing things, but as far as he could tell, the world has no need to fear them. Like all living things they face their own challenges, most of which are the things in life which they have been forced to leave behind because they are in fact different.

From what he has come to understand about them, although different in many ways, vampires share the most basic connection with all organisms on the face of the planet, and that is to navigate through life, whether it be calm winds or heavy storms, but they too have a right to survive as best they can on a path that none of them have chosen for themselves. His biggest challenge has not been the fact that he has a vampire for a girlfriend, nor his selfish demands for the time her job chews up, they literally do not need the money, an argument he had thought he'd had a fifty-fifty chance at winning, but what Robin continues to effectively point out is, that her desire to work has nothing to do with money.

No, his greatest challenge has been accepting the fact that while he continues to age, Robin will remain unchanged. Not one wrinkle. Not a streak of grey hair. It was a subject they tried their best to avoid because of the unpleasant realities.

The love that he embellished towards her was great. So great in fact, that he was willing to endure the unfortunate fate of aging before her while watching her remain unchanged. He checked his watch. The pub would be closing in less than ten minutes. He was making good time.

After counting the money from the register twice for good measure, Robin placed the bills and loose change inside a leather money purse and zipped it shut. She set it on top of the bar near the register so that Frank could pick it up on his way out. Grabbing one of the damp rags she'd been using most of the night, she began wiping down the counter, ridding it of beer glass rings and nuts that had escaped one fate only to find another.

Frank had long since moved from the stool where he had been sitting when she arrived. He now sat asleep with his arms folded in one of the booths. The last customer had walked out over twenty minutes ago. Frank had locked the doors afterward and called it a night, closing the pub almost ten minutes before regular closing time.

She was just about to walk out on to the floor to begin clearing tables, and wiping down seats and chairs when she heard the rapping on the pub's door. She looked up to see Eric peering in through the glass. She flashed him a warm smile. "Oh let him in already will you," Frank yelled from his seat.

"How do you do that, Frank? One minute you're sleeping like the dead, and the next it's like you were never asleep at all." Frank often pretended to be annoyed by the affection that she and Eric displayed for one another, but she had a sense that their sappiness made the better part of his nights.

Robin held up a finger towards Eric, recognizable as be there in a moment, and then rushed over to the booth where Frank sat holding out the keys. "Thank you, Frank." She smiled, grabbing the ring of keys and then rushing over to unlock the door.

"Yeah….yeah," Frank griped.

"Hey you," was Eric's greeting to her as he stepped inside the pub.

"Hey back," she countered, kissing him lightly on the cheek. "Give me a few more minutes. I'll be done as soon as I have wiped down the tables and chairs, and swept the floor."

"I can help if you'd like," he said.

"No I've got it. You take a seat at the bar and relax. I won't be too long."

"Finish wiping down the tables and chairs. I'll take care of the rest," Frank yelled out to Robin.

"Frank, are you sure?" she asked.

"Wouldn't have offered if I wasn't," he shot back.

"Thanks Frank, as always, you're a doll."

"I'm nothing of the sort," he said.

"I don't know, Frank. Old man like you shouldn't be taking on too much. Who's going to come to your aid if you pull out your back," Eric laughed.

"I'm not that old, and for your information, regardless of my age, I can work circles around you, and don't you forget it."

Robin giggled. She loved the way those two carried on. They might go two to three weeks without seeing each other, and then very much like right now, they would make up for lost time by going in on one another. All play of course. *It was cute,* she thought. She returned to the task at hand, while Eric and Frank continued to entertain one another.

When Eric was tired of the playful sport, he walked over and strad-dled one of the bar stools. He spun on it, lining himself up so that he could admire Robin's figure while she bent over and wiped tables and chairs. As she wiped, gravity propelled remnants of food towards the floor. *The big man had his work cut out for him,* Eric thought. *Where would he find the energy?*

Minutes go by as Robin was finishing the last of the tables. She stepped behind the bar and dropped the dirty rag into a bin.

"I'm just about ready, Eric," she said, loosening the straps on her apron, and lifting it carefully over her head. Robin shoved it into the same bin that she had dropped the rag in. Frank would bag the dirty aprons and rags, and then carry them home where he washed them in his personal machine.

"Ready?" she asked Eric as she made her way over to where Frank sat.

"Absolutely," Eric said, rising from his seat and moseying over towards the door. Eric watched Robin shake Frank's shoulder until he returned to the world of the living. The big man opened his eyes, but with some difficulty. Struggling, he tried to clear the booth, but his big frame and huge belly fought him every step of the way.

"Are you good, Frank?" Eric asked from the door.

"Never better," Frank answered. "You'll never find a man in better shape than the one you see standing before you right now. You'll do well to remember that."

Eric chuckled as he watched the big man move as fast as his stiff limbs would permit towards the pub's door.

"Go ahead and get," Frank yelled, "so I can finish up and get home myself."

"Ok already we're going," Eric shot back. They stepped outside the pub and waved good-bye. The big man waved back just as they were turning to walk away.

CHAPTER THREE

A mother muffles the cries of her baby by covering its mouth with her hand. "Shush.....," she whispers, hoping that by some miracle her child would sense the fear in her voice, understand the danger that they were in, and quiet just long enough for it to pass. At present, she was unable to tell whether the blood on her hands was her child's, or her own. With her adrenaline running high it was difficult to tell. One could be seriously injured, yet have no affiliation with the pain that they were in, and what of her baby?

She saw no visible signs of injury that he might have suffered during the crash. Clarification would have to wait. She had to keep moving, their lives depended on it. The car she had been forced to abandon was wrapped around a tree on the next block over. Survive on foot or die. Those were her options. Deep inside, she felt their chances for survival slipping away. *There has to be something that I can do,* she thought. If she was unable to save her own life, then maybe she could save the life of her child.

Kneeling against the side of a residential home, Rosalie stares down at her baby. His tiny lips were curled and set to cry. It was a sure sign that he had needs which couldn't be met. Rosalie tried to fight back her tears, but lost the battle. They came despite her efforts to stay them. She searched her mind for a spell that might save their life or his. Within seconds one came to mind. It revealed itself like a light bulb suddenly turned on. A smile spread across her face, because there was now at least an increased sense of hope. Rosalie stared down at her son. She had given him the name David, after his father.

"I know what I have to do," she whispered softly to her child as she stared into his grey eyes. Rosalie nestled the baby against her cheek and breathed in his sweet scent. After several kisses, understanding that this would probably be a last goodbye, Rosalie smiled, cheeks wet from running tears. "Mommy loves you. Mommy will always love you, don't ever forget."

In that same instance she felt an unearthly silence. It seemed to fill the air all around her. It was the kind of silence that affected everything alike; man, animal, and insect.

Rosalie looked upward towards the night sky and searched it with a feverish fear. Above her was where the danger lay. She didn't need to see it to know that it was there. She held David close. *It is time to move,* she thought.

Rosalie stood up and walked slowly towards the front of the very house that she had taken cover. The streets looked clear, and there was no sign of danger above. With great care Rosalie walked around towards the front of the house and climbed the front steps. She made sure David was swathed snugly inside the tiny blanket, before she knelt down to lay him on the hard wood surface of the porch. She studied his face one last time. Something was definitely not right with him. Her intuition told her as much. Rosalie reached out for the door bell, but stopped short of pressing it, once she realized the commotion that pressing might bring. There was a strong possibility that he was injured in the crash, but still an ambulance arriving on the scene would surely be the death of him. "I have to leave you now, she said in a whisper that barely crossed the threshold of her lips. You have to survive, even if it means my own death."

Rosalie's senses were on full alert. Call it paranoia. Call it an overwhelming sense of fear, but whatever the name for it, it was the same feeling that she had experienced hours ago. Rosalie descended the steps and ran as fast as her energy depleted legs would carry her away from the house.

After running close to two full blocks, she was forced to stop altogether. Rosalie buckled over from the exertion. She was breathing heavily, with both hands resting for support on her knees. She hoped for her child's sake, that she had run far enough to invoke the spell. Rosalie stood up and supported herself against a nearby tree. *It's now or never,* she thought. She reached inside her front left pocket and retrieved a small pouch. On the inside, amongst a few of the other trinkets was a tiny blade. She pulled the object out and stared at it for a brief moment.

A witch's power lies within the essence of their blood. Drawing on that power meant that it was always necessary to spill a little bit, but the younger the practicing witch, the more blood required of her. She was considered young by practicing standards, but not so young that she would be unable to perform the spell that had come to mind.

Rosalie held out her wrist and placed the blade against it. She took a deep breath, and then ran the blade across her wrist cutting flesh and opening vein. Her bodies crimson life force began seeping out through the incision. The act made for a slow death, but what choice did she have? She was already dead anyway. Her death was an obvious requirement this night if her child was to survive.

Rosalie let the blade fall to the ground, and the sound of metal striking pavement pierced through the quiet night. She took her right index finger and ran it across her wrist, bringing away enough blood to suit her need. With it, she drew a symbol across her larynx. It was a simple spell, one that required a small amount of energy to perform. *Please.....Please.....work,* came a desperate plea from within. It was in that moment that she was abruptly shaken by a familiar and terrible sound. Her heart beat so fast, she feared that it would explode within her chest.

Rosalie closed her eyes and recalled the spell that she was all too familiar with. She couldn't have imagined in a million years that such a small spell would be linked to saving a life. Not her own life, but a life all the same. She spoke the incantation. The words rolled off her lips, coupled with an iron will to guide them towards their purpose. Seconds was all that was needed. Rosalie cleared her throat, and then spoke two simple words to see if her magic had indeed taken effect.

The sound that escaped her lips was unnerving because it bore a stark resemblance of David's. Rosalie made a strong effort to control her trembling limbs, but it was no use. She straightened herself upright, trembling limbs and all, and then drew on what little energy she had left. *Now,* she thought, putting the spell into effect. She opened her mouth and the sound of a baby's cry pierced through the night. When she was done, she nearly fainted from exertion and the loss of blood.

She didn't know how close death was, in front, above, or behind her, but she felt certain that it had pick up on the child's cries. There. There it was; the unmistakable sound of terror that had given her cause to take flight with her infant son earlier tonight. Oh how she wished that this were only a nightmare. Then she would awaken to the relief that followed afterwards.

Rosalie searched the sky in every direction, looking for the source that produced a sound similar to a thousand bats flapping in the wind. Her heart beat like the heart of a hummingbird, which made it difficult for her to breathe. She tried to walk, but she was only able to cover a mere ten yards before she was forced to stop. Not fifteen feet in front of her, death hovered above the ground. Its eyes were a terrifying blood red, set deep within the crevice of a large mass of tiny bat like creatures. Rosalie watched in horror as the abomination began taking on a different form. Paralyzed she looked on, but why was she just standing there, when what little strength she had left, could have been channeled towards an effort to escape. She knew the answer to that question. There was no escape, and that was the finality of it all.

Rosalie braced herself, while the creature moved closer and closer to completing its transformation. It hovered, never once coming into contact with the ground, and what was in the beginning a thousand separate entities, was now thousands messed into a single frame. It studied her for a span of three seconds, and then unleashed a sound that chilled her to the bone. It didn't advance on her immediately, which came as no surprise, because she was not the sole object of its desire, nor was her death its primary concern. No, her death would come in the next few seconds, right after she denied the demon what it sought.

"Where is the child?" the demon asked in a muddled raspy voice. Rosalie held her silence. Did the demon really believe for one second, that it had caused enough fear in her heart that she would surrender her child? She was filled with fear, but not so much that she would surrender the one thing that meant the world to her. What in heaven's name was keeping her on her feet? She should have been lying face down on the sidewalk by now. Her eyes wandered to the open wound on her wrist. Oh how she wished that death had come and gone already.

"Where is the child?" The demon screamed, spewing forth hundreds of insects from its mouth. The bugs buzzed around the demon's face as though it were an open wound.

"Some place where you will never find him," Rosalie answered, her words lacking real strength behind them. The demon hovered forward a bit, and then emitted a sound more terrifying than the one before. It pierced the night, and reached into her very soul. The demon's face suddenly sunk inward, leaving behind a disfigured image of what had been there before.

Thousands more insects spewed forward from the sunken hole where the demon's face should have been. They assaulted her like a wave of sand, attacking every inch of her body that was exposed. Rosalie coughed up and spit out the ones that had entered her mouth.

The demon's intent was not to kill her, but torment her, and it was working. Rosalie's strength left her at once, and she fell helplessly towards the ground. She waited in anticipation, for her face to make contact with the cold hard surface of the ground. *Finally, death,* she thought, closing her eyes to meet the greeter of darkness, or of light. *Take me now,* she whispered past an unsupportive tongue, but death kept its distance. Instead she was rewarded by an overpowering smell of rot and stench. It was clear to her that she had never made contact with the ground. Instead she lay unable to move; supported by the demons arms.

Enraged, Entu` manifested a hand lined with jagged claws from the chaos that comprised his body. He stared down at the human with hatred and distaste. His bluish lips parted slightly, as if he were about to speak. The witch was too close to death to retrieve information of any kind, and even if she wasn't near the brink of death her will may have still proven too strong for him to break.

"Your courage may have brought the child some time witch, but I will eventually find him, and when I do, I will finish what I started this night." Entu` plunged claw and hand deep inside Rosalie's chest, forcing a final breath before pulling her heart free.

He held Rosalie's heart firmly in his hand, while droplets of blood painted the surface of the concrete below, leaving a tragic portrait of death. Entu` let Rosalie's lifeless body fall to the ground where it would be found minus one organ. *The child could be anywhere*, he thought. Witches could be as clever as they were stubborn. It is possible, though doubtful that he may have been chasing her magic from the very start. No! He was certain that his eyes had not deceived him. Entu` felt the rage welling up within him again. He was disturbed by the fact that many years could pass before he found the slightest trace of the child's existence. It was but a technicality after all, because he had eternity on his side. He was certain that day would come though. With a thought he willed his form to change, and then took to the sky cloaked by the darkness, where he disappeared into the night.

"Thank you," Robin said, blushing as she walked arm-in-arm with Eric.

"What am I being thanked for now?" he asked.

"For coming all the way down to the job that you wished I didn't have, just to walk me home on this beautiful night."

"It's actually morning, and it's the least that I can do for the woman I profess to love."

She squeezed his arm gently. "It's so beautiful out isn't it? And look, even the moon seems to think so," Robin said.

Eric stared up at the distant mass of soft light. "I suppose you're right," he agreed," but what do you suppose the moon is thinking right now about the couple below?"

"Hmm....That's easy. Its thinking I'm glad to have been noticed by two people so deeply in love."

Eric chuckled, "I'm sure you're right, but I'll bet it's also thinking, what a sweet girl."

"I am aren't I?" Robin playfully joked.

"Well if the moon thinks so then so do I," Eric laughed.

Robin nudged him in his side. "Not quite the answer I was looking for, but it will do." They walked at a slow pace conversing about this and that, but as they neared their home Robin caught wind of a familiar smell. It was one she recognized all too well. She tightened her grip on Eric's arm, though not enough to cause him harm.

"Is something wrong?" Eric asked.

"I'm not sure" Robin answered.

"Okay...but what is it that has you on edge," he asked.

"Eric, I smell blood. The scent is strong."

"It's probably just some animal," Eric told her.

"It's not an animal, Eric, its human. I know the difference between the two." Robin grabbed hold of Eric's hand and forced him to walk at her pace.

"Robin, what is it?" he asked.

"I think someone's injured," she answered. He started to question her, but thought better of it. When she began guiding him into their yard he hit the brakes.

"Are you kidding me?" he asked. Robin released his hand and walked slowly towards the porch.

"Robin, be careful!" Eric whispered, tagging a couple feet behind.

"There seems to be something wrapped inside of a blanket," she said, bending down to examine it. Robin picked the object up.

"Oh my God, Eric," Robin cried out, after opening the blanket up to look inside. "It's a baby," she said, "and it's clearly the source behind the blood that's bombarding my senses. Oh God," Robin said, quickly moving into action.

"What is it?" Eric asked.

"Its heartbeat is barely noticeable. Eric, hurry! Get the door," Robin shouted. Eric quickly reached inside his pocket for the keys to the house. He had the door open in seconds, stepping aside to allow Robin enter. Before closing the door he stared out into the night, looking for signs of life. He stood there and wondered about the type of person who could do such a thing. When he was satisfied that nothing or no one was out there, he closed the door and locked it behind him. "I'll call for help," he said, reaching for his cell phone.

"No Eric, wait!" Robin said.

"Wait! Why? That baby is obviously injured, and in desperate need of help." Eric proceeded to dial the emergency operator.

"No Eric, please!" She pleaded with him.

"Robin, I don't understand," he said, moving the phone away from his ear.

"There's not enough time," she tried to explain. "This baby will probably die if I don't do something within the next few minutes."

"What does that mean? Do what?" he asked, unable follow her meaning. Robin stared at him for a second or two.

"Robin, no," he pleaded after it dawned on him what she was planning to do.

"Eric, this baby doesn't stand a chance if it has to wait on conventional help, but maybe, just maybe I can offer him one."

Eric took a deep breath, and then lowered his head. He stared down at the floor for a few moments; questions circling around in his head. "But I thought…. I mean won't that kill him, or her?"

"Maybe," she answered, "but I have to try."

Eric stood there, shaking his head. She was asking him to be okay with what she was planning to do. "I'm very uncomfortable with this. I need you to know that."

"I know," was all she could say.

"Shit, Robin." Eric waved a hand. "Do whatever it is that….you guys do."

Robin nodded, and then walked over to gently lay the baby down on the sofa. There was no point checking for injuries. The baby's heart beat was too weak to do anything other than what she had planned to do. Anything else would just be wasting precious time. "I think you should leave the room, Eric. You shouldn't have to witness this."

"I'll be fine, Robin."

"Eric, I would prefer it if you didn't watch."

Eric shoved his hands into his pants pockets, shaking his head. "Okay, but I'll be in the bedroom if you need me," he told her.

Once Eric was out of the room, she set her focus on the child. Drawing on will, she forced the talon beneath her index finger to push forward and through the skin. With it she wasted no time opening one of her veins, and after guiding her blood dripped wrist over the baby's mouth and making certain that her life force did indeed pass beyond the child's lips she steadied herself and prayed for a miracle.

Having never attempted this before, she could only guess how much of her blood the child would need for the process to succeed. The next step would be vital to the child's survival, since the child didn't seem to be swallowing the blood. She placed two fingers on the child's neck, and then gently massaged the throat.

Her blood would accomplish one of two things in deciding the child's fate. It would either reconstitute each of the existing blood cells making the child immortal; it's only enemy the sun. Strengthen bone and flesh making the child complete and new, or end the child's life indefinitely. A finality that was sure to take place anyway absent her intervention however small the odds. Robin suddenly remembered the downside to all of this. *Oh my God! What have I done* she thought, recalling her own transformation.

Her transformation had been an excruciatingly painful experience for her, as it is for every human body subjected to vampire blood. She was an adult when her transformation took place. This tiny bundle of pink flesh is but a child. "What have I done?" she said, placing her hands over her mouth. She began to cry, having realized the magnitude of her action, but there was nothing that she could do about it now.

Robin wiped away her tears and waited for a sign, any sign to indicate that her blood was acting in a positive manner on the child's system. What happened next was the very thing that she had wanted to protect Eric from. The baby opened its eyes and a torturous cry burst forth from its lungs. Robin instinctively reached out to pick the child up but stopped herself understanding that there was nothing that she could do except allow the process to run its course whether the child lived or died. She looked on as the baby's skin turned from pinkish white to a bruised blue where the child's veins were. Her blood was acting brutally on the child's small frame. She wanted to cry out but she held her tongue, realizing that if she screamed, Eric would come storming out of the room, and she couldn't have that.

The child's tiny legs stiffened from the strain that was being placed on its body. She could actually see her blood attacking the child's cells where the veins were visibly noticeable. Having experienced the process herself, she would have to agree that the feeling was probably akin to having hydrochloric acid injected into your blood stream, and being made to endure the suffering effect until it either killed, or transformed you. Robin looked on in complete horror, rivaled only by the compassion that she harbored in her heart because the worst was yet to come. Except for the pain, Robin was experiencing every facet of what the child was going through, and because of her heightened sense of hearing she would be forced to listen to the following step of the child's transformation.

She hated herself for having made this choice for the child, but what else was she to do? She wasn't the kind of person who could just stand by and watch a child die. There was no simple solution. It was just about over. At present, bone, tissue, and organs were in the final stages of transformation. The child's body stiffened before her eyes, and its heartbeat stopped suddenly. She held her breath; fist clenched tight. The only thing she could do was shake her head, as she whispered past her lips the word "No." The process had been too much for the child to bear. Robin covered her eyes, and then broke down in tears. She slumped against the sofa, grieving the loss of a child that she had not known. A minute or so must have gone by, she wasn't sure, but what she was sure of was the sudden sound of a heartbeat however weak it was, and the sudden burst of air that had been forced out from the child's lungs.

She removed her hands from her eyes and stared down at what had to be a miracle. *Impossible* was the word she wanted to say, but didn't dare from fear that fate might suddenly renege on the compassionate that it had shown. *Amazing,* was the word she thought. The child's heartbeat was getting stronger. He or she was going to live. The child opened its eyes. Robin was nearly startled by their color.

"Your eyes," Robin said intrigued by their unusual color. She cracked a smile. They were a kind of violet. A string of questions bombarded her mind. Question's mainly about its mother. Like where was she now, and had she suffered injuries as well? And if so was she dead or alive? *I can't focus on that now,* she thought. There will be plenty of time later to ponder her many questions. In the mean time however, something wonderful had taken place, and she would take solace in that.

"Thank you. Thank you God," she whispered. Robin reached down and lifted the baby from the pillow. Holding it out before her, she stared at it and smiled. Amazingly enough he or she smiled back. *How in the world,* she wondered. *It was only minutes ago that you were experiencing what I personally know to be a living hell. How can you bring forth a smile having just gone through all that?*

The child responded to her question by kicking its tiny legs up and down.

"You can't possibly know how happy I am that you pulled through," she said to it. "What are you called?" she asked, in no way hoping for a response.

"So much has happened, that I have yet to discover your sex little one." She placed the child on the sofa, so that it was lying on its back, and carefully removed the diaper. It hadn't been soiled, but it was soaked with urine. "You're a boy," she said, glancing down at the tiny penis between his legs. Robin breathed a sigh of relief. Not because the child was a boy, but because he was alive and well. She had done the right thing.

Eric sat on the edge of the bed, tapping his feet against the carpet beneath them. The anxiety he felt was fueled by fear, concern, and confusion. There were a million questions swimming around inside his head. Questions like, what were he and Robin going to do if the baby died? Hell! What were they going to do if it survived? They were damned either way it would seem. *Jesus!* He thought, *and what about the authorities? Whoever left the child on their doorstep, could just as easily return only the child wouldn't be as they had left it. Fuck!* He thought. The ramifications were playing out like a movie in his head. This was just too much.

He stood up and started pacing the room, but stopped almost immediately when he realized the baby's cries had stopped. He turned towards the door taking a couple of steps, but stopped when he saw the knob turning.

Robin eased the door open and entered the room. She flashed Eric a quick smile thinking it would put him at ease, but he just stood there; his eyes shifting from her to the child that she was holding in her arms.

"I take it he's fine," Eric asked. Robin nodded her head.

"What makes you so sure that it's a boy?" she asked.

Eric shrugged his shoulders. "I just assumed," he said.

"He's fine," she answered, glancing down at the child.

Eric raised his brow. "A boy huh?"

"Yep," Robin answered, walking towards him with the child cradled in her arms.

"I have to be honest, Eric. I was operating on sheer hope out there praying that he would survive. I didn't once think until it was too late, that he was probably too small to be put through what I put him through tonight."

"Well the important thing is that he pulled through. What's going on with his eyes?"

"I don't believe anything is wrong with them," Robin answered. "They may or may not remain the color they are."

Eric studied the child. *This was insane,* he thought, but he had to admit the outcome was a relief.

"He's beautiful, don't you think?" Robin asked.

Eric leaned in to get a closer look. "I suppose," he answered. "Though if I had to argue in his defense. I would probably go with handsome. He is a boy, you know."

"Well I'll have you know, that there is nothing wrong with referring to the male gender as beautiful," Robin argued.

"Okay, whatever, but what exactly are we doing? I mean, what if someone comes looking for him? Even worst, what if we suddenly find ourselves having to wiggle out of questions about the child in one of those interrogation rooms down at the police station? What then?"

Robin walked over and sat on the edge of the bed, holding the child. Up until now she hadn't the opportunity to think that far ahead.

"I'm sorry, Eric. I mean everything happened so fast. I wasn't thinking past trying to save his life, but I am convinced that I did the right thing." He took a seat next to Robin on the bed.

"I am beyond freaked out right now, Robin, but can you blame me?"

"No, but there's no turning back now, she answered. We'll be fine, Eric," she tried to assure him.

"How can you be so sure?" he asked.

Robin shrugged her shoulders. "Just a feeling I have," she answered. "I can't explain it. The mere fact that this baby is alive gives meaning to everything that has happened tonight, don't you think?"

They looked at one another for the longest time before turning their attention on the child.

"Are you sure he's okay?" Eric asked.

"I'm sure enough," Robin answered. "The only thing that matters to me right now is that I was able to snatch him from death's hands. He's alive and well."

"Well let's put aside for the moment, that I am completely freaked out by all of this, and that there is a good chance that we will become fugitives from the law. The truth of the matter is, you did what any person would have done that has half the heart, and that is just one reason among many why I love you so much, Robin." Eric leaned back on the bed. *This is not the way he envisioned becoming a parent*, he thought.

"Okay, what now?" Eric asked.

"Well I have to consider how I am going to care for him, how to feed him. As far as the sun, I'm going to assume that the same rules apply. Beyond that, he will need what every child needs, and that is love."

"Well there has to be more to it than that Robin, what about....."

"Oh my God Eric, I have completely forgotten about my sisters, and the impact that this will have on them. What if what I have done is met with anger instead of understanding?"

"Well I would think that they would all be excited, Robin. I mean this is about as monumental as it gets, wouldn't you agree?"

"I suppose you're right," Robin nodded. "It is rather monumental, any way you look at it. This child goes against everything, and I do mean everything known to vampirism. He is the first male of our kind, and to think that I had something to do with it."

Eric smiled at her. "You really should call, Raven," he suggested.

"Not tonight, Eric. As monumental as this may be, sharing it can wait until tomorrow. Let's just get ready for bed. It's been a crazy night."

"Okay." Eric shook his head. What name do you suppose she gave him?" Eric asked.

"You mean his mother?" Robin answered. "Oh I don't know, but it hardly matters now, does it?"

"We're going to have to give him a new name to go with his new life," she said, "but I would like to put some thought into it, which is why that can also wait until tomorrow."

"Well in light of what the child represents, one name does come to mind," Eric said. Robin turned towards Eric. She was actually surprised that he wanted to remain on the subject.

"I'm listening," she said.

"Well how about Adam? I mean from a biblical stand point Adam was the first of his kind, I don't think it gets any meaningful than that."

Robin smiled as she nodded her head in agreement. "Adam sounds perfect."

CHAPTER FOUR

It was somewhere around 10.00 am when Eric left the house to shop for the list of items that Robin needed for Adam. He and Robin should have realized before turning in to bed this morning that Adam would have a different set of needs then their own. It wasn't like Robin had the means to breast feed. Plainly put, a hungry baby is an unhappy baby. What they needed was a means to feed Adam, ergo the most important item on the list, a baby bottle. For the moment Adam was okay. Robin had had to improvise by transferring blood from her mouth to his in order to satisfy his thrust. It took longer, but with a little patience she was able to pull it off, taking a page right out of bird feeding 101.

Besides baby bottles, the list included a couple of those toy rattles that babies are supposed to be so fond of. Some clothes, using his best judgment in regards to size and fashion, and a pack of diapers just to be on the safe side. She didn't think that Adam would need them, because vampires didn't produce bile, but who's to say that Adam's system would behave like her own, after all, he was different in just about every way.

After some much needed assistance from the store's customer service attendants, Eric returned home with the good's in hand and a splitting head ache to boot. He took two Tylenol gel caps, a shower, and then listened to Robin praise him on the awesome job that he had done in picking out Adam's clothes. Topping it off with how much she appreciated him. It was 4:12 in the afternoon now and far too late for either of them to head back to bed. Besides, Adam was up now, after having only taken a 3 hour nap.

"Can you hold him a minute?" Robin asked. "I feel like I need to feed again."

"We have to get him on a schedule," Eric said, his words slurring as he yawned.

"I know," Robin agreed. She stood up and carefully handed Adam to Eric. She lingered there a bit making sure that they were both comfortable with one another.

"Are you going to be okay with him for a few minutes?" she asked. Eric held Adam with one hand supporting his butt, and the other supporting his back.

"I think I can manage," he answered, producing a counterfeit grin. "You may as well get your shower out of the way while you're at it."

"Are you sure, Eric?"

"Yes, now go," he told her.

"Okay, I'm going," she said. Eric watched her disappear from the room. When he glanced down at Adam, a pair of violet colored eyes stared back at him.

"Why not brown, blue, or black. Hell hazel would have sufficed, but to make things a bit more complicated for all of us you had to go and choose the color violet." Adam just stared up at him.

"Hey wouldn't it be something if your actual name is Adam. Stranger things have been known to happen let me tell you." As he stared down at Adam's tiny face, it suddenly occurred to him that this was his first time holding a baby ever.

"How do you like your new digs?" Eric asked him. Adam turned away from him and stared off in another direction as if suddenly uninterested in what he had to say, but when he turned back around to look at Eric he wore a wide smile on his face. Eric couldn't help but grin. Robin had somehow done the impossible, but the impossible was also unexpected and downright complicated to say the least. Common sense now dictated that they consider selling their house. After all there was no possible way that they could continue living here with Adam. It's not like they can give him back if a parent, or the authorities come knocking; hey here's your baby, he's a little different, but other than that he's fine.

Eric immediately thought of Robin's sisters. It made perfect sense to him that they take Adam in, at least for the time being. Another night here wondering about a knock at the door was probably going to prove stressful. He and Robin needed to take a moment and catch up to reality.

Robin stepped out of the shower and reached for a towel. It was a natural feeling for a vampire to have a paternal connection of a sort to whomever they made, but this was different. It went deeper than the relationship that she and Raven had, even though theirs was an extremely close one. Perhaps it had a lot to do with Adam requiring a lot more nurturing, that and he's only a child. Simple instructions were just not going to do.

What causes a mother to abandon her child so readily in the first place, Robin wondered. She thought about it as she dried herself off. There was only one reason that she could ever abandon her own child; those reasons would have to prove life threatening for the very thing that she was sworn to protect. Adam's existence changes everything. She and Eric were going to have a lot to talk about. Adams arrival had changed whatever future they may have thought they had before tonight. Robin wrapped the towel just above her breast and then turned towards the bathroom mirror to stare at her reflection.

"I am a mother now," she said. "It falls on me to make sure that Adam remains safe, and that he is well taken care of." Robin turned from the mirror and exited the bathroom anxious to return to his side.

After slipping into a pair of sweatpants and T-shirt, Robin headed towards the living room to see how Eric was faring. When she walked into the room it was apparent that he had done just fine with Adam, in her absence. Adam lay fast asleep in Eric's arms.

"Sorry I took so long," she said, "but I see you have everything under control."

"We hardly noticed that you were gone," Eric remarked.

"Ha Ha very funny," Robin responded. She walked around and took a seat next to him on the couch. "I guess we have a lot to talk about don't we?" Robin asked.

Eric shook his head. "Yeah we do," he said, passing Adam to Robin, "but first I need a cup of coffee before we begin." He rose to his feet.

Fifteen minutes later. Eric and Robin were sitting comfortably on the sofa. Robin had placed Adam in their bed so that she and he could talk without distraction. "I think it's probably safe to say that we'll be experiencing daytime sleep interruption on a regular basis," Eric said.

"I think you're right," Robin agreed. "For the most part he displays the wants and needs of an ordinary child."

"Minus the diet," Eric said.

"Yeah, minus the diet," Robin grinned.

"So where should we begin?" he asked.

"I vote we start by talking about the biggest problem we have," Robin said.

"And what would you say our biggest problem is?" Eric asked.

"Well we have to take into consideration, that whoever left Adam on our porch may return."

"Those were my thoughts exactly," Eric said. "I wish we could rule it out but we can't. Staying here another night could be risky you know. Should we opt for a hotel?"

"I really don't want to do a hotel tonight, Eric. Can we stretch another night?"

"I don't know, Robin."

"Then how about this," Robin said. "Let's discuss everything in great length tonight, and on tomorrow we can drive out and introduce him to Raven and the others."

Eric contemplated Robin's suggestion. Leaning forward, his elbows on his knees he said, "I'm going to have to stay behind."

"But, Eric!" Robin began to protest.

"No listen," he said. "Ultimately we are going to have to give up our home. So while you're gone, I'm going to be working on that. I'll stay here for a week or two, three at the most. That will also give us some idea whether or not someone is looking for Adam."

Robin was silent. "Do you hate me?" she asked.

Eric placed his arm around her neck. "I don't think that's possible Robin. Your heart is forever in the right place."

"I love you, you know that? You have always supported whatever decisions that I have made," she said.

Eric leaned in and kissed the corner of her mouth. "You're welcome," he told her.

Eric and Robin talked for hours on end going over the specifics. They covered everything from what they would say if someone came knocking on the door to the price tag they wanted to place on the house. Robin was going to call Frank, and tell him that she had broken her leg and wouldn't be coming back to work for a while. It was the best that she could come up with on such short notice. He would only take tomorrow off, at least for the time being. They also agreed that it would be best if Robin left tomorrow night, and he would try his best to join her in a couple weeks. In the mean time, he was going to focus all his energy on selling the house. "Let's get the phone calls out of the way," he said.

"We may as well," she agreed. As they were about to follow through with the phone calls, they heard Adam's cry from the bedroom.

"I got it," she said, quickly making her way towards the bedroom. Eric leaned back and rested his head against the coach. He thought about sleep. He could feel it there just behind his eyes. He placed his fingers over his temples and began rubbing.

"Tired," Robin asked entering the room with Adam in one hand and a blanket in the other.

"Yeah, I'm just about ready to pass out," he answered. Robin stopped in the center of the living room and spread the blanket out on the floor. When she was done she laid Adam in the center of the pallet on his back.

"Here, let me help," Robin said, walking over to stand between his legs. She placed her fingers against his temples and messaged them in a circular motion.

"How does that feel?" she asked. Eyes closed and near sleep he answered, "Like the right kind of medicine."

"You look like you could use a nap," she said. "Can I make a suggestion?"

"Sure," he said.

"How about I grab another blanket and a couple of pillows from the bedroom and we camp out here in the living room. That way you can grab a nap, and yet still be near me."

"You drive a hard bargain he said, but you have a deal."

"I'll be right back," she told him. Eric stood up and walked over to the living room window. He felt extremely unsettled, and would remain so until he and Robin sold the house and moved for good. He parted the blinds and stared out into the night searching for anything out of the ordinary.

"What is it?" Robin asked entering the room, dragging a blanket with two pillows tucked beneath her arms. "Is there something wrong?"

"No. I was just checking to see if a SWAT team was on our lawn," he said jokingly.

Robin let the blanket and two pillows fall to the floor, and then walked over to where he was standing. "I've been thinking." She wrapped her arms around his waist. "I feel certain that the only person we need worry about at the moment is the person who left Adam at our door, now having said that, given the condition that he was in I highly doubt that they will return. If for some reason we should get a knock at our door, we simply follow through with what we discussed."

"You're probably right," he said.

Robin pressed her head against his chest. "I pray that you will never hold any resentment towards me because of this," she told him.

"I'm one hundred percent positive that I won't," he assured her.

"Come on," she said, leading him away from the window. "Let's find something on TV." When they settled on something to watch, they cuddled up close to one another on the floor with Adam in between them. It was miles away from the comfort of their own bed, but then a solid days sleep was still hours away. Eric was in need of a nap, so Robin suspected that he would be asleep within the next few minutes.

"Are you comfortable enough?" she asked.

"This will do just fine," he answered, adjusting his head on the pillow. Robin leaned over Adam and kissed him on the cheek. "Don't let me sleep too long," he said.

The hours leading up to the following night were summed up in just one word, restless. The broken sleep patterns were something that they were each going to have to get use to now that they had a new family member to look after. The drive to LaVerne would take Robin 3 and a half to 4 hours depending on traffic. If she fed Adam before she left, she shouldn't have to stop for anything. Robin was taking about a third of the clothes she owned, along with those things that a girl just couldn't leave home without.

When he was finally done loading the car, it held the weight of two large suitcases and a duffle bag. The loose clothing was on hangers that lay across the driver's side back seat. Probably the most challenging point in the evening came when they both realized that Adam would need a child's safety seat in order to travel. This meant a trip to the store to purchase in Robin's words, the safest child seat they had in stock while she tended to Adam and packed.

"Do you have everything you need?" he asked as he strapped Adam into the car safety seat.

"I should hope so," Robin answered. "My side of the closet is nearly bare, and I could say the same for my drawers. As for Adam, he doesn't have much. The next time you see him his wardrobe will have flourished."

"Okay then. I guess you're ready to take off," he said. They hugged one another, and as it is when two people who love one another are about to part, their kisses were long and lingering. They separated, each regretting what the next few moments would mean. The beginning of what would be the longest time that they will have ever been apart.

"Call me as soon as you get there," he said.

"I will," Robin answered, sliding behind the wheel of the car. Eric shut the door behind her and then leaned in for one last kiss. Robin obliged, and then proceeded to fasten her seat belt.

"Call me as soon as you get there," he pressed.

"I will I promise," she assured him.

"Drive safely, and you," he said to Adam. "Go easy on your mom." It was probably more the sound of Eric's voice than anything else that got Adam's attention, but had it regardless of whether or not he understood. Robin reached up and pressed the garage door remote that was attached to her overhead visor, and then started the engine to her car.

When the sound of the garage's winding motor finally stopped, Eric stepped out into the night to survey the neighborhood. As he did so, he was hard pressed to settle the butterflies that were fluttering around inside his stomach. He turned around to see Robin backing the car out of the garage and waving a kiss to him goodbye. He raised his hand to wave back to her, but was startled when his attention was drawn away by the sound of someone closing and opening the door to the house next to him.

If the people around here learned that a vampire has been living among them for months, it was hard to say what they might do. Robin and Adam would most likely end up lab experiments, no matter how liberated the world had become.

It wasn't until Robin had completely disappeared from sight that he turned to walk back into the garage. *What a crazy couple of days and nights this has been,* he thought, flicking the switch on the wall to lower the garage door. In the days and weeks to come, he envisioned that things would get even crazier, as this was only the beginning of things to come.

CHAPTER FIVE

Robin found herself periodically glancing over at Adam. Because this was his first road trip, she couldn't help but be overly concerned. She was amazed that he was still awake though given the soft music on the radio, and the motion of the car.

"I see traveling is your thing," she said, smiling at him. He yawned in response. "Now that is a sure sign that you won't be with me much longer," she told him. "In fact, I give you five minutes at the most." Adam stared up at her, his eyelids getting heavier by the second. Robin shifted her focus back to the road for what must have been five seconds.

When she lowered her eyes to check on him again, he had already surrendered to the world of dreams. It was of some relief to her, that he slept in a way that she perceived to be normal for a child of his age. Likewise it worried her that his immortality would never allow him a normal growth. It was a concern that she had neglected to share with Eric, but one that he would be sure to acknowledge given further thought about Adam and the way vampires age. She could hear him now. "Hey Robin I take it back, you really fucked up this time. Your good intentions mean shit."

The only thing that is for certain is that Adam is the first of his kind, and being the first of his kind means that every answer to every question lie's within his makeup. In other words the answers will only come in time. She was dreading the two to three weeks that she would be without Eric. Even a day was sure to feel like a life time without him, and what about the importance of bonding between him and Adam. *Oh stop obsessing,* she told herself. And then there were her sisters. How were they going to react to this big surprise in a little package? She had a sense that not everyone will be happy about Adam; one person in particular Ambrosha. She was the epitome of negativity, hating every-thing and anything that didn't coincide with her own agenda. *Don't stress over Ambrosha,* she warned herself, *because Raven's word, Raven's opinion, and Raven's decision is the only thing that will matter in the end.* Still she was hoping that most, it not all of her sisters would see Adam as a godsend. After all, he is the first male vampire that this world has ever known. Not from the lack of trying, vampires have long since made the effort to mother children, only to discover that the vampire's repro-ductive system is either rendered useless as a result of the change, or the sperm of the human male lacks the potency and compatibility nec-essary to father children to vampire's.

What followed were the detestable and selfish desires of vam-pires in their attempts to change children; each attempt resulting in meaningless and painful deaths. It made her wonder. How had she succeeded where others had failed? Was she the key to Adam's success-ful transformation? Or was Adam? And then there was the question concerning his eyes. *Why violet? What is it about him that gives reason for such an unusual color? Stay tuned for the answer to a question unknown,* she thought.

She had a half hour or so before she arrived at the mansion. She had to constantly remind herself that her actions involving Adam were warranted, but like a coin that has two faces she couldn't help but pay homage to both sides. It was one thing to show up with a couple of suit cases along with plans to parlay for a couple of weeks, but it could prove boarder line catastrophe to show up with a vampire male baby created from her blood. Suddenly, she was happier than she had ever been for the covenant's separation into the two houses, because it meant that it was highly unlikely that she would have to endure Ambrosha's presence tonight.

As soon as she received news though, the witch would surely come running. Robin knew that come tomorrow, it would be in her best interest to develop some thicker skin. She took a deep breath, and then released the air from her lungs. *Maybe I'm overreacting,* she tried to convince herself, but deep down inside she had a feeling that some of her fears were warranted.

Robin turned her car onto the long stretch of road which led up to the mansion. She pulled alongside the mansions intercommunications system and came to a complete stop. A few feet in front of the car were two ten foot tall double-hinged iron gates that were capable of stopping the oncoming force of the average midsize car. Security perimeters were necessary because they were vampires, not the other way around. Robin lowered the driver's side window and then reached over the door seal to press the intercom button. She stared into a camera lens waiting for someone's voice to come over. At last someone spoke.

"Hello stranger." Robin recognized the voice immediately. It was Guiliana. The greeting triggered emotions that were welcomed.

"This stranger has come home," Robin said.

"Well in that case you may enter," says the voice behind the curtain.

Robin heard the motorized sound of the gates electrical system, followed by the sound of a click, and the gate began to open. She shifted the car into gear and drove through. The motorized sound started up again and the gates began closing behind her. She looked over at Adam who was now wide awake, and smiled at him.

"Well we're here," she said to him. Adam stared at her for a few seconds, and then turned his attention beyond the passenger side window to stare out into the darkness. She suddenly had a thought. *Adam is without doubt a vampire, albeit an extremely young vampire.* But the color of his eyes suddenly made her wonder about his sight, would it be the same, or greater than her own? If so, then the images that he was seeing now were as clear as a grey glooming day. That was our gift; a day without sunshine. "Are you ready to meet the family, little guy?" Whether he heard her or not it didn't matter, for the world outside his window still held his attention. "I don't want you to take this the wrong way," she said to him, "but the women that you are about to meet won't see you coming, so I can't begin to tell you what to expect." She smiled at him.

The road to the mansion stretched a little less than a quarter mile from the entrance gate. As she neared her home away from home, she was suddenly reminded of the secure feeling that she had always felt within its walls, and how it was up to her to provide that same feeling for Adam. Robin steered the car to the right of the large circular drive way, and then drove around until she was directly in front of the house. In the center of the circle was a gigantic fountain with outer trimmings of sea shells and other marine creatures, but there was nothing more alluring about the fountain than the magnificent statue of the mermaid towering some sixteen feet out of the water.

The grounds were always well kept. Finding a landscaping crew to keep the grounds was never all that complicated. Back when she lived here two pickup trucks loaded with equipment would entered the gates during the day and provide a fabulous service on the grounds twice a month. In return, the company always received their payments on time.

The mansion's architectural structure was crafted in a contemporary L-shape design, with the vehicle garage extending like an arm to its right. The garage was designed to house six vehicles, and unless something had changed, there were still two cars, two SUVs, and a couple of motorcycles. Nobody laid claim to the vehicles behind those doors. The covenant didn't operate like that. When it came to the vehicles, the girls acted on practicality and mood.

Robin killed the ignition to the car, and then breathed in deeply. Exhaling, she looked over at Adam before opening the driver side door to step outside of the car. She glanced over her shoulder just in time to see Guiliana and Thandie exiting the house.

"It's been too long, sister." Robin recognized Thandie's silk voice.

"My sentiments exactly," Guiliana added. "And where may I ask is your other half?" Her question was in reference to Eric.

"He had to stay behind, long story."

"You guys aren't in a bad place are you?" Guiliana asked.

"No. That's not the reason I'm here," Robin answered." Robin saw that Thandie was going for the passenger side door. "Thandie, Robin held up a hand to stop her. Robin hurried around to the passenger side door. Thandie stared at her suspiciously.

"You're acting real strange," Thandie said, stepping further away from the car. Robin ignored her while she opened the passenger side door. She reached inside and unbuckled the straps to Adam's car seat. What happened next was exactly how she had pictured it in her mind, well almost. Robin removed Adam from the car seat and turned around to show the two women what the real fuss was about.

"What is that?" Thandie asked.

"Are you blind? It's a fucking baby," Guiliana blurted out.

"I know it's a fucking baby, Guiliana. Robin, what in the hell is going on? Why do you have a baby?"

"Like I said before, it's a long story, and of course I will explain everything shortly." Robin looked down at Adam who seemed to be doing okay at the moment. "Robin, have you bumped your head?" Thandie continued.

"She said she would explain," Guiliana said, nudging Thandie's arm.

"What's wrong with his eyes?" Thandie asked, moving in to get a closer look.

"Guys......I said I would explain."

"Where's your luggage?" Guiliana asked.

"I have the two suitcases in the trunk," Robin answered.

"I can't wait to see the expression on Raven's face," Thandie continued.

"Thandie, can you give it a rest. I'm already nervous enough as it is," said Robin.

"And you should be," Thandie responded. Robin handed Thandie the keys to her car so that they could remove the luggage from the trunk. The two women looked at one another and then back at Robin. "So how long are you staying?" Guiliana asked as she pressed the automatic release button for the trunk located on key ring.

"I'm not sure Robin answered. For awhile I guess."

"One thing's for sure little sister. You continue to surprise us," said Guiliana.

Robin entered the house leading the way with Thandie and Guiliana trailing behind. She held Adam in one arm and a duffle bag in the other. The two women set the suitcases down in the hallway where they would collect them later, and then followed Robin to where the rest of the women sat inside one of the larger rooms.

"Is everyone home tonight?" Robin asked.

"Yep, tonight's a full house. We must have been sub-consciously awaiting your arrival, Robin," said Thandie.

"Not much has changed since you left, Robin," said Guiliana. "We lounge around, we party, God, where would we be if we couldn't party."

Thandie cleared her throat. "Things are about to get interesting, and in a big way."

"Thandie, you're acting as if I had a bomb in my hands," Robin said, shaking her head.

"Sorry, I'm just curious to know what you plan on doing with it is all," Thandie blurted back. Robin ignored her and continued to walk ahead. Thandie could be very blunt and straight forward at times, but she was use to it. Adam however, was a sensitive subject.

Of all the rooms in the house, excluding the bedrooms, the great room was the most frequently used. It was the room where everyone gathered when they weren't hanging out in night clubs, or indulging in sexual hit and runs with unsuspecting men or women. Robin push the door to the great room open and was quickly greeted by the closest family that she has know for the last seventy plus years. "Welcome home, Robin," followed the sound of greeting cheers. Six women rose to their feet to greet their young vampire sibling, but as each one of them drew closer, their facial expressions changed, and a joyous and glad moment was quickly replaced by surprise and uncertainty.

"Is that a baby?" the question echoed throughout the room. Robin stood nervous while her sisters gathered around her. It was apparent by the look on their faces, that they had a million questions that they wanted to ask.

"Look, its eyes," some of the women whispered. Robin's eyes traveled beyond those who had been quick to greet her to where Raven sat in the soft white leather chair. It was difficult to read the expression on her face. It was neither hostile, nor joyous, but rather curious like the women who were gathered around her. She eased past the six women, and with child in hand she walked forward until at last, she was standing before her immortal mother.

"Hello Raven," Robin said uneasily. Raven leaned forward to get a better look at the baby that Robin was holding like an over protective mother in her arms. She could definitely see what all the fuss was about. The baby's eyes were like no color that she had ever seen, and she had to admit, she was anxious to hear the story behind them.

"Hello Robin."

"I realize I have a lot of explaining to do," Robin began.

Raven stopped her, and motioned for her step forward. "You'll have plenty of time for that," Raven said. "For now it's just good to have you back home."

"It's good to be back," Robin said.

Raven raised an eyebrow. "Where is Eric?" she asked.

"He stayed behind," she answered. "You will all understand why once I have explained." Robin noticed that all the women were gathering around her again, and they seemed even more fascinated with Adam then they were before. They were taking his presence well, but there were seven other women who still didn't know of Adam, Ambrosha being one of them. The fact that she will be the last to know will only fuel her natural state of being; *that being the bitch I know her to be.*

When the excitement had withered down a bit, and everyone was settled into their seats, Robin began her story at the point where she had first noticed the smell of Adam's blood, and how it had guided her and Eric to their front door. Robin's voice rode on the silence that shrouded the room as she spoke of what had happened from beginning to end. When she was finally finished, the silence was replaced by chatter and whispers. "It's not possible," Natalia voiced. Silence covered the room once again. Natalia had merely spoken the words that everyone else was thinking.

With some reluctance, Robin spoke out. "I'm going to pass him around to each of you. You can then judge for yourselves whether or not I speak the truth." Since Leona was sitting closest to her, she began with handing Adam to her. Leona held Adam at arm's length at first.

His weight was practically nonexistent in her small, but powerful hands. Adam stared up at her for a few seconds and then turned his tiny head to his left where Robin sat. Leona brought Adam in closer so that his face was pressed against her own. "His scent is slightly different than our own," she remarked. "Diluted might be a better word, but perhaps it is a normal scent for a vampire male child. Who can be certain if there has never been one in existence?"

Leona passed Adam to Gelsa who hesitantly reached for him as though he were a soggy diaper. She examined Adam briefly and then handed him off to Natalia, whom apparently was excited to be holding him in her arms. "He's adorable," Natalia said, resting Adam on her knees so that he was lying face up. "His eyes are astonishing; absolutely astonishing. I have to agree with Leona though. His scent is off somewhat." Natalia kissed both of Adam's cheeks and then handed him off to Savana. Raven was the last to examine Adam, and like the rest of the women, she too was in agreement that Adam had a scent that was all his own.

"Raven, you've been on this earth longer than any of us," remarked Guiliana. "Have you ever come across a vampire with eyes remotely close in color?"

Raven's silence accompanied by the tapping sounds that her fingers made on both arms of the chair was a sure indication that her mind was searching through the vast expanse of her existence, for an answer to the question. "No," she said finally. "I have never heard, nor witnessed such a thing. A vampire's eyes; no matter their color before the change, has always resulted in the color black. I would imagine that most, if not all of our questions regarding this child, will be answered in due time."

"He is different," Robin said, "but there is no denying that he is a vampire. I just want him to be safe." She rose from her seat and walked over to where Raven was seated. "He is of my blood."

"You needn't feel like his safety is your burden alone," Raven said. "There is no greater sanctuary for him than under this roof." Raven handed Adam to Robin, and then watched her as she returned to take a seat. It wasn't so long ago; that night when she had found Robin bleeding to death in an alley. She knew then that there was something special about her, and not once has Robin proved her wrong. Robin would give her life for this child; that was apparently obvious. She is further proof that the vampire possesses not only a beating heart, but a heart that is capable of extreme compassion. "It's time for his feeding," Robin said.

"Well there is no shortage of food here," said Natalia." Does he prefer a certain type? We have them all."

"I remember," Robin said, "but to answer your question, he has been on 0 positive since his change."

"Well I wouldn't change it now," Thandie said. "Not unless you want a finicky baby on your hands."

Robin rose from the seat on the couch. "Let me get him fed and settled so that we can talk more. I realize that my actions may still be in question, but I just couldn't stand by and watch him die."

"Have you forgotten?" Raven smiled. "We have all been where you are now."

"Not quite," Guiliana said. "What Robin has managed to accomplish, goes against everything that we know, and have known since the making of our kind."

"I was speaking on the compassion that each of us has felt at one time or another for a human," Raven said.

"I haven't forgotten, Raven. I wouldn't be alive today if not for the like compassion that you showed me so many years ago."

"Well it goes without saying that Adam is the most important development that has happened in the history of vampires," said Raven. "Evolution, if that's what we choose to call it, has new plans for us."

"Well I'm psyched," said Gelsa. The presence of male vampires might be a nice change."

"Maybe," Raven said, "for all we know Adam could be the first and the last."

"Well that would suck," said Savana.

"You guys are getting way ahead of yourselves, aren't you?" Robin was responding to their premature apprehensions. "Will someone hold him? It will just be for a few moments while I prepare his bottle."

Everyone's eyes rested on Thandie. "Why is everyone staring at me?" Thandie barked.

"Give him to me," Raven said. "I really don't see what all the fuss is about." Robin handed Adam to Raven. She was relieved when he didn't put up a fuss, because she knew that he was hungry. Too many hours had passed since his last feeding.

"I'll be back before you know it," Robin assured her. Robin exited the room with a feeling of reprieve. It felt settling to have finally gotten the whole manner concerning Adam out of the way, at least with those who mattered.

She would still have to deal with Ambrosha; probably as early as tomorrow. Robin's ears picked up on sound that she had become all too familiar with. It was Adam's cry. He was making it known that he was ready to eat, and he was ready to eat now. Leona and Gelsa entered the kitchen. "You might want to speed it up," Gelsa said. "Raven is starting to look a bit uncomfortable with Adam."

Thanks in part to the strange sounds and faces that Raven was making, Adam's crying was reduced to a frustrated whimper. In the mean time, Robin was working as fast as she could in the kitchen to prepare his food.

"So Robin," Gelsa leaned across the kitchen island with her fingers crossed. "What does Eric think about all this?"

"Yeah Robin, Leona teased. How does Eric feel about you all's new addition to the family?" Robin knew Leona and Gelsa well enough to know that they weren't going to let up until she answered their questions.

"If you must know, he's okay considering," Robin answered.

"When you say considering." Gelsa scratched her head. "Are you saying considering that he's human? Or because he now has a son, who by the way is a vampire like his girlfriend?" Robin stopped what she was doing and stared off into space. "He's actually scared shitless," she laughed. Leona and Gelsa laughed along with her.

"It's heavy when you really think about it," Gelsa said.

"Heavy isn't the word," Robin added.

"It doesn't matter much now," Leona said. "Adam is a vampire, and that officially makes him a part of our family."

"Ha, we're officially aunties," Gelsa laughed.

"Is that your official way of letting me know that you're okay with what I've done?" Robin asked.

"Yes darling. Now if I were you, I would get my ass moving. Raven probably needs you right about now.

When Robin returned to the great room, Adam was in full swing. Raven no longer had him. At present, he was being passed along to Savana. Robin glanced around the room. Her sisters were obviously in the throes of panic. Robin rushed over to Savana. "Let me take him," she said. "He won't be satisfied until he has this." She held up the bottle. Savana handed Adam over.

"How often does he need to feed?" Savana asked.

"No more than three times a night," Robin answered. "I've become accustomed to his times, but either way he will let you know."

"Oh my God," Gelsa screamed. "I just thought of something. Is he going to be a baby for the rest of his life?" The whole room went silent.

Robin would have liked to have been able to answer her question but she couldn't. Her eyes wandered around the room. "It's possible," Robin said." I mean it's something that we have to consider."

"That would absolutely suck," Thandie pouted. "Sorry Robin, I'm just saying."

"Don't apologize, Thandie," Robin said. "I mean I hope that's not the case."

"Wait a minute," Savana interrupted. "We can all see that Adam is different. What's to say that he won't age like a normal?" Savana stopped herself and shook her head. "No, that wouldn't make sense."

"We have to assume that because he is a vampire, that he has inherited a vampire's gifts as well," Raven argued. "One of which includes the gift of immortality, and we all know what that means." A cloud of silence hovered above the room, and within it, were everyone's thoughts. Robin was probably going to have to accept the fact, that Adam might very well be a child forever. The thought saddened her.

She watched him while he sucked blood from the tiny hole in the bottles nipple. There was that question again at the forefront of her mind. Was saving Adams life a mistake? Had she doomed him to an existence as a child? Her emotions teetered somewhere between what she perceived as morally right, and the decision he might have chose for himself if he had a choice in the matter. "I would like to speak with Robin alone please," Raven said.

"Aww man," Thandie blurted out, like a kid who had just been told to go to bed early on a Saturday night. One by one the women stood up and exited the room, leaving Robin and Raven to further discussion. When the room was finally clear, Raven spoke.

"Robin," Raven began. "Are you prepared to assume the responsibility for Adam, if a child is all that he will ever be?" Robin lowered her head. Mistakenly, it appeared as if she were staring at the white rug beneath her feet, while in truth, Raven's question stood at the center of her mind's eye.

Robin raised her head. "I have to be honest with you Raven. I have questioned a number of times the decision that I made to save Adam, but each time that I have, my doubt is quickly erased. Even if I had had time enough to weigh the pros and cons in all of this, I genuinely believe that the outcome would still be the same."

Raven smiled, and nodded her head. "Robin, your choice was a righteous one. Some might disagree arguing a moral issue, but then how could they possibly understand. We vampires possess a measure of power capable of saving a person's life absent the use of hospital operating rooms, and surgeons. Granted, the chances of a person surviving our mean for prolonging life are next to none, when we do succeed, that person's life is extended a thousand lifetimes; no surgeon can offer that."

"I realize that my responsibility is great," Robin said, "but I feel that I am more than ready to take it on."

"I can see that you are," Raven said. "I was responsible for you after your change, and in many ways I am responsible for you now." Raven placed a hand on Robin's shoulder. "Now that was supposed to be the heavy, and now for the light. I want you to know that you are not in this alone, Raven said. Your sisters and I will always have your back." Robin squeezed Raven's hand.

"Thank you," she said. "I realize that this is not going to be easy, and given the question concerning Adam's fate. Will he, or won't he reach maturity? I worry about Eric and how he will react."

"Your relationship with Eric is about to be tested no doubt, but if he's the man that I believe him to be, he won't leave your side, not even for something as challenging as this," Raven said.

"I hope you're right Raven, I mean, I believe that he is that man, perhaps it is only natural to doubt."

"Just know that no matter what happens, you are not without support. Your sisters and I are here for you."

"To be honest, you guys were the least of my concerns, Ambrosha on the other hand, well you never know with her."

Raven sighed.

"Leave Ambrosha to me," Raven said. "Unfortunately, she is allowed her personal feelings on the matter. She is obnoxiously rough around the edges, and it is sad that she will probably never change."

"I will try to remember, that should she stay true to her character," Robin said.

"Good," said Raven. "I tell you, life is full of surprises don't you think?"

"How do you mean?" Robin asked.

"I mean Adam of course. Each one of us just itching to know the how concerning it all? I mean haven't we been asking ourselves that question since the beginning of time? The question how, when it comes to those things that we have yet to understand? I can't hardly wait, and I suppose I speak for us all, when Adam's how is finally revealed."

"Indeed," Robin agreed. She pulled the bottle from Adam's mouth. "I look at him and think, he has to be special to have survived the change," Robin said. "I can't help but feel that he is important somehow to all of us.

"Robin, you are the youngest of all, the baby so to speak, and quite special as far as I'm concerned. So don't for a single second worry yourself about Adam's safety or his lively hood. I think I speak for everyone when I say that you have our total support."

"Thank you Raven, thank you so much."

"I think it would be a good idea if you called Eric now. He's probably wondering about how things are going."

"Yeah, you're right. I'm kind of nervous about that."

"I don't think you give him enough credit, Robin. You saw something in him from the start that enabled you to trust him with not just your secret, but the secret we all hold. I think he has proved himself thus far. Fate couldn't have chosen a better pair to take care of that child."

"I really hope you're right." Robin closed her eyes and held Adam's face close to her own. "You will always know love," she whispered in his ear.

"I think I can handle him now that he's been fed. Go and make your phone call to Eric." Robin handed Adam over to Raven.

"I promise I won't be too long," she said.

"No, take your time. I'll be fine with him."

CHAPTER SIX

Eric barely took notice of the car chase rolling across the television scene, or the wailing sirens of the black and whites that were in hot pursuit of the mustang. Even though he had seen the movie a countless number of times, he could never quite get use to Angelina Jolie's sexy role as a grease monkey and a car thief, or Eleanor and Nicolas Cage ripping through the streets of LA. Tonight however, the television only served to produce a good background noise, because his mind was currently dealing with so many other things.

He checked the time on his wristwatch. The night had moved well into the early morning. How many times had he looked at the damn thing in the last hour? He sighed and then leaned back on the sofa. Robin had left a little over five hours ago with a child that she had managed to save against all odds. Although saved was probably a term that was somewhere in the grey area in this case. *You're a hypocrite, Eric,* he thought. *Hadn't Robin suffered a similar fate? How is Adam being alive today any different than Robin? Like her, he has been given a second chance and it shouldn't matter the how or the why. Adam was abandoned like he was nothing more than a bag of trash that someone might leave on the side of a road. If I am capable of letting Robin into my heart, I am equally capable of letting Adam into my heart. What matters the most now, is my ability to show compassion where my compassion is needed.*

Have some perspective, he told himself. *You and Robin are physically incapable of having children of your own, so how about you look at fate as a godsend instead of If I am capable of loving Robin without prejudice, then I'm a motherfucker. I now have the complete makings of family.* The more he thought about it, the more he realized that everything was going to be fine. He and Robin had more than enough love to offer a child. *A baby! Shit!* He thought. He was finding it difficult to imagine, what a human male, a vampire female, and a vampire child might do on family outings during the peak hours of the night. He said the word son out loud a few times, just to get a feel for the words as they rolled off the tongue of his mouth. *The word sounded natural enough, even coming from me,* he thought.

He let out a deep yawn, and then stood up to stretched out his arms and legs. *I could sure go for another one these,* he thought, grabbing the empty beer bottle from the table and then making his way towards the kitchen. If he remembered correctly, there were only two bottles left in the refrigerator. While he was reaching for the door handle his cell phone began ringing. *About time,* he thought, realizing that it could only be Robin. He made an about face and then quickly covered the distance between himself and the phone that was lying on the living room table.

"Hello," he answered, taking a seat on the sofa.

"It's me, Robin said. How are you holding up?"

"Okay for the most part. I'm missing you to be perfectly honest."

"I miss you too," she said.

"So give me the scoop. How are things going there?" Eric asked.

"I guess a lot like I expected. There was of course the initial surprise followed by total disbelief, and then the questions that I couldn't answer."

"I kind of wished that I could have been there to see the look on their faces," he said. "I take it Ambrosha is still unaware?"

"How did you guess? Raven assured me that she would not only see to that, but that I had no need to worry where Adam's safety was a concern."

"How is the little guy holding up?" he asked. Robin's heart nearly skipped a beat. Eric's concern for Adam will have to be a key element in their relationship now that Adam was a part of it.

"He's doing great actually", she answered. "The girls were a bit standoffish at first, but that was to be expected I guess. They just have to get use to the whole idea of having a baby around. They will warm up eventually."

"Good," he said. "I take it that not even Raven was able to shed light on how Adam was able to survive the change?"

"I'm afraid not," Robin answered. "Adam is altogether new, so all the questions that have arisen, are impossible to answer right now, even for someone who has lived as long as Raven." There was an uncomfortable moment of silence on both ends of the phone.

"Eric," she said.

"I'm here," he answered.

"Is this too much for you? I mean. Are you overwhelmed?" she asked. Robin felt the silence on his end while he searched his heart for an answer.

"I won't lie to you, Robin. This has been a lot for me to digest, but the fact of the matter remains. I am just as in love with us, as I am with you. Adam has become a part of us, so Fate, or whatever we want to call it, has dropped this kid in our lives. I guess we should look on the bright side. I mean, would we seriously have considered bringing a child into our family? Granted adoption would have been our only option, but I doubt that we would have even considered that. I guess what I am trying to say is that I have begun to see this from a positive point of view." His words were potent source of relief.

"I wish you could see my smile," she told him. Robin wanted to bring up the matter concerning Adam's growth, but she didn't feel like it was the right time. Another day or two won't matter, she reasoned.

"I'm not particularly happy about having to end our phone call," she said, "but I left Adam with Raven. I probably need to get back to them," she said. "I promised her I wouldn't be long."

"Okay, but call me first thing tomorrow," he told her.

"I promise," she said. The phone line went dead, and he sat there tapping his cell phone against his knee. His original plan was to keep working for at least another week or two, but like losing an appetite, another week just didn't sound too appealing. He dialed the number to his job and placed the phone to his ear. The dispatcher picked up after the third ring.

"Concord Security Corporation, Sergeant Caldwell speaking."

"Caldwell, its Taylor. Can you transfer me to A-building please?"

"No problem. Took the night off, did yah?"

"Yeah, I had to. I'm calling in now to request a leave of absence. My department won't be thrilled about that."

"Well I hope everything works out."

"Thanks I appreciate that," There was a brief moment of silence, and then the phone was ringing again on the opposite end.

"Captain Conald speaking." Eric recognized the voice.

"Captain its Taylor."

"Give me a break. Taylor who? I've got three of you guys on payroll, two of you are off tonight, and one called in sick. Which one are you?"

"It's Eric Taylor, sir, the one out sick."

"What can I do for you, son?"

"The reason I'm calling, sir, is because I'm going to need more time off, a leave of absence to be exact."

"How long you been working here, Taylor?"

"Almost three years, sir."

"Well then you must know that your request is short notice?"

"I know, but my situation is unavoidable. I have a crisis that needs my immediate attention."

"Son, if you're sick then that's one thing, but unless someone has passed from this life to the next. I can't grant you a leave of absence on such short notice." He was prepared for this.

"I know that sir, and that's why I'm calling. My grandmother has been ill for a while now. I got a phone call not thirty minutes ago from my relatives telling me that she took a turn for the worst during the night. She passed away this morning."

"I'm sorry to hear that, son." Eric heard the faint sound of a radio playing in the background "I'll go ahead and pull your time card, and I'll make a note of our conversation. Administration will take care of the rest tomorrow. How much time are you requesting?"

"I shouldn't need more than a week I'm guessing," Eric said.

"Okay, I'm penciling in a week, and again I'm sorry for your loss."

"I appreciate that, sir, and thanks." Eric ended the phone call. It was a brutal lie, but it was one that he could afford tell on account that his grandmother was already in the ground. Still, if she were staring out through the windows of heaven right now, she would be less than pleased with his little white lie. Heaven was still a rather grey area for him; its existence and all. In fact, the only reason that he made reference of it at all, was because she believed, but perhaps it was time that he reevaluate his position on the subject, especially when something far more difficult to believe, had become the center most part of his life. If vampires were a solid reality; why not the belief in heaven and hell?

He stood up and walked back towards the kitchen. *I'll have that second beer to top off the night,* he thought. Opening the refrigerator, he removed one of the two bottles that remained of his preferred brand from the container, and twisted the cap off. It was imported and expensive, but well worth the price if you were a stickler for great tasting beer. He returned to the couch where he picked up the television remote. He began to flip through the channels in search for a movie or a program that would possibly take his mind off some of the things that were going on. He finally settled on ESPN.

After a few minutes of listening to sports updates, his mind began to drift somewhere else. This would be the first time that either of them had spent away from one another for more than 24 hours at a time since they met. He pulled his eyes away from the television screen to study the length of the couch. *It sits pretty comfortable,* he thought, *but how comfortable would it sleep?* He laid back and stretched his legs out so that he was horizontal. It wasn't enough to just lie there, so he turned on his side to further test its comfort. *It was an option,* he thought. His sleeping on it would depend on how he felt when it was finally time to go to bed.

CHAPTER SEVEN

Thirty-two miles, that was the distance between the two vampire households. Within the walls of the second, a strikingly beautiful figure moved along a dimly lit corridor. Sconces, mounted and evenly spaced aligned both walls, with lighted candles that protruded from each of them. The light that they provided was neither needed, nor necessary for her to see the detail paintings on both sides of the walls, and even the colors and the patterns which made up the carpets design, were as clear to her as the light of day.

Her name is Ambrosha, spelled slightly different than the godly food of Greek legend, but a myth she was not. Her years in existence were unmatched by all save for one, and it is for that reason only, she was subject to the rules and laws of another. She is not without power; its reach simply has its limits, dampened by the one person who rivals her in strength and years.

There was a time when she and Raven were as close as two sisters could possibly be, and though far from biological, they were still sisters by any claim. The blood they share is alien to about 99.96% of the rest of the population. If that doesn't qualify them as sisters then what does?

The unnatural virus, contaminate, whatever its true name, resides within the blood of only fourteen human beings in all, all females, all strong. It is not a friendly virus, although it is safe to say that it favors the female over the male in this godforsaken world, for there has never been a male who has ever survived; only further proof of mans weak willed mind. It is a favored gift, handed only to those who have been deemed worthy of its full glory. It bestows unimaginable power upon its host, but demands sacrifice in return.

Those sacrifices include secrecy, solid food, and declaring one of creations most magnificent wonders, enemy number one. Yes, that giant yellow ball that humanity has long since named the sun. Their existence as vampires has not gone unnoticed though. There have been, and always will be errors or mistakes to some degree, but they have learned to make fewer, and fewer over the centuries. It is because of past errors that the stories of vampires exist. There has always existed the importance for secrecy, but one thing that she could never agree with, was living untrue to her vampire nature. Without question, the vampire is a step above every organism on the face of the earth. We are super predators, creatures by design, and human blood is the only way that we can survive. There is nothing like feeding straight from the vein. Unfortunately, it is forbidden. Animal blood, there is something about that shit that doesn't agree with us. It won't kill us, it simply makes us sick. A vampire has to be practically near death to consent to the stuff. With fresh from the vein human blood forbidden, packaged blood the law of the land, animal blood was the absolute last resort.

Human packaged blood has become the middle ground for feeding. It has been the method that we have used for centuries, changing only recently for her house. She, and the six women that she has been permitted to have some authority over, have crossed an age old line, which forbids the taking blood straight from the human vein. They have done so, with no regret. In fact, if bothered by anything, it is the further need to hold secrecy of their new found freedoms from Raven and the others.

There is a time for everything though, and when the time is right, she will without hesitation, reveal these liberties which she has always believed were theirs to own. Until then, Raven and her house can continue to live inside their box of rules. Up until recently, she could barely remember what a full-fledged vampire felt like. Never again, she thought, would she allow herself to become a shadow of her true self.

Ambrosha entered a room that was lighted by a single candle. She was completely naked beneath the low-cut see-through nightgown that exposed a great deal of the lower region of her butt. Her ample breast, guided by an erect set of nipples, left little to the imagination beneath the thin material.

The room was one of the mansions smallest, with little to no resemblance to the rest of the rooms in the house. Its location was at the far end, southeast of the second floor. Stepping inside was like stepping into another reality. It bore no furnishings save for the twin bed, that was positioned against the far wall.

As she approached the bed, the slack in the chains tightened, and the prisoner who was bound to them began to squirm on top of the plastic covered mattress. Was he frightened? Yes. Would he scream out? It was highly unlikely since he had done much of that during the early part of the night; yielding not the results that he had expected. The lack of food, and loss of blood, should have already ended her prisoners life, instead he hung on, as if he were waiting to awake from a terrible nightmare.

When Nick Stahl first realized that he was in the middle of something that offered a slim chance of escape, his biggest fear was that his death would come too swiftly, but after having suffered through the last 48 hours, death's mercy was beginning to look like a welcomed friend. His captures were blood sucking demons that had nibbled on him off and on, through the early parts of the last two nights.

Even in his weakened state, there still remained the potent sense of fear. *God...*he prayed, *in what manner of existence is this possible? Vampires cannot possibly be real, and yet here they are.* He would give anything to be ignorant of the truth. The fact of the matter is, he was going to die, this was his new found reality, this and his short lived knowledge that monsters truly existed outside of humans. He would never have guessed though, that they would be in the guise of women that smelled of heaven, and wore skin as smooth as a porcelain statue.

Nick closed his eyes in anticipation of the vampire's approach. It neither helped, nor soothed him to have a premature knowledge of his eminent fate. He felt the mattress sink slightly under the vampire's weight, and his heart felt as though it were beating faster than it had on the previous feedings. It raced, and it pounded inside his chest until finally, his breathing had become labored.

"Shhhhhhhh, don't be frightened," the vampire whispered softly, but any efforts to calm him had come a little too late. He was dying, and the sway of the vampire's voice held little power over the death that was close at hand.

Nick reached for his heart, but the chains that held his wrist secure, would only allowed him to reach so far. In the blink of an eye, Ambrosha's facial expression changed from confident to grim. She had hoped to get a final feeding from this one before he expired. She instinctively moved with the speed of a snake; her precision like reflexes carrying her straight to a vein that would collapse at any moment.

He didn't feel her teeth as they punctured his skin. He was too far gone to feel anything at this point. His body jerked once, and then once more, until finally he lay lifeless in the vampire's arms.

Ambrosha pulled mouth and fangs away from the dead husk up until the very last heartbeat. She stared down into the lifeless eyes of the corps infuriated. Enraged, that she had gotten less than enough blood to wet her throat, she shoved the dead husk away from her, where it struck hard against the headboard. She heard its scull crack, and suddenly wished that the male had been alive to feel her fury. She sat on the edge of the bed willing her anger to subside.

She was in no mood for packaged blood tonight, but if she wanted to feed she would have to accept the only thing left on the menu.

When she felt like she was once again in control of her emotions, she ran her fingers through her hair, and then wiped away any remnants of blood that may have made its way onto her face. The body count had become increasingly large over the past few weeks. It will only be a matter of time before the public is aroused over the disappearances of a few. She neither cared, nor was she concerned, because the bodies of those missing would never be found. These were the ways of the coning domesticated vampire. Feed, but leave no evidence to be found. God, if such a being does exist, has surely given thought to every natural design under his imaginative creation, because the world in which we live, operates strictly on the predator and prey relationship.

When the hawk swoops down to claim the life of an adorable rabbit, or the lioness, absent all emotion except one which was to feed, sinks her teeth into throat of a day old antelope, God doesn't frown on it, because it is the way of life.

The vampire and human relationship is no different, feeding directly from humans is nature's way, and nature's design. Even the numbers are perfect. Take away packaged blood, and we survive easily on the population of humans, because the numbers are right. Raven however, doesn't agree, nor will she be convinced. She, and those who have been content to follow her, can continue living the way they have for centuries, but this house will push all emotion and compassion aside, and live the way vampires were meant to live in regards to food.

So far, all of their victims have been male. It won't always be that way, but why not feed on the one thing you despise the most. There was a time when she was quite fond of males, but that was before she married. She was born Russian, but you wouldn't know it, thanks to a highly adaptable tongue.

Vampires have the innate ability to adapt to any language as though it were their own. She was unmistakably beautiful in appearance. She needed no one to tell her that. Standing at five foot nine, with long blond her, she greatly appreciated the fact that her beauty was the one thing that would never change. She glanced at the dead male whose body lay oddly twisted, and the memories of a time long past came flooding to the present.

When Russia was just a territory of dukedoms, she was an unhappily married woman with two kids, and another on the way. Add an abusive husband to the list and you have a ticking time bomb. The abuse had gotten so bad that she was forced to run away. She left everything behind except for the child in her womb, and she quickly found a way to rid herself of that, by forcing her own miscarriage.

As fate would have it, the smell of blood drew in a nearby stranger, a vampire to be exact. The vampire fed on her, turned her, and left behind a single warning! Avoid the sun! Follow your instincts! Or die! It was a lonely and difficult time in her life, but she survived.

When she finally realized to some extent what she was capable of and what she had become, she paid a visit to her husband. The pain that she inflicted on him was ten times the pain that he had caused her. Afterwards, she took what little blood that remained in his veins, and then snapped the necks of her two children. Some things stay with you no matter how long you live. Murdering her children had been completely unnecessary. At the time however, she didn't see fit to allow anything that bore a resemblance of him to survive.

"God, I'm fucking hungry," she grumbled, rising from the bed to leave the room, and the mess that she had made behind.

A door opened at the opposite end of the hall, and a brunette not nearly as beautiful as Ambrosha, yet attractive in her own right stepped out into the hall.

"Tesa," she called out to the girl.

"Yes Ambrosha," the brunette answered.

"The male." Ambrosha looked over her shoulder back towards the room that she had just come from. "The male is dead. Get rid of the body please." Without words, the brunette removed herself from Ambrosha's presence, and began walking towards the room.

Her name is Tessada, but she has been called Tesa for as long as she can remember. Becoming a vampire has done nothing to improve on her label as a social outcast, but it has made her stronger and more capable to handle whatever society and its degenerates chose to cast her way. Society can lick the shit from her ass for all she cared. She was going to be a bad girl until the day she died.

Her mother knew that early on, and with no father to speak of, her mother, other students, and even teachers became the target of her less than well mannered behavior.

School had definitely been a troubled period in her life. She fought with classmates, students that she didn't know, teachers, and was suspended from school more times than she could count.

When she was expelled for the remainder of her sophomore year, she didn't see fit to return. She quit her mother as well; that bitch and all her religious beliefs. Her mother's relentless efforts to force that shit upon anyone that she felt was up shit creek without a paddle, had gotten on her last fucking nerve. Oh, she thought about her mother from time to time, and when she did, she would always ask herself that age old question. Was she, if there really is such a place, in heaven? Well, fuck her; that was always her response. If that place is filled with idiots like her mother, then she would do whatever it took to avoid it.

Tesa entered the room, and approached the bed where the dead man lay. Like a painter transferring an image of expression onto a piece of canvas, Ambrosha's expression was shown in the manner in which she had left the corpse. His body, neck and arms, told the disturbing tale of his tragedy.

She stood there staring at the lifeless husk and wondered by chance, if he would see her mother in passing. "Wherever you are now," she said to the corpse, "if you happen to see my mother in passing, let her know that her daughter says hello. You'll know her when you see her. She's the one you'll want to strangle." Tesa flipped her middle finger up at the corpse. "Make sure you give her this," she said. Tesa removed the restraints, grabbed the lifeless body by the ankles and pulled it towards the foot of the bed, so that it lay horizontally on its back again. She climbed onto the bed, straddled the figure, and stared into its open eyes. She held her gaze for the longest time, holding back her urge to blink. She imagined her mother somehow rushing at the opportunity, to stare back at her through this man's eyes from the grave. She quickly looked away. Nonsense, she thought. Once you're dead, you're dead. It's as simple as that.

Then why do you cower like some weak thing? She asked herself. She stared back into the corpse's eyes as if she were challenging an unseen force.

"You will not have my soul." She gritted her teeth, and with a fury that took her back to the days of fighting both students and teachers, she struck the corpse across the face until its eyes were partially closed.

"Fuck it." She began striking the corpse across the face repeatedly, again pushing eyeballs and eyelids further into the sockets of its head. Feeling her sense of power returned, she grinned sinisterly at the corpse and then crawled off the bed. She lifted the dead body with next to no effort, and tossed it over her shoulder. From here, she would carry it to the basement, where she would toss it into a raging hot furnace. It was a highly practical method for the disposal of dead bodies.

At five foot four, and one hundred and five pounds, Tesa looked impressive carrying the one hundred and eighty pound hunk of dead weight over her shoulder. At the bottom of the staircase, two of her sisters were chatting about their previous night experiences, but they fell silent as Tesa approached. One of the women, a brunette named Constance, smiled at Tesa before saying,

"That one stayed alive longer than any of us expected."

"I agree," Maxine added. "He had a very strong will."

"I can't even begin to describe, what filling up on warm blood does to me now after not having it for so long." Constance said wickedly, caressing herself with her two small, but powerful hands. Maxine grabbed the stiff by the hair, causing Tesa to immediately stop her forward progress, and studied its battered face.

"What happened to his face?" she asked. Tesa gave the two women a blank stare. "It almost looks as if someone had a problem with his eyes," Maxine said.

"Excuse me," Tesa said taking her leave and stepping past them. She heard the two women pick up where they left off, as she put some distance between them. Maxine and Constance had her by a number of years. She was the youngest out of all the women with the exception of Robin, who almost didn't count because she may as well be human. That little bitch has managed to get around nearly every rule that has applied this covenant. She is, and always will be Raven's soft spot. How careless can you be; a vampire exposing her true self to a human in hopes of love? Didn't make sense then, and it doesn't make sense now. Eric, or whatever his name is, will eventually shrivel up and die, there's no getting around that. And Raven, what a fucking hypocrite. She is forever preaching the importance of masking our true selves when we are in the presence of human beings. Robin's single selfish act is capable of doing far more harm than would there regularly feeding on this vast population of human beings. She didn't understand what Ambrosha is waiting for. Tesa believed that if she were in possession of Ambrosha's strength and power, she would have dealt with Raven and Robin a long time ago. Then again, if it were that easy, Ambrosha would probably have done it already.

The iron furnace creaked and groaned from within, as the flaming tongues of fire licked at the inner walls. Tesa made her way down the basement stairs, taking care to watch each step. Once down she placed the corpse on top of a metal roller, and guided it towards the cast iron door of the furnace. She took hold of the handle which was warm to the touch, and pulled the door open. The flames jumped out at her, but they were unable to leave their confine. She grabbed hold of the corpse's feet, and shoved it inside. The flames engulfed it immediately, and the smell of burning flesh quickly spread throughout the basement. The sun would be coming up in a few hours she thought, but somewhere out there were two men with fates already sealed. Come tomorrow, they will be duped, and deceived with a promise of pussy into running to their own deaths. *Hail to the V,* Tesa thought.

By the time she had returned up the steps, both Maxine and Constance had disappeared. She had one more thing that she needed to do before she could call the rest of the night her own. She still had to scrub down the mattress in the feeding room. There were only two feeding rooms. The other had already been cleaned the night before after that food had taken its last breath. Her youth more than guaranteed her the shit jobs around here. It was the only thing she despised about being under Ambrosha's rule. These women were well capable of cleaning up behind themselves, even Ambrosha, yet it would be foolish for her to challenge any of them. Challenge Ambrosha if you wanted, and see if your head wasn't laying on the ground staring up at you. Every woman that resides under the roof of this house has pledged their loyalty to Ambrosha for one reason and one reason only. We were all promised the freedom that is due to us. Freedoms that at the present go against our covenant formed laws, laws that may have been appropriate at the time, but laws that we as vampires should have out grown. She was nearing the feeding room when Ambrosha called to her from behind. Tesa turned around. "Yes," she answered.

"By chance have you seen Victoria?" Ambrosha asked.

"No," she answered. "Come to think of it I haven't seen her at all tonight." A sound escaped Ambrosha's mouth, and Tesa knew that beautiful blond bombshell was impatiently annoyed.

Ambrosha turned around and headed back towards the direction that she had come. There were times like this that the enormity of the mansion got under her skin. She needed to look into getting an interior intercom system installed. Victoria was easily the closest friend that she has ever had in her long existence. They had a relationship that seemed to develop without strain or effort of any sort, and it continues to do so despite the past, the present, and what may lay over the horizon. Their views on the subject of food and the male species mirror one another's as if they were one and the same. There are other things of course, but these two in particular, act as the catalyst that has strengthened their bond. She would need Victoria's strength and friendship in the coming months, as she and those who have chosen to follow her move further and further away from Raven's laws. Her insurrection will yield dangerous consequences for her entire house if she and her women are not prepared, but there was no turning back, not after having tasted the long overdue freedoms that are supposed to be theirs.

Ambrosha entered one of the least frequently visited rooms in the house and found that it was being occupied by Vanessa and Sabrina. Both maker and made were lounging across a five piece sectional sofa that took up about a quarter the space of the room.

"Have either of you seen Victoria?" Ambrosha asked.

"She's in the library," Vanessa answered. Ambrosha raised an eyebrow, and then turned to exit the room. Vanessa and Sabrina were twins. The story went that Vanessa was turned first, and because they were so close, Sabrina practically had to beg Vanessa to turn her. What they didn't realize at the time was that they were taking a risk that could have cost Sabrina her life. They got lucky, and it may have had everything to do with them being twins.

When she entered the library, Victoria was standing some twenty feet away from her facing a book shelf. She was on her cell phone, but as she turned to face her, Victoria's phone conversation had obviously ended as she lowered the phone to her side. She didn't knock herself for not having tried Victoria's cell. The only time these women bothered with their phones was when they were going out. Half the time none of the phones had a charge.

"I've been searching all over for you," Ambrosha said. Victoria held up her cell phone.

"Don't remind me." Ambrosha waved a hand. "Anyway, I wanted to speak to you about adding another male to our weekly food supply."

"It might have to wait," Victoria said. "That was Raven on the phone."

Ambrosha raised an eyebrow. "Well what did she say?"

"Not much. It was a summons. However, she did say that it is of the highest importance and that she needs all of us to show."

"A summons," Ambrosha repeated. There was no need for her to ask when. A summons always meant at the earliest convenience; in this case tomorrow night.

"Well why didn't she..." Ambrosha thought about what she was about to say, but decided to let the thought pass. "She said she tried the house phone, but got no answer."

"Well how did she sound?" Ambrosha asked. Victoria paused for a moment to reflect on the short conversation that she'd had with Raven. She knew what Ambrosha was asking. Ambrosha wanted to know if there was a hint in Raven's tone that may have suggested that this sudden summons was brought about by their un-law abiding activities.

"I don't believe we have anything to worry about, Victoria said. We have been more than careful. However, caution should always be regarded as an ally."

"Of course, Ambrosha agreed. It has been awhile. I believe the last time that we were all gathered together, was on account of Robin."

"Please, don't remind me," Victoria said. "I have never been more nauseated in my life, than I was, when I was being forced to accept that bullshit." Ambrosha remember all too well what they had all been forced to accept that night. She clearly remembered thinking, *I can't believe my ears.* Robin had carelessly gone against covenant law, and had fallen in love with what's his face the human, but even worst, she had revealed to him what she was. Instead of reprimanding Robin and ordering her to clean up what could have been a potentially fatal mess for all of us, Raven gave Robin her blessing and asked that each of us do the same. The argument that she used, was that Robin's situation was unique. She had confided in a human male, and he had guarded her secret. *Horse shit,* Ambrosha thought at the time.

"Jesus, if we're being summoned on account of that spoiled little brat of hers I can tell you right now, I won't be pleasant to be around.

"I wouldn't be surprised if this was about Robin, Victoria smiled. Perhaps she's announcing plans to be married, but again we need to be prepared for anything."

Ambrosha sighed, and then voiced her final opinion on the matter.

"I hate gathering together with Raven's bunch, under the pretence that we are all one big happy family. Inform the other girls, because I would hate to walk into something unprepared."

Victoria nodded, and then turned to walk away. Ambrosha however, remained where she stood.

CHAPTER EIGHT

Robin laid Adam across the bed in between two pillows to limit his range **of** movement. He was already turning over, so she didn't want him rolling towards the edge of the bed. She had no sooner wrapped a little blanket around him when there was a knock on the door. There was no mistaking the scent. It was Raven who stood on the opposite side of the door.

"Come in, Raven," she said. Robin turned around just as the door was opening. Raven entered the room wearing a warm smile. "Hey, I was just putting him to bed, and contemplating a hot bath for myself."

"A hot bath is a sure remedy for getting away from it all, Raven said. If only for the short time that it takes to get in, relax, and get out. How is Eric?"

"You were right of course. I wasn't giving him the credit that he deserves. He's doing okay, and he is handling this much better, than he did when I first told him that he was crushing on a vampire." Raven laughed. "That's funny. See, I told you," Raven gloated.

"Yeah...yeah," Robin blushed. "Have you spoken with Ambrosha yet?"

"No, but I did however speak to Victoria," Raven walked over and stood next to the bed. She studied Adam while he lay sound asleep.

Robin raised an eyebrow. "Victoria? Where was Ambrosha?" Robin asked.

"We're terrible when it comes to phones," Raven answered. "Not to worry, she'll get my message."

"Of course, I knew that I would have to face her eventually."

"Don't concern yourself with Ambrosha and her moods. They won't have any bearing on tomorrow night."

"Believe me, I'm trying not to," Robin said. Raven held her arms out, and Robin messed with them feeling that she could really use a hug right now.

"I'm so glad that you're here Robin, your presence has been missed by all of us."

"I have missed you guys too, she said, and I am happy to be home."

"Okay then, if you need anything, anything at all."

"I will of course let you know," Robin said. They released one another, and Robin watched Raven exit the room.

The following evening was met with tired eyes. Despite a vampire's attributes, the heightened senses, and increased strength, sleep was as necessary as breathing air. The little sleep that she had gotten was measured in cycles rather than a straight line. Adam had awakened twice during the day, and with each time, Robin had found it increasingly difficult to find sleep again. It wasn't difficult to pin point the cause. Her one night of insomnia, and the absence of Eric's warm body had much to do with her getting very little rest. The evening was already looking grim. She and Eric hadn't missed a single day sleeping together up until now. As for Adam, he was a precious gift that came with an abundance of sacrifices that she was more than willing to accept.

Her needs were of little importance now. If she wanted to be a good mother, his would have to come first.

"Are you enjoying your bath, Handsome?" she said as she lathered him up with a bar of soap. This was only the second time that she had bathed him since he had come into her life. One thing was for sure, he enjoyed every minute of his time spent in the water. Robin picked up a glass that she had gotten from the kitchen, and dipped it in the water. She used it to rinse off the soap, first by pouring over his head. *He was amusing,* she thought; the effort he made to keep his eyes open while the water rushed over them tickled her.

"You're funny," she told him. He wasn't the only one enjoying himself. She was enjoying the simple moment of motherhood, while he was enjoying the simplicity of a child.

"Let's enjoy this moment while we're able handsome, because the company that we are keeping tonight, is probably going to suck the life out of the atmosphere." Adam smiled at her and kicked his tiny legs like babies do when they are excited. "Look at you trying to cheer me up. Are we done? Mommy is going to have to ask one of the girls to watch over you while she takes a quick shower. Now which auntie will it be?" Robin lifted Adam out of the tub and wrapped a towel around him. Ambrosha and the others would be here in a couple hours, she thought. She could literally feel the butterflies dancing in the pit of her stomach, as she visualized the probable outcome of this evening's gathering. *Both houses will be joined together. One will come to find out what the other already knows. Ambrosha will be no less than her usual self; that is an air of negativity, and everyone will be curious about her response once Adam is unveiled.* She sighed. *The sooner we get this over with the better,* she thought.

Robin stared into the full-length mirror. Her attire this evening was a pair of white leather pants, and a sleeveless vest to match. Hanging in the closet of her room, were at least sixteen other outfits that were either similar, or close in style, but varying in color. She thought about Eric, and wondered what his opinion of her might be, if he saw her dressed like this. She would never openly dress this way in his presence, because this style of dress, just didn't agree with who they were. These clothes were a representation of the person that she had left behind, and that is why they remain here inside her bedroom closet. She lingered awhile longer in front of the mirror, studying herself from every angle imaginable. She had almost forgotten how sexy and empowering these clothes made her feel. *There is just something about leather and latex. It creates the feeling that you are donning a sensual and sexual costume. It is the absolute perfect look for the female vampire, because we are the absolute embodiment of strength and power.* Robin smiled, satisfied with her reflection in the mirror.

You look dangerous tonight, she told herself. She glanced over at the clock that was on her nightstand to check for time. 8:16 pm. Ambrosha and her crew would be here within the hour. At present, Gelsa was looking after Adam, an unexpected surprise if there was one. It just goes to show, that you can't judge a person by a single layer. Gelsa may be a little rough around the edges, but she was certainly warming up to Adam. As she was exiting the room, the unpacked suitcase in the corner on the floor reminded her of a task not yet done. It was highly doubtful that she would get to it tonight, so it would have to wait until tomorrow. Robin stepped out into the hall butterflies and all, and closed the door behind her. *Breathe,* she told herself, *just breathe.*

Robin entered the great room to find everyone present, with the exception of Raven. Thandie, Gelsa, and Leona, had formed a triangle on the floor around Adam. He was lying on folded blanket that they had spread out over the floor. Robin noticed that Thandie's outfit was cut much like her own. The major difference was the color. Gelsa wore powder blue latex leather pants, with a tube top to match. It was a top that further complimented her huge rack. Leona wore blue too, only a darker color. Her top was tux like in appearance; short sleeved with a collar and a penguin tail. Guiliana, Natalia, and Savana represented as well. Robin walked over and sat in between Gelsa and Thandie. "Hey little guy, how you doing?" She playfully rubbed his little tummy. Adam produced a smile, and then turned to look over at Gelsa.

"I think he likes you, Gelsee," Robin teased.

"Am I unlikeable?" was Gelsa's response. Robin and Leona looked at one another.

"What? A twisted expression formed on Gelsa's face.

"You can be a pain in the ass sometimes that's what," Savana blurted from behind the magazine that she was reading. Gelsa flipped Savana the bird and went back to what she was doing.

"See what I mean," was Savana's response. Robin giggled.

"It feels good to be home," she said. "I had almost forgotten how amusing you guys can be at times." Robin reached down and picked Adam up. "And thanks for looking after him you guys, I really appreciate it, and I can tell that he does too."

"Don't mention it Sis, he's pretty easy to look after," Gelsa said. Robin fell silent. She must have been silent for some time to have warranted the concern from her sisters.

"What's bothering you, Robin?" Leona asked.

The question jogged at Robin's conscious, awareness of her feelings towards Ambrosha. "A few things," Robin answered. "Why do I have such a bad feeling about tonight?"

"You're just a little nervous, that's all," Leona said.

"I really don't feel that I am up for Ambrosha's bullshit tonight," Robin confessed.

"We all know that Ambrosha can be a pain in the ass sometimes, well most of the time," Leona said. "At the end of the day though, she is the Ambrosha that we have always known. There are no surprises, and therefore we always know what to expect. She'll walk in here with a snotty attitude acting like her being here is a waste of her precious time, but boy is she in for a shock tonight. I for one can't wait to see the expression on her face after she has been made aware of Adam."

"And that is exactly what I am afraid of," Robin argued. "Adam is not some object to be used to get Ambrosha going. What I absolutely don't want is for her to see him as any type of threat. We all know how much Ambrosha despises males, and therefore I am not inclined to believe, that her sudden knowledge of Adam is going to make her day. It won't matter to her that he is nothing more than a helpless child."

"I didn't mean it like that Robin. I just meant, that Ambrosha will just have to accept the fact that Adam is now part of our world, whether she agrees with it or not."

"Well I will be watching her like a hawk," Robin said, "and I will decide for myself whether or not she is a potential threat to Adam."

"We will all be watching Ambrosha closely," Natalia added.

Two Cadillac Escalades, one black, the other silver, pulled up in front of the mansion, and came to a complete stop. Inside the first vehicle, behind deeply tinted windows, sat four women. Vanessa, a five foot four inch beautiful redhead with freckles, was sitting behind the wheel, with her twin sister Sabrina occupying the seat next to her on the passenger side. Constance, the dark-haired brunette, and Maxine, the brown-skinned African-American beauty with short hair sat in the rear seats behind them. Tesa, Victoria, and Ambrosha were the occupants of the second vehicle, with Tesa behind the wheel, Victoria in the passenger seat, and Ambrosha in the rear seat behind her.

The vehicle doors began to open successively, and the women began emerging, stepping into the night. Their movements exuded a confidence, and their beauty marked the simplicity of their deadly lure. Six female vampires led by a seventh, made their way towards the two hostesses that awaited their arrival. Guiliana, who stood at five foot seven with chestnut colored hair and of Italian descent, was one of the hostesses standing by. Savana was a native of Georgia, who stood almost at equal height to the woman that was standing next to her. She had pale skin and strawberry blond hair, that if not for her light brown eyebrows, she could probably pass for an albino. They stood like sentries between their guest, and the entrance which lead inside the mansion. Savana, who had a knack for breaking the ice, leaned over and whispered in Guiliana's ear.

"If I didn't know you so well, and we had just met, I would definitely fuck you for looking so good," she said jokingly. Savana was a far cry from a lesbian. The remark was just a simple attempt lighten their mood.

Guiliana had to literally bite down on her lip to keep from laughing. Savana had a way of saying the wrong things at the wrong time. She did have to admit that. Tonight she was dressed to the nine in her peach-colored leather pants. She wore a simple white blouse with peach colored boots that she had paid a handsome amount of money to have specially made.

"I would fuck me if I had just met me," she whispered back to Savana. Now it was Savana's turn to restrain her laughter. The seven female vampires formally of the same house, stopped within two arms lengths of Guiliana and Savana.

"Hello Guiliana, Savana," Ambrosha greeted the two women.

"Savana and Guiliana returned the greeting. It's been awhile hasn't it?" What seemed like what might have been a question was merely a remark.

"The fabric of time and its memories was Ambrosha's response; some pleasant, some not so much."

Savana grinned. She for one enjoyed these games of cat and mouse with her sister house. They were fun and games, and never any real harm behind them. Like many relationships, theirs was a love hate. Guiliana sensing the playful tension between the two women stepped in and spoke, before either of them could utter another word,

"We've wasted enough time out here," Guiliana said. "Let's go inside where the others are waiting."

"Lead the way," Ambrosha hissed.

Guiliana and Savana turned around and led their guest inside. Ambrosha trailed, with the other six women following close behind. She despised these gatherings. It was simply a matter of time before she would figure out a way to be completely detached from Raven's rule. The divide had allowed her to exercise certain freedoms that would have been impossible, had she remained in the same house. Unfortunately, those liberties weren't enough.

With legs crossed, Raven waited patiently in the soft white leather chair for her guest to enter the room. With the fingers of both hands, she caressed the arms of the chair in small circular motions. The great room was exactly what the term implied. It measured a little over three hundred square feet with adequate ceiling space. The floor furnishings were white and grey speckled diamond polished tiles, with throw rugs ideally placed to support the contemporary European style furnishings. The paintings that hung on the walls, along with the vases which varied in **sizes, gave** the room its rich but unique appearance. There was enough sofa and chair space to easily accommodate the fifteen women that would be present in the room. It was nothing new. This was something that they had done many times before.

Raven glanced around the room. It had been more than eight months since the two households had come together, and Ambrosha and her household were becoming more and more antisocial, and more and more irritable between each gathering. Before the divide, both she and Ambrosha had agreed, that the two houses would come together no less than four times out of the year. It would be a sure way to remain connected. She had supported the divide with an understanding that fifteen women living under the same roof, was beginning to take a toll on some of the relationships. Too many personalities tethered to an immeasurable amount of time, could take a toll on any family. She personally hated the fact that the girls' relationships were suffering.

When last they'd come together, the two households had sat on opposite sides of the room. Tonight though, she had insisted that her house occupy seats on both sides of the room, forcing Ambrosha's house to have to fill in the spaces between them. Hopefully it will force them to have some civil conversations with each other.

Guiliana and Savana entered the great room with Ambrosha and the six other women behind her. The room suddenly fell silent. Raven rose from her seat to greet her guest. Her outfit for the occasion from head to toe was black. It was a fitting color that complimented the tone of her skin. The rest of the women stood to their feet also. Guiliana and Savana walked over and stood in front of chairs that they would be sitting in, while Ambrosha and her house studied the seating layout. Ambrosha smiled in Raven's direction and then winked an eye as if to acknowledge touché, and then she instructed her women to sit wherever there were seats available. She however, would not be one of the maneuverable pieces on Raven's chessboard.

With respect to the position she held, Ambrosha always sat in a chair on the opposite side of the room facing Raven. Tonight, her attire closely resembled that of Leona's. The only difference being that hers was white as was the majority of her outfits. White was an absolute favorite color of hers. She felt that it was the only color that truly accented her full head of long blond hair

Ambrosha took her seat in the soft leather chair, and casually threw a leg across one of its arms. The rest of the women took their seats as well. Ambrosha studied Raven for the span of a few seconds. The mood in the room seemed less than hostile. *What exactly was this summons about?* She wondered. It hardly mattered now. Whatever this was about, she and her women stood prepared.

"It's been a while," Raven began. "It's good that we are once again under the same roof, so welcome, and I am glad that we are all here. First, I would just like to say, that the only reason I agreed to this divide was because I believed that there was wisdom in it, but I also feel that we haven't gathered enough. Also, an increasing amount of tension has developed between your house and mine Ambrosha, and it is only getting worst. Am I mistaken?"

You're hardly mistaken, Ambrosha thought. "Whatever tension you may sense between our two houses, may be large in part to the personalities that differ between us, nothing more, nothing less. Fifteen women under a single roof was simply becoming too much."

"In that I have always agreed, Ambrosha, but if tensions continue to rise between us, we will find ourselves in this room again until we figure out exactly what to do about it. You can expect to be summoned more frequently in the future." Raven studied some of the women's faces.

"Was this the only reason that we were summoned, to discuss the tension between your house and mine? No wait, I'm sorry, your house and the house that I oversee," Ambrosha said sarcastically.

"Always the attitude, Ambrosha, and no that is not the only reason that your house was summoned here tonight."

"Let's just skip the formalities, the lectures, and even the lessons where you put me in my place, Raven, and get to the reason why we are all here."

Raven leaned forward in her chair, and for a moment, it appeared as though she would lash out at Ambrosha to in fact put her in her place, but silence held her tongue. The biggest problem was, that she and Ambrosha both possessed alpha personalities, but there was only one alpha bitch in the room that possessed the years, wisdom, strength, and therefore the right to lead this covenant.

For the moment, silence ensued between the two, and the only noise that could be heard were the subtle sounds that the leather made when the women shifted their weight on the leather sofas. Raven's eyes were like blazes of fire that could have burned holes straight through Ambrosha's flesh, and against her better judgment,

Ambrosha dangerously stared back. Right now she was bordering on the line of a challenge, the very thing that she was not prepared to do.

Fool! She thought. This was hardly the time to be pissing Raven off, so she conceited, and shifted her gaze from Raven to her freshly manicured fingernails.

"My apologies," Ambrosha said, breaking the silence. "And you are right. We can all do without the tension, and if that means that we gather more then so be it. Now can we get to the real reason why we are all here? I would like to be in the comfort of my own home before sunrise."

"Of course," Raven answered, leaning back in her chair. In the past, she had found little harm in Ambrosha's antics, because Ambrosha was always quick to remember her place, but of late, her attitude had become more and more sinister.

"Listen to me," Raven spoke, her alpha tone traveling evenly across the room. "I mean it. We have known one another far too long to let our personalities and what not come between us. It stops now, am I understood? And for those of you insistent on the idea of challenging my authority…" Her eyes rested on Ambrosha. "Don't play with the idea, produce the courage. Otherwise bury the idea deep enough so that it will not be mistaken for something else."

The women from both houses glanced around the room at each other, and then nodded in agreement.

"Good," Raven said." Now we can get down to business. The reason I asked you and your house here tonight Ambrosha, is because something amazing has happened in our mist that will no doubt have a future impact on this covenant as a whole. I would ask, that your perspective on what you are about to witness, not be clouded by decades or even centuries of the way things have always been. We are all living proof that evolution has created something different in us, but that doesn't mean that she has ceased to create." There was some unsettling movement on the sofas, as the women from Ambrosha's household glanced at one another with curious expressions.

"What is this?" Ambrosha demanded.

"You will see soon enough," Raven answered. "Just remember what I have said." Raven gave Gelsa a signal to go upstairs and bring Robin and Adam down. Ambrosha straightened up in her chair. She was suddenly more alert than she had been. *What in the hell could she be talking about?* Ambrosha wondered.

Moments before Ambrosha's arrival, she had been instructed to take Adam upstairs, and remain there until summoned, but now came the knock on the door. "Come in," Robin said.

Gelsa opened the door to Robin's room and stuck her head inside. "It's show time sis." Robin stood up with Adam in her arms. "How's the atmosphere down there?" she asked.

"Not as friendly as we would like, but Raven has asserted control."

"No surprise there," Robin said.

"No, you're holding the surprise in your arms," Gelsa reminded her.

"He's much more than that," Robin argued. "I believe that Adam's existence is somehow meant to make a difference, or at least set a balance."

"I can see how that would make sense," Gelsa said, "since we are the only organisms on the face of the planet without males. Come on let's get downstairs, and be prepared. Ambrosha has been her usual self. Raven has already had to put her in her place. Try not to worry so much. Everything is going to be fine."

"I hope you're right," Robin kissed Adam's forehead. "I hope you're right."

The doors to the great room opened, and nearly every vampire in the room shifted in their seat. Gelsa entered the room, with Robin following close behind. Ambrosha, who sat in the only chair facing away from the door, was almost completely turned around in her seat, while the women from her household leaned around one another to get an unobstructed glimpse at Robin and what she held in her arms. There was chatter and whispers, much like there had been when Raven and her house first set eyes on Adam. Ambrosha looked on with curiosity hammering at her brain, while Gelsa, Robin, and the baby that she was carrying, made their way towards the center of the room. Robin kept a watchful eye on Ambrosha as she walked past, but Ambrosha hardly noticed her as she was too focused on the child. Gelsa walked over and sat in one of the open seats. Robin however, continued to walk until finally she was standing next to Raven. "What's the meaning of this?" Ambrosha shouted.

"This." Raven held out her arms to take Adam from Robin. He was completely swaddled save for a portion of his face. "This wonder is what happens when nature is having one of her creative moments. This is what happens when nature has been traveling on the same road for too long. It is a sign that signals that she has grown bored with a single species of vampire, for how else could something so fragile survive the change?"

The creases on Ambrosha's forehead deepened as she allowed Raven's words to sink in. *It's not possible,* she thought, but the word vampire in whispers echoed throughout the room. She felt compelled to challenge Raven's claim, but what difference would it make since Raven was not prone to lie. Amazingly, she had paid little attention to Robin, because it was the presence of the child that had commanded so much attention. But it was all coming together now. Why else would Robin be here? For all intents and purposes it was virtually impossible for something so fragile to survive the change from human to vampire, and yet this small and weak thing has managed to do just that. Ambrosha stood up, and as if it had been choreographed, her house was suddenly on their feet with her.

"What is this? She demanded a second time. This!" (Bitch) is what she wanted to say, pointing a finger towards Robin. "She continues to go beyond the boundaries and laws that you yourself have established, Raven. First she places us all at risk, by callously running off to play house with a human. Now she's out there sharing her blood with infants, and for what? So she and her human lover can take it up a notch?"

"Ambrosha makes a valid point," Victoria argued.

"Ambrosha's point would only be valid if she were right," Guiliana said. "There is more to this than you can possibly imagine, Victoria. I say this for reasons you have yet to discover." Ambrosha went and stood at the center of the room.

"Fine, a sister has been added to the fold. I suppose we can count our blessings for that, considering how nearly impossible we are to make, but It still doesn't change the fact that our youngest and least experienced sister is out there sharing blood with children."

"I agree with Ambrosha," Victoria said. "So do we," the rest of her house chimed in. Ambrosha pointed a finger towards Adam, as she began to address Robin.

"Did you even once consider the fact that this child will never be anything more than a vampire infant?" Ambrosha said. Robin wished that she could completely lose control and say everything that was presently on her mind to Ambrosha.

"I've heard enough," Raven shouted; her voice, like a cannon that had suddenly gone off inside the room. The entire room fell silent, everyone except for Adam. Raven had inadvertently startled him so now he was crying. Robin reached out to take him from Raven.

"My apologies," Raven said, handing him over. "Ambrosha, if you will take your seat please," Raven asked in a much lighter tone.

Ambrosha hadn't realized it until now, but her fist had been so tightly clenched that she had driven her own fingernails into the palms of her hands. She relaxed them slowly, and then backed away from the center of the room. When she was firmly seated back in her chair, those who were of her house regained their seats as well.

"This child is not the product of a vampire and a human seeking to fill a void in their relationship. This child was left for dead on a door step, Robin's door step to be exact. She only did what came natural to her, which was to make an effort to save its life, knowing full well the consequences that her effort might yield. For reasons we have yet to discover, this child survived the change. It matters not if its existence is to forever be an infant vampire, if that is its fate. What matters is that it is vampire, and that it did survive."

One of the women from Ambrosha's house started to speak, but Raven held a hand up to wave off the interruption. "There is more," she said, her eyes coming to rest on Ambrosha. "The child will not be called sister, as you may have imagined, but brother." The information was absorbed instantly, by those from Ambrosha's house. The commotion that followed took the form of a barrage of questions that seem to travel at the speed of light.

"Brother?"

"What do you mean brother?"

"It isn't possible."

"It can't be true."

These were just a few of the questions that were circulated throughout the room, by vampire's who in seconds would require far more information than Raven had given. "Show us," some of the women from Ambrosha's house began to demand. "Yes show us," said the rest. Ambrosha said nothing, but sat there in her chair contemplating the ramifications that this would have on their future as a covenant. She thought about her own agenda, and the impact that a possible male species might have on it. She still had the loyalty of her women, unfortunately that might not be enough. They were curious just as she was. Still the one thing she dared not do was pretend to care. They were idiots all of them, blind to the first signs of a future of enslavement; a sign that this child was perhaps the first male vampire to signal a future for many. Guiliana and Gelsa walked over and stood next to Robin as the women from Ambrosha's house gathered around to get a closer look. Robin held Adam close to her, though she had removed the blanket that was wrapped around him. Like a mother ensuring the safety of her young, Robin studied each of the women's faces as they drew nearer. If she sensed any danger, she was prepared to react. Robin glanced down at Raven who remained seated. Because she held Adam facing her, the women from Ambrosha's house had yet to lay eyes on his gender. When Robin finally turned Adam around so that they could view him, there reaction was nothing less than what she had expected. "It's true," the women started to whisper. "And look at his eyes." They sounded completely amazed. "They are the color violet."

Victoria, who had seen just about enough, turned her back on what had become the center of attention. She walked over and stood next to Ambrosha, who too had remained in her seat the whole time.

"It's true," Victoria whispered. "It is a male, and its eyes. Its eyes are unlike any that I have ever seen, violet."

"Look at them all," Ambrosha said bitterly. "They are like children unaware of the danger before their own eyes."

When the room was settled down once more, and the insistence of proof long faded, Ambrosha, displaying more control than she had thus far broke her silence.

"So what now?" she asked Raven. "Are we to suddenly believe that the virus has taken a liking to males?"

Raven entertained Ambrosha's question for a moment. "It's possible," she answered. "Adam is a complete mystery. But you know as well as I do that the world is forever changing. It is not farfetched to believe that vampire males will one day walk among us."

"I see that you have already given it a name, Robin."

"I have," said Robin, "and in the future I would appreciate it if he wasn't referred to as it." A sinister grin lined Ambrosha's lips.

"Well I for one do not look forward to an existence of male vampires," one of the twins blurted out. "Neither do I," the other twin added. "Men are pigs, and if this is true of the human male, then we can only imagine how awful the vampire variety will be."

"We are all entitled to our feelings on the subject of males, whether human or a potential vampire race," said Guiliana, "but at the end of the night, opinions mean nothing once nature has decided."

"You speak of nature as though she were incapable of being thwarted, Ambrosha argued. Nature's hand can be guided like every other thing in this world. We can decide whether or not we choose to be overrun by males. That is what we can expect you know, should they one day rise to even half our numbers. They will seek dominance because that is their way. What position can we possibly hope to hold then? I will tell you, a weakened one."

"What exactly are you saying, Ambrosha?" Raven asked. "I hope that it is not what I think you're saying, because regardless of what the future holds for a vampire male race, surviving the change is a rite of passage. This is the way it has been for every female, and so shall it be for every male beginning with Adam."

Ambrosha forced a smile. She had nothing more to say on the matter. "Are we concluded here?" she asked.

"If no one else has anything to add, then yes we're done," Raven answered. Ambrosha rose to her feet and the women of her house followed suit. "Until next time," Ambrosha said, as she and the women from her house made their way towards the door. Guiliana and Savana were following close behind; they would see their guest out.

The gathering had gone about as well as Raven had expected. Ambrosha was her usual predictable self, but all in all the tone was normal. They were all still gathered inside the great room, mainly because each of them was curious about how the house as a whole interpreted the things that had been brought to light. Robin was the first to speak, and she didn't hesitate to say what was on her mind.

"She can't be trusted, she can't," said Robin.

"We know, Guiliana said, at least not for the moment."

"Not for the moment!" Robin unintentionally raised her voice. "It sounds to me like she can never be trusted where any male is a concern."

"Relax, Robin," Gelsa teased. "Ambrosha can be a real bitch at times, but she'll come around, she always does. Only in this case, it may take a lot longer."

"Gelsa's right," Savana added. "If we make reference to Ambrosha not being able to be trusted, in this case for example, we only mean that you can't count on her for babysitting." Robin could hardly believe it. How could they joke at a time like this? Why was it so hard for them to see what she was able to see behind Ambrosha's mask?

"You guys, I'm serious," Robin argued. She looked over at Raven for support, but not even Raven was taking her seriously.

"Robin," Raven said. "If it's Adam's safety that you're worried about, you shouldn't. He is perfectly safe here believe me. It would be foolish for any of us to ever believe that Ambrosha will someday bond with Adam. I know her, and the one thing that we can be sure of is that she will keep her distance. Just think of her as the distant aunt who doesn't do well with children or males for that matter."

"That's right," Gelsa said.

Robin listened, but she didn't agree. It's true, they've all known Ambrosha far longer than she has, and maybe that was the whole problem. Maybe they've become too relaxed. It didn't matter. She wasn't going to allow herself to be fooled to the point where she would let her guard down. She felt something from Ambrosha that went way beyond their description of her as the typical bitch. No, the vibes that she got from Ambrosha were pure hatred and disdain, accompanied by an anxiousness to destroy whatever got in her way.

"You're allowed to feel the way you feel towards Ambrosha, Robin, only trust us when we say that no harm will come to that little guy that you are holding right there."

Robin sighed. "Okay," she said finally, but she had only done so to appease them.

"Can I hold him?" Leona asked.

Robin stood up and walked over to where Leona sat. "Sure," she said, carefully handing Adam over. "As a matter of fact, it's almost time for his next feeding. Will you be okay with him while I prepare his food?"

"Of course," Leona answered. Robin excused herself and then headed for the kitchen. After Robin had left the room, Natalia spoke. "I for one find it hard to believe that males have suddenly become capable of surviving the change, even though my eyes tell me different whenever I look at Adam."

"Well you're not alone," Raven said.

"Then how is he possible?" Leona asked.

"Again, I don't know," Raven answered. Raven stood up and walked over to where Leona sat with Adam. Let me have him Leona," she asked. Leona handed Adam over to Raven. The women watched with curious expressions on their faces to see what Raven would do next. Raven breathed in Adam's scent.

"What is it, Raven?" Thandie asked.

Raven shook her head. "It's nothing."

"But there was a reason behind what you did, was it not?" Guiliana asked.

Raven smiled. "I don't know what I was hoping to find," she answered.

Robin entered the room. "So what did I miss?" she asked, holding Adam's bottle up.

CHAPTER NINE

Ambrosha's mind worked overtime from the back seat of the SUV, as it traveled along the highway headed back towards home. *They are fools! All of them to believe, that there is a place in this world for a race of male vampires.* If it was up to her, she would strangle the child and be done with it. *From the very beginning, our beginning, only one gender of vampire has existed. I for one see no reason why that should ever change. If that child is allowed to live, he will ruin everything.* Ambrosha wanted to believe that if Robin and the child met their death, then it would be feasible to believe that whatever secrets they may hold, would surely die with them. That little bitch has done nothing except to complicate things from the moment that she was changed, but killing Robin and the child would surely mean that she would have to kill Raven and her lot as well. She had made the statement not two hours ago regarding nature, and how simple it would be to thwart her hand in this. *She is well known for stirring up the existing balance of things. I say fuck her. For one, her plans do not coincide with my own. Nothing has ever pleased me more than the male's rejection to the change, and I refuse to have my perfect harmony snatched away. If it weren't for the fact that Raven possessed a total control over the covenants resources, I wouldn't have to go through all this shit. I had hoped to one day in the near future demand a portion of the covenant resources, which would have given me the means to put some distance between our two houses.* The light bulb lit up inside her head, and she suddenly realized that there was something that she had to do, and do so as soon as possible.

"I'm going to need men," Ambrosha said, breaking the silence, "at least ten of them to start with."

Tesa took her eyes off the road to stare into the rearview mirror at Ambrosha. "Care to share?" Victoria asked.

"A test," she answered, "a test that I am hoping will give me some piece of mind, while I contemplate what I plan to do about Robin and that child."

"What do you mean?" Victoria asked.

"What I mean is that child can't be allowed to live, but killing the child would also mean that we would have to kill Robin along with the rest of them." Tesa tightened her grip on the steering wheel.

"You're talking all out war," Victoria said. "Are we ready for that?"

"Nobody is ever ready for war, Victoria, but wars are fueled by purpose, and isn't ours clear?"

"It is," Victoria shook her head.

"Well then it is final," Ambrosha said, turning her attention to the distant trees outside the window.

The unpleasant memories that followed last night's gathering, was indisputably the cause behind her poor day's sleep, she thought, and as the crown of the sun ducked just beneath the horizon, Ambrosha slid from beneath the covers of her bed. She dug her toes into the thick rug beneath her feet while she reached over to switch on the lamp next to her bed. Eyes barely open she studied the painting on the wall in front of her. The longer she stared at the piece of art, the more she came to realize that she had never really looked at it until now. There were colors and shapes that she hadn't noticed before.

Ambrosha sighed and then removed the strand of hair that was hanging over her left eye. Rising to her feet, she walked over to the bedroom window and slid back the locking mechanisms to the solid oak shutters. They were an absolute necessity, used to stay those harmful rays of the sun and protect the creatures that resided on the other side. As the fresh night air forced its way into the room, her vision began making the adjustment to the darkness beyond her lighted room.

About twenty yards away to her left, a rabbit took off suddenly over the open grounds. It ran in a straight line at top speed for about 30 yards or so before making a hard right, but the sudden turn had proved just as costly as it would have been, if the rabbit had maintained a straight line. Nature was at work yet again. She wondered. Would the outcome have been the same if the rabbit had turned left instead of right? It was a question that would never be answered now that its lifeless body was hanging limp from the talons of a horned owl.

Strange, she thought. *These are two creatures who have probably shared the same territory for the better part of the rabbit's existence, so it would stand to reason that the owl wasn't oblivious of the rabbit's presence. How then, had the rabbit managed to survive for so long, only to have met its end this night? Does it really make a difference now?* She thought. *The rabbit had met its end, end of story.*

Ambrosha stepped away from the window and headed towards the bathroom. A nice hot shower, some breakfast, and then there was the business at hand. She could hardly wait to attend to the later though. She felt like she should at least consider the possibility, that the relationship between man and the virus which has been so deadly to them up until now, has suddenly evolved, but what could she really hope to gain? It was unrealistic to think that an answer would suddenly materialize because a few men were infected with vampire blood now. Wasn't the child enough proof? Somehow she didn't think so. If males have truly become candidates for a successful change, then it would stand to reason that their rate for survival was much like their own. So was tonight really about finding out the truth, or was it simply a means to direct her frustration onto to the one thing she despised the most? Whatever the reason, it would not go undone.

The hours rolled by with little respect given to what was transpiring beneath the pores of reality. Lighted candles, soft music, and nine of the ten men that Ambrosha had requested stood, oblivious to their plight within the large great room. They mingled and held conversation, with some of the most alluring women they had ever met. So far, Sabrina and Vanessa were the only ones who hadn't returned. It shouldn't have been that difficult to find one male, and then lure him back to the mansion. The witching hour had long passed, so chances are they were goofing around.

These men were here because they desired something. They wore expectation like a mask, and in doing so it revealed their very souls. Their nature was ultimately their weakness, and therefore their down fall. They were obviously thinking, *surely to drink and socialize is not the only reason why we have been brought here.* Ironically they were right. Few could neither control nor hide the noticeable erections beneath their pants. So to divert attention, they either kept their conversations colorful or moved to take a seat on one of the sofas or chairs.

Ambrosha signaled, and the women began herding the men out of the great room towards predetermined destinations upstairs. Life can be quite shitty on its own, but nothing comes close to be led to your unsuspecting death wearing a smile. How disappointing they were all going to be, with the decisions that they had made this night.

"You know she's gonna kill us right? We should have been out of here a half hour ago," Sabrina said. "Let's stop screwing around, so we can get what we came for." The two vampires sat at the center of the bar facing outward. From this view point they were able to check out most of the men that were prancing around in the night club. Pussyfooting around, trying to figure out what to wear had gotten them off to a late start.

"Time sensitive, Vanessa," Sabrina barked.

"I know," was Vanessa's response. "Look, how about that one over there?" Vanessa pointed to a fairly good looking guy. Sabrina tilted her head to inspect Vanessa's choice.

"He'll do." She shook her head. "He has the look of the hunter about him. I say we educate him, what do you think?"

Vanessa turned to her sister and grinned. "Well let's get to it then," she said.

Ben took notice to the two women staring in his direction from the bar. He whipped his head around expecting to see their boyfriends, but the only thing he saw was a club full of people doing their own thing. He turned back around to see if the two women still had him in their sights, and he was surprised to find that they did. One of the girls raised a finger and pointed it in his direction. Ben smiled, and then pointed a finger at himself. The girl smiled back and then signaled for him to approach. *I'll be damned,* he thought. *These girls were not only hot, they were twins. Don't fuck this up,* he told himself. Tonight he was well dressed. His haircut was fresh, and his mustache and beard were barbershop trimmed. Why wouldn't they be interested in him? He was as about as good-looking as they came. He started walking in their direction. As he approached, he couldn't help but notice how they were staring him up and down. It was a look that he was all too familiar with, and one that came natural to men whenever women were viewed as sexual objects to be devoured. *Hell yeah,* he thought, *my shit will have to be on point tonight if I hope to have any chance of getting these two bitches into bed.* From his standpoint he was standing face to face with lady luck, and he was experiencing more generosity from her than he had ever known.

The two women were on their feet now and moving slowly in his direction. The way they glided across the floor seemed to suggest, that their bodies and the clubs music were a union of harmony. The twins stopped just short of him, and like a pair of cobra's seduced by the music's vibrations they began to dance, one in front, and the other behind him. Ben could only stand there where he had stopped; his head on a swivel as he attempted to follow and meld with their every move. He was like putty in their hands as they reduced him to nothing more than a mindless hunk of flesh bent on one thing; sexual gratification. Strangely enough, he had completely forgotten the crowd of people that surrounded him the club. The influence that the two women held over him was over powering. So much so that he began to question his current position. Was he still the predator in this hunt? He felt that he would be lying if he answered yes. From the moment that he had laid eyes on them, they had been in complete control. They were the shepherds, and he was the lone sheep. *This is where you ask yourself does it really matter, Ben? And the answer would be hell no.* He leaned in and whispered his name into both of their ears.

"I'm Ben," he said, turning his voice box up a few notches to compensate for the clubs rumbling music, "and your names are?"

"I'm Vanessa," she whispered in his ear, "and the pretty girl to your left is Sabrina."

"Vanessa, Sabrina? Those are two beautiful names, for two beautiful women," he told them. "I'm not at all disappointed."

The two women smiled at one another. It was the kind of smile that had immoral intent written all over it. What in God's name, his lips moved, but were absent of sound. They weren't finished yet. The one called Vanessa took her hand and cupped her sister's neck. He watched as she guided her twin's lips towards her own. *You got to be shit'n me,* he thought, as he watched the two sisters kissed one another with a passion that seemed to transport them to another place in time. He felt an uncomfortable ache in his dick because it literally felt like the muscle would rip through the coat of skin that incased it. An image of the Hulk ripping through his outer garments suddenly came to mind. *You'd better not fuck this up,* he told himself.

"Can I buy you both a drink?" he yelled over the music while stealing a quick glance at Vanessa's breast. Vanessa shook her head and told him that it wouldn't be necessary. Ben raised an eyebrow and said a silent prayer, praying that this wasn't the beginning of a string of no's ending with the most dreaded no that a man could face after experiencing a long night of hard- ons. The one called Vanessa took him by the hand, while Sabrina leaned forwards on the tips of her toes to whisper in his ear.

"Would you like to get out of here?" she asked. The words were felt deep down in his loins.

"Sure," he answered, his perfect white teeth forcing their way past a smile. "Shall we?" he asked, leading the sisters towards the clubs exit. He was feeling VIP as he walked across the clubs floor with a woman on each arm. This had been too easy, he thought, not that he was complaining, but things like this didn't happen too often, and yet here it was happening to him. Pussy lottery, that's what the fuck this was, he thought. Like he had walked into the club tonight, asked for a pussy scratch off ticket and bam! Jackpot! Now all he had to do was collect, and collect he would.

Loud music, cigarette smoke, men trying their damndest to get laid, that's all behind me for the moment, he thought as he stepped out of the night club and onto the sidewalk with the twins. *Hugh Hefner, eat your heart out.* He grinned. The club's location was smack dab in the middle of downtown LA. Traffic could be a motherfucker on any given night of the week.

As Ben walked towards the parking lot with a girl on each arm, he couldn't help but feel that fate had smiled upon him. He had a sense that these two could be a hand full, and that was ok because his life could use a little spontaneity. Ben took a quick look at Vanessa, and then at Sabrina. *Oh yeah,* he thought now that he was able to view them in better lighting. It was a known fact that a combination of club lighting and alcohol could play tricks on your eyes, and more often than not, the person or persons that you were going home with dropped a couple of notches on your rating scale. But on a scale of one to ten, these two were an easy nine.

The thing about redheads is there is no in-between. They are either beautiful, or butt-ugly. The red hair, pale skin and freckles, didn't jive too well below an eight rating, you could settle for a seven and in some cases a six with blonds or brunettes.

Ben guessed that the twins stood anywhere between five foot four, and five foot three inches in height. Their beautiful black eyes; an unusual color for redheads, were surrounded by a light shade of freckles and an umbrella of curly red hair. When they reached the clubs parking lot, without skipping a beat Ben launched the million dollar question.

"My place or yours, ladies?" he asked.

Sabrina tugged gently on his arm. "You're coming with us," she told him with a smile that promised a pleasured-filled night.

The club's L-shaped parking lot allowed for five rows of cars on one side of the building, and three rows in the back. He suddenly realized that he was being lead to their car, because they hadn't questioned him about his own car or where it was parked. "FYI ladies, I did drive you know, so why don't I follow you guys, and that way I can avoid a towing cost."

"Leave it," Vanessa said. "We'll cover the expenses and then some."

"That's right, and then some," Sabrina added, flashing him a sassy smile.

"In that case, I promise not to give my $40,000 dollar BMW another thought." Vanessa squeezed down on his hand.

"Trust me," Sabrina said. "In another hour or so, any thoughts you may have concerning worldly possession will be far from your mind. We promise to show you things that even you'll have trouble wrapping your mind around."

"Oh I highly doubt that," said Ben with a confident smile, "although I'm not opposed to being surprised." Sabrina removed a set of keys from her pants pocket, and pushed the unlock button on the remote. There was a single chirp, and then the headlights flashed on to revealed the vehicle the twins were driving.

"Sweet," Ben said. The girls were driving a black Cadillac Escalade with ivory bone and dark wood grain interior.

"Thanks, we're Cadillac kind of girls," Vanessa remarked.

"You guys must have some pretty rich blood then?"

"That would be an understatement," the twins giggled. Ben made a motion for the rear seat, but Vanessa waved him off. "The front seat's all yours, big guy." Ben gave her a quick glance.

"Thanks, I could use the leg room." Vanessa pushed the passenger seat forward and climbed into the car.

Once they were all inside, Sabrina turned to Ben and asked, "Will this be your first experience with two women? I mean, two women at the same time?"

The question caught him off guard. *Play honest on this one,* he told himself, believing it would count for something this night. An honest answer might even excite the twins if felt they were popping his cherry. "There is a first time for everything ladies, and I thank God for all of them," he said.

"Then fasten your seatbelt," Sabrina laughed, "we wouldn't want anything to happen to you, at least not before you've had your fill of us." I have died and gone to heaven, he thought. Ben fastened his seatbelt while Sabrina started the engine.

"Wew....Wee," Vanessa screamed from the back seat. "Let's get this show on the road."

CHAPTER TEN

They had gone through a total of nine males in less than two hours, and not one of them had survived the change.

"Where in the fuck are they?" Ambrosha screamed. "They should have been here by now." Her frustration had reached a high.

"They just pulled up," Maxine answered from one of the doorways.

"Those two have wasted a lot of precious time tonight," Ambrosha barked. "Tesa, see to the male. Maxine, I'll join you shortly." Maxine nodded and then disappeared from the doorway. Only Ambrosha, Tesa, and the dead male remained in the room. The rest of the women had already begun disposing of the other eight bodies. Ambrosha stared down at the dead male who had taken his final breath only moments ago. Tesa had mixed her blood with this one, and to no surprise her blood had proven just as lethal as her own. *This is a massive waste of time,* Ambrosha thought. She would have to go through hundreds of males, maybe even thousands to put her fears and suspicions to rest.

"I'm handling this all wrong," she told Tesa. Tesa kept silent. She rarely responded to Ambrosha's comments when she was angry.

"Clean up this mess, Tesa." Ambrosha was referring to the corpse that was still tied to the bed.

"I'll get to it as soon as I take care of..." Before Tesa could finish her sentence Ambrosha was on top of her. Ambrosha struck Tesa with an open backhand. The blow lifted Tesa completely off the floor sending her flying across the room towards a wall. Tesa instinctively shifted from solid, to her mist form before impact. Her body had become nothing more than scattered molecules that now hovered some eight feet above the floor. As the mist began to slowly take on its natural form, gravity was forced to serve its purpose, and in a matter of seconds, Tesa was whole again. Ambrosha stormed past the unharmed vampire without uttering so much as a word. After Ambrosha left the room, Tesa tightened both fists into balls. Ambrosha had never struck her before, so in doing so, a wave of uncontrollable emotions had been released. Clearly she sympathized with Ambrosha, because Ambrosha's anger was understandable, but there had been no cause for such actions. Tesa relaxed her fists and proceeded to do what Ambrosha had ordered.

Words like wow, incredible and amazing came to mind as he beheld the beauty that was the mansion before him.

"I'm impressed," Ben said, "but isn't this a bit much for the two of you?"

Vanessa looked at him and smiled.

"Who said it was just the two of us?" Sabrina parked the SUV in front of the house and then turned off the engine. "Home sweet home," she said, glancing back at Ben. They exited the car and headed towards the front entrance to the house. As Ben walked, he couldn't help but form opinions about the two women that walked beside him. If he had to take a guess, he would probably conclude that the twins were just two spoiled little rich girls with trust funds. This house obviously belonged to their parents, who at present, was on a yacht somewhere in the Bahamas. Ben wondered what it would take to squirm his way into their money. Whatever the order, it would no doubt be tall.

Awe was the word that came to mind once he was inside. His one bedroom apartment would never be the same to him now. Wherever his eyes rested, was a reminder of the money he only wished that he had. He could probably eat off the high polished floors, they were that clean, and the paintings, one could probably real in a small fortune by selling just one. The furniture, what he had gotten a glimpse at so far, looked as though it had never been sat on.

"Do you guys ever sit on this stuff?" he asked.

Vanessa gave Sabrina a look and then said, "Honestly, I can't recall ever sitting in any of the rooms we just passed. If we're not in our own rooms, we're either in the great room, the library, or the kitchen."

"So you guys cook?"

"Hell No! Don't be silly," Sabrina said.

Ben laughed. "I just assumed," he said, "but now that I think about it it's right up there with all the stupid questions ever asked. The rooms are beautiful, he added. It's hard to imagine living inside a place like this. It's too damn perfect."

"Wait until you see the room that we're taking you to now," Vanessa said. "I swear it's going to blow your mind."

He caught the smile they shared with one another. *Mischievous devils,* he thought.

"I can only imagine," he said in response, "and I look forward to being utterly surprised." He tried to imagine that room and all the things that were about to take place in it. Visions of acts that guarantee pleasure were the images that came to mind.

"Not that my mind isn't where it is should be right now, but can I get a complete tour of this place before I leave?" he asked.

"Of course," Sabrina answered. The twins were leading him up a flight of stairs now, and as he neared the top, a beautiful blonde stood waiting on the landing. "I must be dreaming," were the words escaped his mouth.

"Just so you know, her mood is poison," Victoria said, standing there with her arms folded. "What took you guys so long?"

"Sorry," was Sabrina's response.

The blonde smiled at him and said, "I'm Victoria." She held out her hand, and Ben gently reached out to take it. Her skin was amazingly soft.

"I'm Ben, and it's nice to meet you," he said.

Victoria pulled her hand away just as Maxine was walking up beside her. "Ben?"

"Yes," he answered.

"I hope you enjoy the rest of the night," she said.

"I promise to try," he told her. The twins grabbed him by the arms and led him down the hall.

"Who was that?" Ben asked. "And who was she referring to when she said 'her mood is poison?"

"Stay focused." Sabrina shot him a smile. "And try to remember why you're here."

Ben nodded. "You're absolutely right," he said. *There will be plenty of time for questions later,* he thought.

The twins led him down a poorly lit corridor. The only source of light, were the candles that illuminated lining both sides of the walls. One of the doors opened, and a female stepped out into the hall and began walking in his and the twin's direction. He glanced at her as they passed, and he could swear that her eyes flashed blood red against the lighting. It startled him. Has to be the lighting, he tried to convince himself.

"Why do you keep the hall so dark?" he asked.

"We find it comforting," Vanessa answered.

"Oh," Ben responded. They stopped in front of a door, and as he was standing there, something began to nag at him. So far he had seen a total of three women, not including the twins or the one that the blond had referred to. If this was some high class whorehouse then his luck was about to change. Not once had there been a mention of money, and he doubted that he could afford the price tag if the conversation suddenly shifted in that direction.

Vanessa opened the door to the room and entered. Ben followed her inside with Sabrina close behind. His first thought was that the twins were playing some sort joke on him. It was as if he had stepped into the twilight zone, because this room looked nothing like the world on the opposite side.

"Okay, I'm confused," Ben said.

Vanessa turned around and faced him. "What were you expecting?" she asked.

Ben noticed the straps that were located at the four corners of the bed. "Well I'm not at all surprised by those." He pointed towards the straps that in his mind indicated they were at the least into bondage. "I guess I'm just thrown off by the overall appearance of the room, after having experienced what I have so far of the house." Another woman;

one whom he had not yet met entered the room. *She was decent looking,* Ben thought, *but not as attractive as the twins.*

"If I were you two I would stop fucking around and get him strapped to the bed, she'll be here in a few seconds;" the female addressed the twins.

Ben glanced at one of the twins and giggled nervously. "Who'll be here in a few seconds?" he asked.

"Well hello to you too, Maxine," Vanessa addressed the woman who was sporting a rather sinister grin.

"Wait, how many women live here?" Ben asked.

Vanessa rubbed up against him. "I'm sorry Ben, but we're going to have to cut this short."

Ben stared at the three women with a blank expression on his face. "You mentioned strapping me to the bed. At one point I might have been comfortable with the idea, but I'm not so sure now."

"Oh come now Ben," said Sabrina. "You're not frightened by a few women that happen to have a fiendish appetite are you? After all, we did promise you the time of your life did we not?"

Ben was hesitant in how he should respond, and that troubled him. "I had a bad experience as a child, he lied. Let's say we do without the straps this time." What happened next happened before he had a chance to register. The one called Maxine grabbed him with one hand by the throat and lifted him off his feet. Ben's eyes lit up with surprise as he was being slammed onto the bed. *What the fuck* he wanted to say, but his airway was cut off by the female's vise-like grip.

"If you two know what's good for you, you'll have him strapped and secured before she gets here," Maxine addressed the twins. The two women walked over to the bed and secured Ben by the arms and legs.

"You two should take this more seriously," Maxine said. "Just leave - I've got it from here."

"Fine," Sabrina said. "Bye, Ben." The twins wiggled their fingers at him as they were exiting the room. Maxine released her grip on Ben's throat, and he coughed as he welcomed the return of oxygen into his lungs.

"Who the fuc.." .He continued to cough uncontrollably. When he was finally able to breathe normal again, he asked, "Who the fuck-are you women, and what in the fuck is going on?" he demanded, yanking at his restraints. "Fuck!" He yelled at the top of his lungs.

"Shut your fucking hole," Maxine said sternly. "Answering your questions won't do you any good."

Ben's mind flashed back to how easily she had lifted him off his feet.

"How were you able to lift me so easily?" he asked. "The last time I checked I weighed in somewhere around 180 pounds. That has to be twice your weight. So how is it that you were able to do what you did?"

"You'll understand soon enough," Maxine told him.

Ben yanked at the restraints again. "Stop fucking around," he said, his face turning bright red. "I'm serious – get these fucking things off me." Someone entered the room, and Ben turned his head towards the door to see who it was. He was hardly surprised to find that one she was a woman, and two that she was beautiful. More beautiful than any of the women he had seen so far.

"Are you the one that everyone's talking about? Ben asked. "Okay, you can let me go now. I don't know what's going on here, but whatever it is your secret is safe with me."

"Leave us," Ambrosha waved a hand at Maxine. Without a word, Maxine turned and exited the room. Ambrosha stopped next to the bed and stared down at what she was certain would be another failure.

"Who are you?" Ben asked. Ambrosha didn't answer. Instead she inspected him from head to toe. Finally she said.

"My name is Ambrosha."

Ben locked eyes with her. "Be straight with me, he asked. Are you going to hurt me?"

Ambrosha smiled. "As a matter of fact I am," she answered." Ben jerked at the straps again, but his efforts continued to prove futile. Ambrosha's eyes traveled along Ben's torso eventually stopping at his groin region. She noticed that he had formed an erection. Ben had been so concerned with the terrifying thoughts that were running through his head that he hardly noticed himself.

"You men are all alike, which is to say pathetic," Ambrosha said, "but I'll make you a deal. If you survive what comes next I will not only let you go, but I will take care of that." She motioned towards his erection. Ben turned away from her and gazed up at the ceiling. *She was right,* he thought. Even though he knew that his life was in mortal danger, the blood continued to pump through his sexual vein demanding that he stay erect. The fact that she was beautiful and barely clothed didn't help the situation much.

Ambrosha raised the see-through nightie up over her hips, and climbed onto the bed. A clear view of her unshaved pussy, curved hips, and thin waist, sent an army of sensations south of his thinking brain, causing more blood to pump through the already expanded blood vessels in his cock.

Ambrosha unzipped Ben's pants, and freed his erection. She straddled him, taking care to keep his stiff shaft out front of her vagina to avoid penetration. Part of her wanted to take hold of the object and rip it clean away from his body, but she had other plans for him.

"What did you mean when you said if I survive was comes next?" Ben asked. Ambrosha leaned in so that her face was just inches apart away from Ben's. She parted her lips and revealed two rows of straight white teeth. Ben stared up at Ambrosha, uncertain of her intentions. Was she really going to hurt him, or was he just a part of some great big prank. These women didn't look like killers, not that he was an expert on the subject, and then there was the one called Maxine. He didn't imagine the pressure that he had felt around his neck, or how she had lifted him off the floor with no effort. He was about to pry further when he was taken aback by the sudden change of expression on Ambrosha's face. Ben watched in disbelief as Ambrosha's lips began to spread even further around her otherwise perfect set of teeth. What happen next though was unnatural. It was subtle, but he was seeing movement beneath her gums, and then the teeth appeared, only different than the others. These curved slightly inward, resembling the fangs of a poisonous snake or something similar to it. Ben tried to put some distance between his face and Ambrosha's, but he was only granted inches, one maybe two at the most.

"What the fuck are you," Ben yelled as he attempted to press his head even further into the mattress.

Ambrosha reached forward and grabbed a hand full of Ben's hair. She angled his head so that she would have a direct line to the thick vein just beneath the skin on the right side of his neck.

"Wait! Stop," Ben cried out, but his words meant nothing to whatever this thing was. Ambrosha honed in on the vein, and like a hungry animal she struck; sinking her teeth into flesh and blood. Ben jerked aimlessly at his restraints, even though he knew that his efforts would yield no results. *Why do we fight, knowing that there is no hope?* he wondered. Seconds passed by, and as a result his strength began to wane. The seconds turned to minutes, and the minutes began to feel like a life time.

Ambrosha released her grip on Ben's neck, and then wiped the remnants of blood from her mouth, using the back of her hand. The room was spinning now, and there was nothing that he could do to stop it. He was alive, but barely. Ben stared with some difficulty into the eyes of something that his mind was finding extremely hard to grasp. The room began to spin even faster, but isn't that what happens when a person loses most of their blood? *It was all so strange* he thought, yet there was only one explanation for what was happening to him. These women, this house, they were all vampires. Ben closed his eyes. *I just need a moment,* he thought, *a moment's rest; my eyes are so heavy.*

Ambrosha reached down between her thighs and grabbed hold of Ben's deflated penis.

"Have I frightened your manhood?" she asked. You men place so much value on your penises. Well where is your strength now?" Ambrosha raised a hand and brought it down across Ben's face.

"Open your fuckin eyes," she yelled. "There's one more thing yet." Ben forced his eyes open. *The moment of truth,* he thought. This is the moment where she would end his suffering.

"That's it," Ambrosha whispered, turning her wrist up to expose the vein beneath her skin. She held out her index finger and began pushing forth a second finger nail, rendering the one that allowed her to pass for human of no further use. These nails were a lot harder; as hard as the hardest bone, and as sharp as a set of kitchen knives. She sliced open her wrist and immediately the blood began to flow out. If not for her will, the wound would have closed almost instantly.

"This is going to hurt," she told Ben. Ambrosha grabbed hold of Ben's face and forced his mouth open. She placed her dripping wrist over his mouth and watched the blood trickle down his throat. Ben tried to push the foul-tasting substance back with his tongue but he was unsuccessful. When he began to cough, Ambrosha removed her wrist from his mouth and she gently began to massage his throat. "Swallow," she hissed, "or I will kill you and be done with it."

The self-inflicted wound that Ambrosha had made to her wrist began healing the moment she removed it from Ben's mouth, and the deadly finger nail was once again beneath the skin of the index finger. Ambrosha sat up and watched patiently for her blood to take effect. Ben's eyes were closed now, but she detected movement behind his tightly closed lids. She shifted a bit on top of him and felt his hardness beneath her. If it were not for her blood coursing through his veins, his ability to be erect would not be possible.

Ben had fallen into a state of nothingness. He may as well have been inside of a cloud, because he could see nothing beyond the cloud like fog that surrounded him. Was he dead, he wondered? He must be. There were no shapes of any kind that he could tell. No people, no buildings, or cars. He must be dead. Suddenly, the nothingness began to move before him, like it was clearing a path for something, or some-one. Finally a shape began to take form. With its features still unclear, he was tempted to move forward to get a closer look. *There was no sense in being frightened,* he told himself. *No need to be frightened if you are dead.* As he drew closer to blurry object, its form became more and more recognizable. The form was without doubt, that of a woman. She was wearing what looked to be a white evening gown that began to bleed out like a spreading stain, until finally the gown was red.

"Ambrosha?" he heard himself say. She wore her hair pinned up, and the earrings that dangled and sparkled alongside her slender neck appeared to be upside down crucifixes. If the devil were to take on flesh for the sole purpose to entice man, he could do no better in choosing this form. She was smiling at him now, and he could clearly make out the set of fangs which did nothing except to further enhance her beauty. Ben ran his tongue across his own set of teeth, and was beside himself to find that his own teeth had taken on a change. He was like her now. He was a vampire. He had no idea what this meant, and he was oblivious to the possibilities and limitations that he would possess, now that he was a vampire. *Not to worry,* he told himself, *because she will teach me what I need to know to survive.* Ben glanced down at himself, and was surprised to find that he was in dress shoes and slacks. He held out his arms, a tux? Strange, he thought. This was all so strange. Ambrosha leaned in and whispered into his ear.

"How does it feel to be immortal?" she asked. Before he could answer, she took his hand into her own and led him through the cloud like fog. It was as if the puffy white vapor had a mind of its own. It parted created a path, that as far as he could tell led nowhere. Still, he followed her purpose driven strides, until finally they stood in a clearing. The floor beneath his feet was like a marble tile. It was white, and had what looked to be the patterns of doves, black doves to be exact. Out of nowhere came music. Powerful, like the sound of opera. Ben took one of Ambrosha's hands in his own, and placed the other on the small of her back.

"I'll lead," he said. They danced, and they danced, the whole time staring into one another's eyes. He felt as though she were staring into his soul. He hoped that she could, because if she could, she would know that there was no other place that he would rather be, and that there was no other woman that he would rather be with. He suddenly felt the overpowering desire to kiss her. *Surely she wouldn't deny me,* he thought. After all, she had made him. Ben reached up and gently clasped Ambrosha's chin. He leaned in and passionately kissed her on the corners of her mouth, moving slowly towards the fullness of her lips, but what took him over, was the pleasure that he experience once he found her tongue. *Perhaps it was a little too domestic,* he thought. He guided his lips along the slope of her neck, until he reached a certain spot. He couldn't help himself. It was as if he had lost all will. He bit deep into Ambrosha's flesh. *It was not like I remember,* he thought, tasting her fluid of life. Her blood no longer tasted bitter, but pleasantly sweet. He knew that he should stop, but he was unable. With each drop he felt more and more powerful. So good, he thought, and suddenly, out of nowhere it happened, like something gone terribly wrong. His body began to jerk uncontrollably. He released his hold on Ambrosha's neck and clung to her for dear life.

"What's happening to me?" he asked. Ambrosha didn't respond. What she did offer was a blank stare. The pain he felt was excruciating. It was as if he were being attacked from the inside out.

"Help," he heard himself say, but Ambrosha just stood there, making no effort to aid him. Violently his body jerked. Ben stumbled backwards and away from Ambrosha, and he watched as the cloud like fog began to engulf her. He reached out for her, but her form began to fade away as quickly as it had appeared.

Ambrosha watched as the male began to experience a series of convulsions. Within seconds his heart flat lined, leaving him just as dead as the other nine men. She removed herself from on top of the dead thing and slid off the bed. She stood there for a moment with her hands on her hips. *What now?* she wondered. In light of Robin's male child it would stand to reason that there will one day be more of them, unless she dealt with the root of the problem, that being Robin, the child, hell Raven's whole house hold. With every last one of them gone, her problem would be solved. To do this it was going to require careful planning on her part. There would be no room for mistakes. Any mistakes and the death of her covenant would surely follow. Ambrosha glanced one last time at her experiment gone wrong.

"So much for that," she said as she turned to exit the room.

CHAPTER ELEVEN

Robin was awakened by the subtle pressure of Adam's feet kicking her in the side. She looked over and smiled at the sight of him gnawing at his tiny tight clinched fist.

"Good evening," she said to him. Adam turned his head to face her. "How's my little man?" She rubbed her finger gently across his nose. "I take it you're teething? Adam just stared at her before he finally decided to smile.

"What's so funny? She rubbed his nose again. "Mommy didn't make a joke. Come here you," she picked him up and lifted him into the air. She continued to nurture his good mood by showering him with kisses, that and speaking to him in the universal baby language.

"What would you like to do tonight besides your usual eating and napping?" She giggled. Doesn't that get boring?" She laughed a little harder. She really enjoyed their bonding. It was important that he know happiness and safety in his surroundings.

"I wish papa Eric could be here to enjoy moments like this. You remember him don't you; the strikingly handsome guy? He's going to be a big part of your life. He'll be joining us soon." The expression on Adam's face looked too intense for a child of his age.

"You have the most beautiful eyes she said to him, and you're much too young to have such a serious look about you." Robin scrunched up her nose to see if she could draw a smile from him and it worked.

"There we go," she said. "The girls are going to be like putty in your hands." Robin laid Adam down next to her and climbed out of bed.

"What do you say to some breakfast?" She smiled his way. Robin stepped into the bathroom to grab the robe that she had hanging on a hook behind the door. She was only in the bathroom for a few seconds before she heard his cry. It started out like a typical hunger cry. "I'm coming luv," but when his crying turned into an all out scream she quickly became concerned. Robin exited the bathroom to find Adam right where she had left him, but what alarmed her the most was the obvious pain that he was experiencing, and her not knowing the reason why.

"Adam!" She screamed out as she rushed to the bed.

"Adam, what is it?" Robin began to cry while she attempted to soothe him. The door to her bedroom opened, and Gelsa entered with the rest of her sisters following close behind.

"Something's wrong with him," Robin cried out through a rain of tears. Adam continued to scream from the top of his lungs. His body stiffened in her arms, and that made her cry even harder.

"Dear God help him," Robin called out. Robin looked up at Raven and the others, but their expressions revealed how helpless they were to offer any aid to the situation. Adam's body stiffened again, and Robin could feel a difference this time.

"Oh my God what's happening to him?" Robin cried. Robin heard the sound of something akin to bones popping, and she could literally feel Adam's weight begin to increase in her arms. She stared down at him in horror while bone mass and flesh slowly stretch before her eyes. Meanwhile Adam was still screaming in agony. Whatever it was that was happening to him was taking forever to end.

"Please God make it stop," Robin screamed. She prayed and she prayed to a God that for the most part she had never lost faith in, despite who or what she had become, but when no relief came to Adam, she reason that God might not be so inclined to help a child vampire, no matter his pain and suffering. Finally she laid Adam down on the bed, but she dare not leave his side. She felt the mattress sink. It was Gelsa. She had come over and taken a seat on the bed. Adam's size had increased significantly. He was looking more and more like a little boy now, around four or five years old. A few more seconds went by and his body began to relax. "Thank you God, she prayed. Thank you." She caressed his forehead. "You're going to be okay," she whispered softly in his ear.

"My God Robin, he looks like a five year old child," Thandie said. Robin stared down at the little boy who had only moments ago fit snuggly into the crevice of her arms. He was unconscious, but breathing normally.

"I want to believe so bad that this won't happen again, but in my heart I know that it will."

"Robin," Raven said. "Are you okay?"

"No." Robin shook her head. "I'm not okay. Whatever this is that's happening to Adam nearly broke my heart in two."

"I believe he's alright for now," Guiliana said. "It took a lot out of him." Robin stared past her sisters. She should have known that there would be some sort of price to pay for what she had done. She couldn't help but feel that what Adam, no what they had all experienced tonight was anything but over, and worst yet would it stop? Would it continue until it finally killed him? Was Adam doomed to a life cycle of days or months?

"He's so handsome," Leona said. Robin looked down at Adam. He was exactly that, she thought. His hair was as black as a night sky without a moon, and his facial features were strong for a boy of such young age.

"What if this kills him? Robin said. "I'm not ready to part with him. He just came into my life." Her sisters offered up a warm smile. It was comfort that fell short of what she was actually praying for, but it was the only comfort that they were able to give for the moment.

Eric stared up at the ceiling from the living room sofa. He had been awake for the better part of the night, and was unable to think about anything other than what had happened over the last forty eight hours. Things were happening so fast, but if he knew anything, anything at all, it was how life could move at the speed of a snail one minute, and at the speed of a NASCAR race the next. He was still questioning his resolve. Still questioning whether or not this new chain of events would have enough of his heart to work. He sat up and swung his legs over so that his feet were touching the floor. His bladder was beckoning him to empty it at once. He had managed to hold it for the last ten minutes, because he had been too lazy to get up from the couch.

He stood up and immediately questioned whether or not the couch had been such a good idea. He was definitely feeling the decision that he had made in his lower back. He tried loosening it up with a series of side to side motions. "There," he said with a groan. "I would be asking for it if I slept on it another night." He entered the half bath that was located off the hallway and flipped the light switch on. He struggled at the task of loosening the tie string on his pajamas, while he rushed over to the toilet.

"Shit!" he cursed. The string had somehow made its way into a knot. He danced in front of the toilet before abandoning all hope of loosening the knot.

"Shit," he swore again reaching for the waist band. With some difficulty he managed to pull the pajamas down over his waist, and they hit the floor around his ankles.

"Ah......," was the sound that he made in triumph, as he released a stream of urine towards the bowl of water. When he was finished with that bit of business, he grabbed a piece of toilet tissue to wipe around the toilet seat, because his aim had initially been untrue. After flushing the toilet, Eric flipped off the light switch and headed towards the bedroom. On entering, he paused for a moment to stare at the empty bed that hadn't been made since he and Robin last slept in it.

He shook his head before entering the bedrooms full bath to start his shower. Afterwards he would make himself something to eat and then call Robin.

Robin entered the great room, guiding Adam by his hand. Less than four hours ago he had to be carried everywhere, but now that he was able to walk on his own was beyond freaky to everyone in the house. Adam wore a large T-shirt that stopped just below his knees.

"Aw..., he's so cute," Gelsa said from one of the sofas.

"How is he doing?" Raven asked. Robin looked down at Adam.

"He seems to be doing okay," she answered.

"Bring him," Raven said, motioning for her to come. Robin guided Adam over to where Raven was seated.

"I'm curious. Has he spoken?" Raven asked.

"No. He hasn't said a word," Robin answered. "I've asked him questions, but he just looks at me." Raven studied Adam.

"Adam, my name is Raven." She pointed towards herself. "Do you understand?" Adam didn't respond, at least not in the way that she had hoped. Instead he glanced around the room a few times occasionally fiddling with his fingers. Robin placed a hand over her chest and turned to everyone in the room.

"All I'm asking for is your best guess on this," she said." Besides the obvious, what are your thoughts on what is happening to him?"

Thandie cleared her throat and then said, "What if this is happening because he's male?"

"I don't think he would have survived the change if that were the case," Guiliana said.

"No wait, maybe Thandie has a point," Natalia interrupted. "Let's think about it for a moment," she said. "What if Adam is nature's way of catching up to the rest of us? Wouldn't it stand to reason that because Adam is the first male vampire, that it would do little good for the natural order of things, if he has to achieve adulthood natural the natural way?"

"Oh my God, Guiliana," Robin said. "I would give anything if that were true, and let's say that what you are saying is correct. The question that still remains, is will his growing stop?" The room fell silent, while everyone contemplated Guiliana's theory. The silence was rocked however, when Adam out of nowhere uttered the word Raven. Robin covered her mouth with both hands.

"Adam, you spoke!" she said, barely able to contain her excitement. Gelsa, and Leona, practically leaped out of their seats, while the rest of the women leaned forward in awe.

"Adam, can you say my name?" Robin asked excitedly. He stared at her for a moment before uttering the word Robin.

"Oh my God, he's talking, he's really talking," Robin said, kneeling down and placing her hands on Adam's cheeks.

"Adam, I want you to try a sentence for me, okay? A sentence is more than one word. One word is Robin, or Raven, like you said, but a sentence is more than one." Adam glanced over at Raven, and then around the room before giving Robin his complete attention.

"Can you say, my name is Adam for me?" Adam thought the words in his head. However something didn't seem quite right. Did Robin want him to say all the words in a sentence? Something inside told him no. He thought the words in his head again and instinctively spoke the words. "My name is Adam." Robin stood up and looked from Adam to Raven.

"He learns quickly," Raven said. "It's probably an innate ability of his that is necessary to balance out the rapid growth that he's experiencing. For now, I think we should all cling to Guiliana's theory. If he continues at this rate, I estimate him reaching the age of an adult in less than a month." Leona and Gelsa walked over and placed a hand on Robin's shoulder. The rest of the women stood up and joined them.

"Don't worry," they each said to Robin. "He's going to be fine." Robin shook her head in agreement. It was the only thing that she could do to have a positive perspective on Adams situation.

"Do we share this information with Ambrosha?" Guiliana asked. The women all looked in Raven's direction.

"No. We'll keep this to ourselves for the time being," Raven answered.

Robin sighed. She really didn't need the added stress, but suddenly she thought of Eric. "What about Eric? Robin asked. I can't keep this from him."

"I agree," Raven said. "He should know what's going on."

Robin turned to Adam. "Are you hungry?" she asked him. Adam knew these words. He reached up and grabbed Robin by the hand. She could hardly believe what was happening. Hours ago he might have weighed in at nineteen pounds. Now his weight had to be somewhere close to forty-five. She smiled at him as she led him out of the room.

Ambrosha sat at the vanity, staring at her reflection in the mirror. There were too many reasons to count, why she felt her transformation into a vampire had been a blessing. Privileged is how she felt. If not for the sun and the harm that it was able to in flick on her she would view herself as a god, but she was not a god, only god-like, and the sun was a means to remind her and her kind of that. Still, she had her beauty after so many years, and her strength among other things.

Another night in the presence of Raven and those who would continue to have their nose up her ass, but at least tonight would be short and sweet. She would say what she had to say, state her reason as to why, wait for the response that she knew would come, and then make it known that she would be assuming total control of her house. Victoria and Maxine would be the only ones accompanying her. Even though she would be challenging Raven's leadership, she didn't want it to seem like she was ready to go to war on the spot. There would be harsh words for sure, and even threats, but not war, not yet. Ambrosha stood up and walked over to the walk-in closet. *What to wear*, she thought, sliding clothes that were on hangers along the chrome plated bar. She pulled an outfit off the bar and held it up.

"You'll do," she said. To her left were shelves that supported some of the most expensive brands of shoes in the world, but as many as there was to choose from, she knew exactly the one's that she wanted to wear. She removed the pair of shoes from the shelf and exited the closet. Perhaps after the dust settled, she would consider turning a few more females. The only downside was how many women that would have die before she succeeded in creating a single vampire. The female fatalities didn't bother her, however the number of women that she would have to go through, and the amount of energy involved did. The sacrifice would be well worth it though, if only to create more of her kind. She would ponder over the matter at later time. *First thing first*, she thought; *Raven!*

"He needs clothes," Robin said. "I'm thinking that I should hit a store tonight and purchase a few things."

"That's probably a good idea," Raven said. Guiliana stuck her head inside Robin's bedroom door.

"Ambrosha just pulled up."

"Is she alone?" Raven asked.

"No. She has Victoria and Maxine with her."

"Robin, I want you and Adam to stay up here. There's no reason for you to come down."

"Raven, if you don't mind, I would like to be present," Robin said.

"Are you sure?" Raven asked. Robin shook her head.

"I'm positive," she answered.

"Well in that case – Guiliana let Gelsa know that she is to keep Adam up here."

"I'm on it," Guiliana said.

"Shall we go see what this is about?" Raven asked, turning to Robin.

Raven addressed Ambrosha, Victoria, and Maxine with a raised brow. "I'm surprised to see you again so soon, Ambrosha. What brings you, business or pleasure?" she asked. Ambrosha took a seat in one of the chairs. Robin stayed especially close to Raven. From Ravens house, everyone was present for the exception of Gelsa, and of course Adam.

"This is business," Ambrosha answered.

"I take it that you're still holding on to your difference of opinion concerning Adam?" Raven asked. Ambrosha raised her hands above her head in a manner that showed that she was irritated by something Raven had said.

"What's with the fuckin name," Ambrosha hollered. She lowered her hands. "The reason behind my being here tonight is that I raise serious concerns about your judgment on the issue of this child."

"We all do," Victoria added.

"This child poses a serious threat to our future," Ambrosha continued. "Kill it and be done with it."

"Do you even hear yourself?" Raven asked. "So let me get this straight, Ambrosha. You would have me kill an innocent child simply because he's a male? Are you really that insecure? Well I have news for you. You have lost your mind. It's not going to happen."

Robin felt her blood boiling on the inside. Physically she was no match for Ambrosha, but she didn't need physical strength as long as there were others who were willing to protect Adam. "I've heard enough Ambrosha," Robin spoke. "You're not going to lay a finger on him. Why isn't that sinking into your head?"

"Shut the fuck up," Ambrosha said sternly.

"Your threats mean nothing here," Robin said, and she was about to speak further, when she was interrupted by the gentle pressure of Raven's hand on her own.

"Ambrosha, your opinion is your own. It belongs to you and you alone. My advice to you is to go home and work out your male issues. Adam is under my protection, and will be as long as I have life in me."

"Oh please Raven," Ambrosha said. "You're all so high and mighty. You act as if you don't already have blood on your hands. There is no amount of good that any of you can do now that's going to make a bit of difference for the lives that you have taken over the centuries. God! Oh yes, I could care less about your rooted belief in him. If he does exist, you will never be accepted into his arms because of what you are. If you allow this child to live, he will one day become a man. What do you think will happen when there are suddenly two, and then three? I'll tell you what will happen. It will get to the point where we are over-run by them. Open your eyes Raven, if the world around us has taught us anything, it is that men have a tendency to fuck up everything when power is in their hands."

"I see," Raven said. "This is you laying out flat in front of one of nature's vehicles and telling it over your dead body will it progress any further. You're upset and angry over something you have no control over. You're foolish if you think for one second that you are bigger than nature's intent. Adam is a perfect example of that." Ambrosha shook her head.

"You know what, fuck Adam, and fuck nature. Futures can be decided. As long as I have life in me, I will not accept the existence of male vampires. From this point forward, and as long as that child lives, the meaning of the word sister no longer applies."

"Do be careful, Ambrosha," Raven said with a stern voice, "or are you so quick to forget your place and mine."

Ambrosha stood up. So did Victoria and Maxine.

"We stand with Ambrosha on this Raven," Victoria said. Raven dug her nails into the armrest of the sofa. Ambrosha is clearly out of control were her thoughts, and so were the women who have decided to side with her. Raven straightened in her seat like someone who had suddenly stuck by a revelation. How could I have been so naïve? She thought. Challenging her right now would be like falling into her hands. No. I need time to think, especially if my instincts are right.

"We're leaving now," Ambrosha said. "We'll see ourselves out."

"Ambrosha," Raven called out behind her.

"What is it, Raven," Ambrosha said, halting in her tracks.

"Just this," Raven said. "Regardless of what you might think or feel, I lead this covenant. You thinking otherwise will not negate that. Test me any further on this, and I will be forced to remind you of my claim. You are no match for me on your best day. I would hate to have to prove that to you. There's just one more thing. Dare I find out that you and those who you have been given the privilege to lead, have strayed from the basic rules that govern our survival; Adam will be the least of your worries." Raven motioned to her house to remain seated as she rose to her feet. She wanted to send a message to Ambrosha to clearly state her strength and prevalence as covenant leader. She closed the distance between herself and the three women.

"If you want the mantel, Ambrosha, then you know what you have to do to obtain it," Raven reminded her. Ambrosha turned her nose up to Raven and then turned to exit the room. This was her way of telling Raven that she could kiss her ass as far as she was concern. The women stood up and gathered around Raven. "What now?" Natalia asked.

"It's worse than I thought," Raven said.

"What do you mean?" Leona asked.

"They're feeding on humans," Raven answered.

"Are you certain?" Guiliana asked.

"I am," Raven answered. "Adam is not at the center of their aggression. The fact that he now exists only amplifies it."

"Again, what do we do now?" Natalia asked.

"I don't know just yet," Raven answered. "Any accusations would require proof for which we do have."

"Well I'm going up to check on Adam," Robin said. "And about his clothes; I can wait until tomorrow." Some of her sisters offered up a smile, some a pair of sympathetic eyes. Robin walked away leaving them to ponder over the blonde lunatic who had only moments ago threatened the life of her child. She quickened her pace. She couldn't believe how much she was missing the little guy. It was already bad enough that she had missed some of the most important stages of his life, and that she would probably miss more behind the freakish growth spurts. She also felt the need to call Eric. *What an interesting conversation that's going to be.*

Maxine pushed the SUV slightly above the speed limit along the four lane highway. Victoria sat quietly in the back, while Ambrosha stared out of the passenger side window. Ambrosha lowered the window slightly to allow warm air to enter the cabin. She cursed Raven under her breath for being a fool. How long would she have to wait for an opportunity to snap both Robin and the child's neck? There has to be a way to get to them short of suicide.

A vehicle pulled alongside, interrupting Ambrosha's train of thought. She recognized the make and model. It was a Dodge Caravan. It lingered alongside traveling at the same speed. She could see every occupant inside the van, almost as clearly as if it were daytime in spite of its tinted windows. It moved forward slightly, and then maintained that speed. A little boy sitting all the way to the rear was staring up at the starring sky outside his window. When they had failed to hold his gaze any longer, he shifted his focus onto the vehicle next to him. Ambrosha watched the little boy and wondered how long it would take before he lost interest in the vehicle that she was in to focus his attention on something else. *He looked to be no more than ten years of age,* she thought, running the tip of her tongue across the edges of her teeth. She pushed the electronic button on the door panel and her window lowered all the way down. Maxine glanced over at Ambrosha for a second or two, and then resumed concentrating on the road. Ambrosha watched the boy as he moved his face closer to the window. She smiled at him and was pleased when he had smiled back. She leaned out of the window slightly and bared fangs resembling that of a striking cobra. The little boy's eyes squinted as he pressed his face closer against the window. His eyes grew wide before he scurried away from the window and disappeared. *Coward,* she thought.

"Having fun?" Victoria asked from the rear seat.

"Hardly," Ambrosha answered, raising her window. "Fun would have been feeding on the entire family."

"I suppose, but on another note, you do understand how impossible it's going to be to get near the child without taking losses." Ambrosha didn't respond. She wasn't a complete idiot. She just didn't believe in the impossibility to get to the child. For starters, Robin has weaknesses that can be taken advantage of. Her love for the male human is one of them.

"Not impossible," Ambrosha said. "That Robin is a stupid one. Her desire to have a normal life is all the advantage we'll need to get to her and the child. I'll bet my life that her human lover is sitting inside their home as we speak."

"It's possible," Victoria said, "but do you really believe that she would offer the child's life for his?"

"No. I do believe that she would offer her own though," Ambrosha answered.

"Hm...You may have a point," Victoria said. "Further proof, that having a conscience is overrated."

"I agree," Ambrosha said, "and if I know Raven, and I do, a rescue attempt is in her blood. She'll do anything for Robin's benefit; exposing her own weakness that we will be able to act upon. Now all we need is a fuckin address."

"And that's where I come in," Maxine said. "I visited her home once. When she moved out she left something behind. I graciously drove out to her place to deliver it to her. I say graciously, because at the time I was happy that we were being rid of her. She never fit in."

"We won't chance it tonight," Ambrosha said. "There's not enough time. We'll drive out tomorrow, and hopefully get lucky."

CHAPTER TWELVE

"**H**ey where have you been?" Eric asked. "I've been calling you."

"I'm sorry Eric. It's been fuckin crazy here, and disturbing!"

"Okay, what's going on?" Eric asked.

"Where do I start," Robin answered, taking a deep breath. "I guess I'll start with Ambrosha, and how she is dead set on Adam's nonexistence, and not just her but her entire house."

"You can't be serious," Eric said. "Why? I mean I know that Ambrosha can be a bitch most of the time, but why would she want to harm Adam?"

"She's twisted, Eric. She somehow believes that Adam will ultimately be our down fall. She harbors a deep hatred for men, so you can only imagine her position on a future where male vampires might exist."

"What's Raven's stance on this?"

"She more or less told Ambrosha to go fuck herself, but I still get a sense that Adam will never be safe as long as Ambrosha lives, and breathes."

"Try not to worry too much. She'd be a fool to go up against Raven and the others," Eric said.

"I'm not so sure about that," Robin said. "Something happened just hours before Ambrosha arrived; something that could put Adam at even a greater risk."

"Okay, I'm listening," Eric said.

"I know you're listening, I just hope that you're ready," Robin said hesitantly.

"Will you tell me already," Eric said impatiently.

"Adam went through something that has all of us worried and baffled, and if you though that we were baffled before, then you're going to have even a greater time wrapping your mind around what I am about to tell you."

"I'm listening," Eric said.

"To put it mildly he's no longer the little boy that you remember," she said.

"Get to it already," Eric insisted.

"His body went through some kind of a metamorphosis."

"Metamorphosis," Eric repeated the word.

"Yes," Robin said. "He's grown about two feet. Eric, he looks like a five-year-old boy."

"You're kidding me," was Eric's response.

"I'm afraid not Eric, and to be honest with you I'm worried sick about him."

"There was complete silence on both ends of the line for the span of about ten seconds.

"Is he fine now?" Eric asked.

"He's okay," Robin answered. "I just hate the fact that I have missed out on four or five years of his life. Those are the most important stages of a child's development." Eric wanted to console her, but he didn't know how.

"On the bright side of things he's fine," Eric said. "We can be glad for that."

"I am, but it still doesn't change the fact," she said.

"Well just so you know I put in for a leave of absence. There's really no need for me to continue working," Eric said.

"You're right, there isn't. In fact I see no reason for you to be there at all. Can't you handle most of what needs to be handled from here?" Robin asked.

"As a matter of fact I can," he said.

"Well why don't you pack most of your clothes so that you can head up this way tomorrow? No, scratch that. I'll come up tomorrow, and you can tail me back."

"Why do you need to come up?" Eric asked.

"Okay, don't take this the wrong way, but you'll have your hands full packing your own things. I left some stuff there that I wouldn't want you to forget."

"Ouch!"

"Sorry."

"It's okay."

"I love you, Eric."

"I love you too. Hang in there, okay? I'll see you tomorrow."

She had to admit that she was somewhat surprised that Raven hadn't put up a fuss last night after she had explained to her that she would be driving home to pick up a few more of her things. She seemed to be more excited about Eric coming up. His presence in the house would cause everyone to have to make an adjustment. A human male living under the same roof with eight female vampires was going to be tuff. Eric was probably going to feel the most uncomfortable, and that sucked, because there was no telling how long she and Eric were going to have to remain under Raven's protection. How long would it be, before she and Eric felt safe enough to venture out on their own with Adam? And then there was the instability surrounding his growth. Oh God! What if he suffers another one in her absence? She hadn't thought of that.

It seemed like she had a million things to worry about, and not one of them was going to give her lesser cause to worry anytime soon. Robin applied a little more force to the accelerator paddle, and the needle on the gage move from sixty miles an hour to seventy. She was suddenly wishing that she had stayed with Adam.

Eric reached down and grabbed the television remote that was lodged between two sofa cushions, and placed it on the coffee table. He scanned the living room once more. *It looks good,* he thought. He had started cleaning over an hour ago. The house hadn't looked that bad; he just knew that it could stand more cleaning. Robin was already under enough stress. Walking into clean familiar surroundings might alleviate some of that. He walked into the kitchen and removed an apple from the fruit bowl that sat on top of the counter. He'd eaten a decent breakfast, but that was over two hours ago. His stomach was looking forward to lunch.

Eric glanced down at his watch. *I'd better shower and get dressed. Robin is going to be here soon.* He bit deep into the apple while heading towards the bedroom. He had no sooner taken a few steps when the door bell rang. He raised an eyebrow. *That can't be Robin,* he thought. *It's a little too early, and the only reason she wouldn't use her own key, would be if her hands were occupied.* He checked his watch as he made his way towards the front door. When he opened the door, he immediately regretted not having first looked through the peep hole.

"It's Eric, right?" the female asked from the other side of the door-way. He felt his heart as it began to pound faster in his chest. This was no ordinary woman. He recognized her for what she was; a vampire. He was in trouble. Worse yet, Robin would be here soon, but he doubted that he would have the opportunity to warn her.

"Hi," the female said, shaking him out of his trance. I'm Maxine, do you remember me?" Eric stood there contemplating what he should do. *Nothing,* he thought. There was nothing that he could do that would get him out of his current predicament. He did remember her however. Robin had accidently left a gold bracelet behind when she'd moved out of the mansion. She'd given Maxine the directions to their house, after Maxine had told her that she had no problem making the drive to deliver it to her.

"Um...what can I do for you?" Eric asked.

"Well for starters, you can let us in," Maxine answered.

"Us?" was Eric's response. He looked past her, but saw no one else.

"Yes us." Another woman accompanied by two more stepped into view. *Fuck me,* he thought, recognizing one of the women to be Ambrosha. Maxine stepped across the doors thresh hold brushing against his arm as she pasted. This was nothing like the movies where he would have been safer, after denying them entrance into his home.

"Um...Where's Robin?" he asked, believing the question might somehow throw them off. It didn't. It lingered in the air and was quickly forgotten. The four vampires walked around the living room like they were casing it. Meanwhile his heart was still beating a mile a minute.

"What do you want, Ambrosha?" Eric asked. Ambrosha walked over and stood inch in front of him.

"And how is it that you remember me or my name?" Ambrosha asked. *He would be damned if he answered that question,* he thought.

"Now you've got me curious," Ambrosha said.

"Why?" Eric asked.

"Well for starters, you're asking questions about Robin's whereabouts. Are you saying you don't know where she is?"

"No. I was just wondering if something happened that I wasn't aware of, but now that I know different, I just want to know why you're here."

Ambrosha smiled. "Well if you absolutely must know, we need your help with a problem."

"I'm not following," Eric said. "How can I be of any help to you?"

"It'll be easy," Ambrosha answered. "You won't have to lift a finger, I promise."

"Look, whatever you guys are up to, can you just please take it somewhere else?

"I'm afraid not," Ambrosha said, "and I must insist on your help."

Curious, Eric asked. "What is it that you want me to do?"

Ambrosha backed up a few steps and then studied Eric for a moment. "What is the child worth to you?" Ambrosha asked. "Would you sacrifice Robin's life for it? Would you sacrifice your own?"

"If you lay a hand on Robin…" Before he had time to realize how stupid and dumb his bravado had been, the one called Maxine charged in and delivered a painful blow to his chest. The force behind the blow lifted him clean off the floor, leaving gravity to take care of the rest. Eric landed hard on his back. When his vision had finally cleared, and his breathing was somewhat stabilized, Eric found himself staring up into Maxine's face. She was standing over him with her legs apart. He blinked twice for affirmation. Maxine wasn't wearing panties beneath the short leather skirt that she had on.

"See something you like? He heard Maxine ask. "Now what would Robin say?" That was enough to snap him out of the trance that he'd been in.

"Too late, you already looked," Maxine giggled.

"Quiet!" Ambrosha whispered, pushing the hair away from her ears.

Maxine lowered herself onto Eric, so that she was straddling his waist, and then she placed her hand over his mouth.

"There's a car pulling into the driveway," Ambrosha said. Eric knew that it could only be Robin. I have to do something to warn her, he thought. He reached up and put both hands around Maxine's neck, thinking that a surprise attack might be all he needed to create a ruckus. She might even remove her hand from his mouth long enough for him to call out. Maxine grabbed Eric's wrist with her free hand and twisted it slightly. His eyes widened from the immense pain. He even felt a tear run down the side of his face, and a whimper was all the warning that he could muster beneath the vice like grip that Maxine had on his mouth.

"Be still or I'll snap your neck," Maxine whispered. They each heard the sound of the key being placed in a lock.

Robin turned the key and then froze. There were vampires inside. How could she have been so careless? We should have anticipated this. I should have anticipated this. They had under estimating Ambrosha, by not accounting for Eric's safety. She considered phoning Raven before she entered the house, but she had already turned the key. Eric was her main concern now. Robin turned the doorknob, and then stepped inside of the house.

"Hello, Robin," Ambrosha greeted her. "Close the door behind you, please." Robin scanned the room for Eric. He was pinned to the floor on his back with Maxine sitting on top of him. She was outnumbered four to one.

"Why are you here, Ambrosha? And what gives you the right to come into my home?"

"Save your breath, Robin. Your questions mean nothing to me. I'm more anxious to know how you're going to answer mine," she said, walking over to take a seat on the living room couch.

"Let Eric go," Robin demanded.

"I can't do that, not yet anyway," Ambrosha said. Robin took a deep breath and then made a B-line towards Maxine. She had begun mapping out in her head the moment that she had entered the room how she would attack if it came down to it. Well it had come down to it. Constance and Tesa reached out to grab both her arms, but she instinctively shifted to a mist form, leaving her would be capturer's nothing but air to clutch onto. It took her less than a second or two to shift back, and when she did she revealed just how deadly she could be when backed into a corner. Nails as sharp as a set of kitchen knives were exposed. Robin felt a hand on her shoulder. She instinctively lashed back at her assailant cutting into flesh. When she adjusted her angle towards Maxine, Ambrosha was suddenly between them. Robin froze in her tracks. Further attempt to aid Eric was pointless with Ambrosha standing before her. Constance grabbed one of Robin's arms and Tesa grabbed the other.

"Let him go Ambrosha, he has nothing to do with this," Robin pleaded.

"That's not true," Ambrosha responded. "He is a part of this and he has you to thank for that."

"Why are you doing this?" Robin searched each of their faces. "You act as though I am an enemy. Are we not the same? Are we not sisters of a kind?"

"Sisters of a kind yes, but we are not the same, Robin. We are different on almost every level. You can't see far enough ahead to appreciate what I am trying to do for all of us. What kills me the most is neither can Raven. She is supposed to be so wise, but I believe wisdom agrees with me on this."

"But Adam is just a child," Robin argued.

"You're naïve, girl. You're viewing him much like a child views a puppy. He's small, cute, and adorable right now, but that will change as soon as he reaches adulthood."

"That's where you're wrong," Robin argued. "Have you forgotten that we don't age? Robin wanted to try and take advantage of what Ambrosha was still unaware of concerning Adam's recent growth spurt. So you see, Adam is not a threat to any of us."

"Sorry," Ambrosha said, "but it's not something that I am willing to risk. Every trace of him will have to be burned."

"You really need to think about what you're doing, Ambrosha; when Raven finds out…"

"Fuck Raven. Raven this, Raven that. As far as I'm concerned Raven is without a clue. I'm done with her. I'm done with all of you. None of you are able to see the negative impact that this child will have on us twenty or so odd years from now. So this is a fuckin mutiny. I want my own goddamn ship."

Robin held her silence. She knew that her words meant nothing to Ambrosha. She relaxed her arms, hoping that Constance and Tesa might do the same with the pressure they held on hers. It appeared to be working. Ambrosha's rambling bullshit might even be helping her cause. Unfortunately, phasing from a stand still position was useless. Shifting to her mist form was at its most usefulness in motion.

Ambrosha walked over to the bar stool counter and grabbed an apple from the bowl. "I can't remember the last time I tasted one of these," she said, "and so I can't say that I miss it. What about you, Robin? Do you miss the taste of food? Don't answer that. The question is irrelevant."

Robin readied herself for another attempt at Maxine. She would hardly be expecting it. Meanwhile, Ambrosha was standing off to the side twirling the apple around in her hand. "Enough talk," Ambrosha said. *Now*, Robin thought, raising both arms and bringing them about to break free. With all the strength that she could muster she shoved both women away and darted for Maxine. She hadn't taken two steps when she felt the searing pain in her back. It was either Constance, or Tesa, but one of them managed to slashed open her back. Her plan was already failing. What if she achieved nothing beyond getting herself and Eric killed? If Ambrosha's plans were to kill them both anyway, then she may as well make the effort. Adam was safe, and that was all that mattered. Robin reached out for Maxine, but was thwarted. She found herself on the floor near the kitchen with Constance on top of her. She struggle against the vice like grip that her sister vampire held on her wrist. Robin bared her fangs, and Constance returned the treat with a catlike hiss. The two vampires were at each other like a pair of rabid dogs. Robin managed to get one arm free, and she used it to slash open Constance's jaw. She raised her hand to deliver another blow, but her arm was quickly seized by Tesa. Robin hissed, but the animal like sound was quickly quieted once she felt Constance's hand around her throat.

"Hold her," Ambrosha yelled. Robin looked up to see Ambrosha bearing down on her with a wooden stake. With every ounce of strength that she had left, Robin attempted to lift her shoulder. The stake breezed past her, missing her by an inch.

"Damn it!" Ambrosha screamed. Hold her down!" Tesa pinned Robin's shoulder to the floor. Ambrosha raised the wooden stake high above her head. This time she brought it home. Robin screamed out in agony. Through sheer reflexes, she attempted to shift to her mist form. The woods properties however, would not allow it. In the end, she was forced to relax and seize her struggles, but Constance and Tesa maintain a tight hold on her.

"It hurts like hell, doesn't it?" Ambrosha said, kneeling down beside her. Robin looked over at Eric to make sure that he was still okay. Maxine was still straddling him, but she had removed her hand from his mouth.

"Are you okay?" Eric asked. Robin nodded to let him know that she was. Robin locked eyes with Maxine. She wished that she could knock the smug expression off her face. She was never one to hold grudges, but if the opportunity presented itself, she would torture Maxine and remind her repeatedly of the reason that she was doing it.

"Bind her," Ambrosha ordered, tossing Tesa a roll of rope. Tesa started with Robin's ankles and finished with her wrist. Meanwhile the flesh around the wooden stake had begun healing but with difficulty. Ambrosha ran a finger along the length of the wood causing Robin to winch with pain. She couldn't believe the amount of discomfort she felt just at the slightest touch.

"You thought going in was a mother. Pulling it out feels worse," Ambrosha said.

"What do you want to do with him?" Constance asked. Ambrosha walked over and knelt down beside Maxine and Eric.

"Try not to leave out anything. Put him to sleep," Ambrosha ordered. Maxine leaned in close to Eric.

"This is going to hurt," she told him. "You can close your eyes if you like."

"Just get it over with," Eric said.

"If you say so," Maxine grinned. She raised her fist and brought it down across Eric's chin. His body went limp immediately. Ambrosha looked over at Constance and Tesa. "Take her to the truck. The two vampires lifted Robin off the floor, and then headed towards the door. Robin glanced over at Eric and was relieved that Ambrosha had allowed him to live. "You didn't have to hit him so hard," she said to Maxine.

"I know, but I wanted to."

CHAPTER THIRTEEN

Dawn was less than an hour away, and Robin still wasn't answering her cell phone. Her frustration had only mounted when she realized that she didn't have Eric's number. Robin's overwhelming concern for Adam was even more reason enough for her to have called by now. She reached for her phone; it wouldn't hurt to try again. She would try as many times as it would take until she figured out what was going on.

Tesa pulled the SUV up to the front of the house and parked. A noise erupted from the third row seat where Robin lay on her side.

"It's her cell again," Constance said. Robin's cell phone had begun ringing about thirty minutes after they had left her home. Ambrosha knew that it could only be Raven or Eric calling. Her initial thought had been to remove it from Robin's pocket and toss it out the window, but then it dawned on her that she might receive some pleasure counting the number of times that it would ring. Ambrosha turned around in her seat.

"Give it to me," she said. Constance reached inside Robin's pocket and pulled out the phone. She then handed it to Ambrosha. "Take her inside," Ambrosha said. Maxine stepped out of the driver's seat and headed towards the front entrance of the mansion, while Tesa and Constance removed Robin from the SUV. Ambrosha checked Robin's call log. Four calls within the last hour and each of them had been made by Raven. Eric must be unconscious still. She would allow Raven's concern for Robin to build a while longer.

A sound in the far distance guided Eric towards consciousness. It was the sound of a phone ringing; faint at first, but growing louder with each ring. He opened his eyes slowly, but by this time the ringing had stopped. He rolled onto his stomach and pushed himself up using one hand because his wrist was broken on the other one. He had to steady himself once he realized that the room was spinning. *Got up too quickly,* he thought shaking his head. He took a few steps forward; stopped; balanced himself again and then continued in the direction where he believed his phone to be. He spotted it on the coffee table lying next to the television remote.

Eric reached down and picked the phone up to identify the missed call. It was a 1-888 number; hardly the number that he was expecting. There was no questioning what he should do next. He walked over to the refrigerator to locate Raven's cell phone number. He was thankful that she had written it down before she left. He dialed Raven's number and then waited for her to pick up. Raven answered on the first ring.

"Hello!" Her voice sounded close to panic.

"They took Robin," Eric heard himself say. The words were so uncomforting he had to fight back tears. "They drove a stake through her and knocked me unconscious. They were gone when I woke up."

"Okay, calm down," Raven said. "Tell me what happened from beginning to end." Eric explained to exactly what had taken place to Raven.

"I promise you that we will get her back Eric. Are you okay to drive up?"

"I think so, he answered. What are they planning on doing to her Raven?"

"I don't believe that they are going to do anymore then they have already done, Raven answered. It's obvious what Ambrosha wants. What we have to figure out is how we're going to proceed."

"You have to figure something out and quick, Raven. Ambrosha is clearly psychotic. They all are."

"Like I said, we'll get her back even if we have to end lives to do so," Raven said.

"I know that you'll do everything that you can. I'm already packed and ready to go. Will there be someone to greet me when I get there? The sun will be up."

"Yes there will be, and I'll phone you if anything changes."

"Okay, then I'll see you soon."

"Eric?"

"Yes, Raven."

"My apologies, we should have known that something like this could happen."

"You couldn't have known. I don't believe that any of us would have thought that Ambrosha would go this far. Let's just focus on how we're going to get Robin back," he said.

"Okay, then be safe on the road."

"Ambrosha has crossed the line," Guiliana said, pacing back and forth across the great room's marble tile floor.

"That is an understatement," Gelsa said in agreement, "and even worse, they've cut off all communication. They aren't answering their phones."

"They can afford to keep us worrying, and guessing. There is nothing that we can do now; the sun rises in an hour," Raven said.

"What do we do in the mean time?" Leona asked. "It's going to be especially hard to sleep knowing that Robin is in serious trouble."

"We wait," Raven said. "It's the only thing we can do now. Eric will be here in a couple of hours. I'll wait up until he arrives. How is Adam doing, Gelsa?"

"What he experienced seems to have taken a toll on him, but otherwise he's fine. I put him down for bed a half hour ago."

"Good, he's been through a lot. Has he asked for Robin?"

"He called out her name as I was tucking him in. I told him how much Robin loves him and that he would see her again soon. I think he understands well, and that he's capable of saying a whole lot more. He's probably just a little reluctant to speak as freely as he is able."

"Robin would be happy to know how well you are caring for him, Gelsa," Thandie said. He's taken a real liking to you."

"I'm not doing much. Robin is the one that he needs. Let's focus on getting her back to him."

"We will," Raven said. "Okay, so we wait, and for Robin's sake we try diplomacy first."

"And if diplomacy doesn't work?" Guiliana asked.

Raven fell silent. "If diplomacy doesn't work, then they leave us with no other choice," Raven answered. What Ambrosha has done is unforgiveable, and when the smoke finally clears; after Robin is safe, and if Ambrosha is still alive, she will still have to answer for her actions. I don't have the proof, but I'm convinced that they're all on warm blood."

"That in itself is more than enough cause to bring their whole house down," Guiliana added.

"I agree," Natalia added.

"Then let's hope that we hear something soon," Raven said.

Gelsa entered her bedroom and quietly closed the door behind her. She glanced over at her bed to see Adam curled up and sleeping peacefully with the sheet just above his ankles. She walked over to the bed and pulled the sheet up to his shoulders. The thought of going to war, with the women that she has known forever was unsettling for all of them, yet hands were being forced, and this little guy was in the center of it all. *If Raven is right about their new feeding habits, then war would have probably been an inevitable reality. Victoria, Constance, Maxine; hell each of them have personalities that mesh perfectly with Ambrosha's own misguided way of thinking. If they are feeding on warm blood they won't want to stop, not even if Raven commanded. Add a recently made vampire male child to the equation, and we're talking gasoline to a fire. Who knows how this will all end, but whatever the finale, may we not be robbed of the severing of Ambrosha's head from her body.*

"I'm not going to let anything happen to you Adam, and we're going to do whatever it takes to get your mom back to you safely." The way that she'd taken to him surprised even her; perhaps because she had always clung to what she now realized, were nothing more than negative images of what it might be like to have to raise a child. It was nice to finally find out that she was wrong.

Eric turned his car onto the road that he had taken only two other previous times in his life. He rolled down his window as he pulled alongside the telecommunications box. It seemed sort of funny that vampires would need this much security. He buzzed the alarm twice. Raven assured him that there would be someone waiting up for him when he arrived. The temperature outside was blazing hot. Even with the air condition running he could still feel the heat trying to force its way inside the car. It would be a gratifying feeling to be able to drag Ambrosha and her entire household kicking and screaming out into this scorching sun. He'd find great pleasure in watching each of them burn.

Eric heard a click followed by the motorized sound that the gate made as it opened. He raised the window up and proceeded to drive through.

"Here we go," he said, driving down the long stretch of road, making his way towards his temporary new home. Eight female vampires and one male human, was going to make for an uncomfortable living situation. Eric pulled up to the front entrance and switched off the car engine. He picked up his cell phone and dialed Raven's number, because her number was the only number that he had. Raven answered on the second ring. "The door is open," she said. Eric opened the car door and stepped out into the midday heat. The majority of the things that he had brought with him were inside the trunk of the car. He would have to make a minimum of two trips, so he would grab whatever he could carry on the first one.

Eric stepped inside the house, pulling two suitcases on wheels. He didn't expect to be greeted at the door; not while the sunlight was beaming through. He placed the suitcases in a corner, and then headed back out to the car to get the rest of his belongings. When he returned with his things, he locked the door behind him. When he turned around Raven was standing at the end of the foyer.

"Would you like some help?" she asked.

"No I've got it, thanks."

"You remember which room is Robin's, right?"

"Up the stairs take a left; second room on the left."

"Correct," Raven said.

"Still no word?"

"No, and I doubt that we will hear anything before nightfall." Eric grabbed the handles of the bags and followed Raven up the stairs.

"How's Adam doing?" Eric asked as they ascended the stairs.

"He seems to be doing okay, considering," Raven answered.

"That's a relief. Robin filled me in. Have you figured out why this is happening to him?"

"No. We can only speculate."

"Where is he now?" Eric asked.

"Gelsa has been caring for him in Robin's absence."

"Hm…. Look I know it's late, but would it be okay if I looked in on him?"

"I would prefer that you waited until tonight. Gelsa is no doubt sound asleep."

"That's fine," Eric said. He stopped in front of Robin's room and set the suitcases down. "I guess I'll see you in a few hours then." Raven nodded, and then headed off towards her own room. Eric opened the door and peeked inside the room. No light shown through because the windows were designed to block out sunlight. Still the room provided enough light that he was able to see what he was doing. He grabbed the suitcases from the hall, and set them down on the floor next to Robin's dresser. The duffle bag that contained his deodorant and toothpaste were still downstairs next to the front door. He exited the room and headed back downstairs to bring up the rest of his stuff. When he returned he shut the door to Robin's room, and then placed the bags at the foot of the bed. He removed the toothbrush and toothpaste from the zip pocket and stepped inside the bathroom. The bathroom looked especially clean. The only place that showed any evidence of its use was the shower, where soap film had adhered to the glass. He did a half ass job on his teeth and then laid the toothbrush on the sink counter after he had rinsed it off. Eric stepped out of the bathroom and crawled onto the bed fully clothed. His thoughts circled around Robin, and the emotional as well as the physical pain she must be experiencing at the moment. He wasn't able to think about anything else. More than a half hour went by before he finally dozed off to sleep.

When Eric opened his eyes, he was amazed by how dark the room could truly get. Again, the room reflected the life of a vampire. He felt his way over to the bedside lamp, and with some difficulty he was able to switch it on. The room lit up around him, and he immediately looked down at his watch. 10:00 pm. He crawled out of the bed and walked over to the bedroom door, where he opened it and stuck his head out into the hall. Not a soul in either direction. He closed the door; picked up the suitcase and laid it on top of the bed. After a quick shower he would head downstairs and find out what was going on.

Eric stepped inside the large room. "Why didn't anyone wake me?" he asked, shutting the doors behind him. Everyone seemed present; still no one answered. The room was covered by an awkward silence.

"I felt you could use the sleep," Raven said. "Regardless, I was just about to send someone to see if you were up."

"You've heard something?" Eric asked, hearing a hint of excitement in his own voice.

"Yes. A few minutes ago," Raven answered.

"So tell me. What's going on? Is Robin okay?" Eric asked.

"I spoke with Ambrosha of course. It turns out that there will be no reasoning with her. Robin is fine, but Ambrosha promised me on her own life that she would make Robin suffer before killing her, if we didn't hand Adam over. She wanted me to understand that it would be a total shame if I didn't comply, because she would get what she wanted eventually anyway. I told her that I needed some time to consider her offer."

"So what do we do now?" Eric asked." We can't let Robin suffer anymore then she has, and we can't give them Adam. Speaking of Adam, where is he?" Eric glanced around the room. When he didn't see him, he assumed that he was with Gelsa because he didn't see her in the room.

"He's with Gelsa," Raven answered. "To answer your other questions, Eric, we're going to have to go get her."

"I'm definitely down for that," Leona said, cracking her knuckles.

"So am I," Thandie added.

"We all are," he heard Guiliana say.

"All we have to do now is figure out how we are going to get it done," Raven said.

The doors opened, and everyone in the room suddenly shifted their attention in that direction. Eric couldn't believe his eyes. *No way,* the two words seemed to play over and over in his mind. Even though Robin had given him forewarning, he simply couldn't believe his eyes. It was hard to believe, that this was the same kid that Robin had driven off with three nights ago. Eric walked over to where Gelsa and Adam were standing, and knelt down to get a better look at him.

"Hi Adam, do you remember me?" Eric asked. Adam just stood there staring back at him, while he held on tight to Gelsa's hand.

"He's a handsome little guy, isn't he?" Eric said.

"He is that," Gelsa agreed.

"My God, I get where Robin was coming from, when she was trying to explain to me how she feeling about the years gone by. He looks like a five-year-old, yet despite the time gone by, I'm just thankful that he's alive," Eric said.

"He's clearly a special boy," Guiliana said, "and though we struggle with the fact that we have missed some of his years, with the possibility of more to follow, I believe that whatever it is that's going on with him, it will eventually stop."

"I hope you're right," Eric said. "Anything else just wouldn't be right."

"You must be starving, Eric," Natalia said. "There's food for you in the kitchen. Obviously we don't cook, so we ordered in for you."

"Thanks, I appreciate it that, and you're right I am starving." Eric placed his hand on top of Adam's head and ruffled his hair.

"I can't get over how big you've gotten," Eric said to him. He turned towards Raven. Please keep me in the loop," he asked.

"Of course," Raven answered. Eric nodded and then exited the room.

CHAPTER FOURTEEN

She had tested the restraints several times, before she had finally decided to just give up. They had proven too strong, and the pain that accompanied her shoulder too much to bear, whenever she placed a great deal of strain on it. The stake of course, was still where Ambrosha had placed it. Had they removed it, she would have easily escaped her bonds.

Her situation was bleak. There was no escape, and the room that they had placed her in was filled with the scent of blood. *Ambrosha's been busy,* Robin thought; *busy feeding and killing humans inside this very room. The room where I will probably meet my own end, but at least Eric and Adam are safe.*

Stop! she told herself. *Stop focusing on death as if it were your impending fate. This is far from over, and there are seven other vampires who no doubt share her sentiment. If nothing else, I know that I can rely on them to keep that which is important to me safe.* Robin's body tensed when she realized that someone was approaching.

The door opened and Tesa entered the room. The expression that she wore on her face was emotionless; without feeling, but that was normal for Tesa. The dark-haired she-devil closed the door behind her, and approached the bed carrying a glass filled three quarters to the rim with blood.

"She has a heart after all," Robin said, referring to Ambrosha. "I was beginning to think that her hatred towards me extended to depriving me of food." Tesa sat down on the bed next to Robin, and lifted her head so that she could drink from the glass. Robin downed half the substance greedily.

"I want to speak with Ambrosha," Robin said, running her tongue across her lips to remove the excess blood. Tesa stared at her for a moment and then grinned.

"Tesa, say something, will you?" Tesa lifted the glass to Robin's lips so that she could finish what remained. Robin lay her head back down on the plastic-covered mattress and stared up at the ceiling.

"You're all going to fail," Robin said. "The only thing you might manage to do is take the life of one or more of your sisters for a meaningless cause, but some of you, if not all, will die."

Tesa stood up and smiled at Robin. "You're all weak," Tesa said, looking down on Robin. You wouldn't be here if your house was strong." Robin closed her eyes. She dared not look into Tesa's eyes from fear that perhaps she may be right. She simply couldn't afford to have her hope shattered by a few spoken words. Was Tesa right? The thought clung to her like unwanted gum on a shoe. *Did we classify as weak; the old adage that good guys finish last? Did Ambrosha have the upper hand, because she was willing to operate with less conscience?* She closed her eyes, and attempted to focus on something that wouldn't shred what little hope remained.

It had taken him less than ten minutes to shower and get dressed. Robin's abduction had introduced him to a level of anxiety that he'd never felt before. He knew that it was important for him to continue functioning properly. It was just difficult to do when Robin's life was hanging on the line. He walked into the library after having been told, that it was where he would find Gelsa and Adam. He spotted them sitting at one of the tables, where Gelsa was reading a book to him. Eric walked up to the table and stood next to Gelsa.

"How's he doing?" Eric asked.

"He's doing as well as one could expect given his circumstances. Despite all the years that he has missed, he has an increased learning ability watch. Adam, can you read this sentence?" Gelsa pointed to a spot on the book. Adam looked up at Gelsa, and then at Eric and began reading. ["Gareth watched Adele as she went about arranging her new quarters at the museum."]

"Isn't that amazing," Gelsa said, overly excited.

"It is amazing," Eric agreed. "What book is he reading from?"

"A favorite of mine; The Vampire Empire," Gelsa answered. Eric grinned.

"I'm not surprised," he said.

Gelsa looked down at Adam. "Adam, I have to leave you for a couple of hours, but I'll be back. Can you hang out with Eric until then?"

Adam looked up at Eric, and then Gelsa. "Yes," he said.

Gelsa smiled at him. "We're meeting to discuss how we're going to go about fixing our problem," Gelsa said, looking up at Eric. You two could use some time together, don't you think?"

"Absolutely," Eric agreed.

"Okay then, I'll find the two of you when we're done with the business," she said.

"Okay." Gelsa stood up and ran her fingers through Adam's hair.

"I'll see you in a little while, okay?" Adam looked up at Gelsa and shook his head. Eric took a seat next to Adam, and Gelsa turned to leave the room.

"Looks like it's just the two us," Eric said. "Do you want to read some more?" he asked Adam. Adam nodded his head, indicating that he did.

"Okay then, let's start where you left off."

Robin opened her eyes to the sound of a doorknob turning. She turned her head to see Ambrosha entering the room. "You brought this on yourself, Robin," Ambrosha said, taking a seat at the edge of the bed, "but you are not the only one at fault here. Raven is as much to blame as you are, but honestly Robin, you are as selfish as they come. Think about everything you've done so far that could have easily put our covenant in harm's way, and then you fuck up even more by turning a child."

Robin shook her head in disbelief. "You're fuckin one to talk, Ambrosha. You have been feeding on humans. You are seriously fucked in the head, and I solemnly swear, that if you lay a finger on Adam, I will make a deal with the devil if I have to exact my revenge on you."

Ambrosha raised her hand high above Robin, and then slapped her hard across the face. The nerve endings in the left side of her face felt as though they were on fire, but it was a small price to pay for having threatened Ambrosha's life. The message was worth the pain she felt. "Care to threaten me again?" Ambrosha asked. Robin set her mouth to say something that she was sure would earn her another lick, but decided against it.

"That's more like it," Ambrosha said. "Let me paint a clear picture for you," she continued. "I'm going to kill you, that child of yours, and because I am sure that Raven will stand in my way; she'll have to die also, along with etc. etc. Get my point? That is how serious I am about this. You can make a deal with the devil, God, whomever you want, I won't be thwarted from my convictions, which are to see the child dead. Rest up. It will all be over soon." Ambrosha stood up to exit the room.

"How long, Ambrosha? How long have you been feeding on humans?"

Ambrosha smiled. "See, that's another reason why you all need to be ghost. I have lived this way for far too long. I am a vampire, and it pisses me off that I haven't been living as one. That must be very uncomfortable for you?" Ambrosha asked, pointing at the stake in Robin's shoulder.

Robin had to bite down on her lip to keep herself from saying something she might regret.

"Don't fret," Ambrosha said. "I'll remove it right after I've severed your head from your body." With that, Ambrosha left the room, leaving Robin to wrestle with fears of the unknown. Robin yanked on her restraints in frustration. *It can't end this way. It just can't,* she thought. Robin closed her eyes and made an attempt to empower her battered spirit, with thoughts centered upon hope.

"So we are doing this tomorrow?" Guiliana asked.

"Yes," Raven answered. "We don't have much of a choice. Time is not on our side."

"How do you want to do this, Raven?" Natalia asked.

"I have an idea," Raven answered. "I just hope that it doesn't get any of us killed. Gelsa, you and Thandie will remain behind. If something should go wrong, it'll be up to you guys to get Eric and Adam to safety."

"Roger that," was Gelsa's response.

"As for the rest of us, we'll all meet in the weapons room in one hour; plan on being there for a while."

He had spent the past hour with Adam inside the library, completely amazed by his capacity to learn, and at such a rapid rate of speed. His only regret was that Robin wasn't here to witness it all. "Adam, would you like to take a break?" Eric asked.

"Yes please," Adam answered.

Eric smiled, and then ruffled Adam's hair. "You know I think Gelsa is going to be surprised by what you have accomplished in her absent." Eric looked up to see Gelsa entering the library.

"Speak of the devil, here she comes," Eric said. Adam pushed his chair away from the table, stood up, and then ran towards Gelsa. Gelsa knelt down, and lifted Adam into her arms.

"I'm hungry," Adam said.

Gelsa smiled. "Wow! That was really good, Adam."

"It's amazing how fast he's learning," Eric said from the table.

"He's an amazing little boy," Gelsa added. "Your mom is going to be real proud of you, Adam. We'll head to the kitchen in just a minute," Gelsa said, setting him down. Eric pushed himself away from the table and stood up. Gelsa raised a hand towards Eric to stop his forward progress, and then walked over to where he stood.

"Eric, they're planning the rescue for tomorrow."

"They, aren't you going with them?"

"No. Thandie and I are staying here with you and Adam in case something goes wrong. We need to be prepared to leave at the drop of a dime."

"Where would we go?" Eric asked.

"No place in particular, just far away from here."

"Right," Eric said, "but I have to admit that I would feel a whole lot better if all of you were going. You guys would have a better chance at rescuing Robin."

"That may be true, but unfortunately we do not have that option. We can't leave you and Adam unprotected."

Eric lowered his head. "Why do I have a bad feeling about this," he said.

"Don't," Gelsa said. "With the exception of Ambrosha and Victoria, we are stronger and more skillful in the art of engagement."

"Well that makes me feel a lot better," Eric said.

"I'm hungry," Adam tugged at Gelsa's arm.

"Hunger calls."

"No, that's fine," Eric said. "I'm in need of food myself. It's just a pain to have to keep going out for it."

"Eric, you live here now, which means that you are free to cook. You may as well buy enough food to last let's say a week. Keep in mind that we do not have pots and pans, so you will also have to purchase what you will need in order to cook."

"Good advice," Eric said.

Eric and Gelsa left the library; Gelsa on her way to the kitchen to feed Adam, and Eric up to Robin's room to grab his keys so he could head out and do some shopping. He was just about to ascend the stairs when he spotted Raven coming down the hall. "Gelsa filled me in," he said. "I can't believe that it has come to this. Robin has a good heart. She wouldn't harm a fly, yet this is happening to her."

"I know. The worst things seem to happen to good people."

"Raven, I'm terrified. I can't lose her."

"Believe me when I tell you that I understand. Now listen to me. Even if we should lose the element of surprise, Ambrosha will have her hands filled with us. Our goal first and foremost will be to locate Robin wherever they're holding her. If we can do that our chances of rescuing her will be greater. Getting Robin to safety is our primary goal. When and how we chose to deal with Ambrosha will be at later time, unless she forces our hand."

"What is your plan?" Eric asked.

"Manipulation of course," Raven answered. "I'll phone Ambrosha when we are at the halfway mark, and ask for another night to consider her offer. If she believes us to be a hundred miles away instead of fifty; that may be all the surprise we need to get Robin out of there safely." Eric sighed. "I know. We have to keep a positive attitude about this. Look, I'm heading out to pick up a few things; need anything while I'm out?" Raven smiled.

"Of course not," Eric said. "I'll see you when I get back." Eric started up the stairs. "Eric?" Raven called behind him.

"Yes," he answered, stopping halfway up the stairs.

"She'll be back with us in no time," Raven said. Eric nodded, and then continued up the stairs. He told himself that Robin would be in his arms by late tomorrow.

CHAPTER FIFTEEN

Guiliana held the custom-made staff in both hands. "It's been a long time," she said, tightening her grip on the weapon. She felt her adrenaline rise slightly at the thought of wielding the weapon for a purpose other than training. They were a single design; four and a half feet long and crafted from strong oak. They were hollowed out with tempered steel pipes running through the center.

The handle grips at each end were made from pure ivory to give the staff both balance and ease in handling. Each of the ivory handles bore an engraved image of the sun representing certain death for the wielder's enemy. The internal spring mechanisms served two purposes. At one end a silver tipped wood stake could be released with the correct maneuver of the handle, and launched with enough force behind it to knock a two hundred pound man clear off his feet. It was anchored by four feet of tempered retractable chain capable of immobilizing a vampire for a final blow.

The opposite end of the staff housed a different type of weapon, but it was equally effective. A seven inch canister supporting about fifty or so one inch wooden shards, that acted similar to an aerial grenade, but having a more controlled radius proved highly effective against two or three vampires. The weapon proved very uncomfortable for a vampire or vampire's who couldn't phase fast enough.

The staff's deadliest feature was the two short blades hidden within the staff's belly. When pulled apart the blades were a foot and a half in length; long enough to sever a vampire's head from their body.

Savana and Leona were off to the side of the training room, getting reacquainted with their own weapons. They wielded the staffs as though they were extensions of themselves.

Natalia was at center floor, sparring with an imaginary foe. She focused intensely and with purpose rolling the staff through the fingers of one hand, and transferring it to the fingers of the other like a baton. Leona twirled her weapon above her head a few times before dropping into a battle stance. "Is that an invitation?" Guiliana asked from across the room.

"No, but since you asked," was Leona's response. The two vampires were poised to spar, but then Raven entered the room and waved them off.

"Cool your jets for a moment and listen up," she said. Leona and Gelsa lowered the weapons to their side. "I spoke with Eric a moment ago," Raven began, "and he said something that really hit home. So close in fact that it weighs heavy on my heart even now. He said I can't believe that it has come to this. I can scarcely remember the last time a vampire has had to be put down. Our numbers have always been so few, that we have more than not managed our existence well, but things change. Unfortunately that change is upon us. So get the cobwebs out knowing, that by getting reacquainted with your weapons, it is but another advantage that we will have."

"Then what are we waiting for?" Natalia said, raising her staff. "Anybody?"

"Why not." Savana smiled, raising her own weapon. Half of the women appointed a target and then rush in.

The sparring sessions went off without a hitch. The only thing left was to follow through with the plan. Thandie and Gelsa had also been permitted to join the training session, but only after the proper preparations had been made concerning the orders that Raven had given them.

Eric had been gone for hours, but when he finally returned he wasn't empty handed. He walked into the house carrying two grocery bags, which didn't include the box of pots and pans that he had to go back to the car for. When he had finished putting his purchases up, he sat down and went over some of the things to be prepared for on tomorrow with Gelsa and Thandie.

"There's just one more thing," Gelsa said to Eric.

"What else is there?" Eric asked.

"Adam," Gelsa answered. "You weren't here the first time it happened. It was terrible. It was an experience that none of us will ever forget, and my heart goes out to him still, because none of us believe that what happened is the end."

"It has to stop at some point. You do believe that don't you?" Eric asked.

"We're all prisoners of hope," Thandie answered. "Hope is all we have."

"So much is happening," Eric said, "yet very little of it is positive."

"Well if we succeed tomorrow, that will be a positive turning point for things to come," Gelsa added.

"Well I'm going to turn in," Eric said, "but first I'd like to check in on Adam before he hits the sack."

"Leona was giving him his bath earlier. I'm sure she finished by now."

"Well if I don't see you again tonight, it will be bright and early tomorrow evening," he said.

"Sleep well," Gelsa said. Eric stood up and left the two women where they sat. It was going to be a long restless night for all of them, he thought, and he didn't know about the rest of them, but come tomorrow he was going to be a nervous wreck. If he found sleep to be out of his reach today he had an unread book packed away. Something told him that he was probably going to need it.

Eric climbed the stairs stopping at the very top to look in both directions. He had no idea which room was Leona's, and the corridor was completely empty. He stood there for a second hoping that a door would open so he could ask one of the girls. A few seconds went by with no luck. He headed to the right and stopped at the first door that he came to. He knocked twice and waited. A few seconds went by before the door opened, and there stood Savana dressed in a pair of men's pajamas with a scarf around her head and a toothbrush sticking out her mouth. She gave him a look; one he recognized as curious. "I didn't mean to disturb you, Savana, but I'm having trouble finding Leona's room."

Savana took the toothbrush out of her mouth. "Two doors down on the left," she said.

Eric pointed towards the room. "That one?" he asked. Savana nodded her head. "Thanks. I guess I'll see you later on this evening," he said. Savana smiled, and then closed her door. Eric shook his head. *This is what I have to look forward to,* he thought.

Eric knocked on Leona's door and waited. Within seconds she answered. "I just wanted to look in on him before he laid down for bed, if that's alright."

"Adam," Leona called his name from the door. "Come and speak with Eric." Adam leaped off the bed and walked towards the two grownups.

"Hey Adam, I just wanted you to know that I had fun spending time with you tonight. You sleep tight and I will see you tomorrow, okay."

"Okay." Eric knelt down to one knee. "Would you mind giving me a hug?" Eric asked. Adam stepped out into the hall and wrapped an arm around Eric's shoulder. Eric pulled the boy to him and gave him a big hug. What he had to realize was that Adam barely knew him. He barely knew any of them really, but of all the people in the house, his relationship with Gelsa was the closest. He only hoped that Adam's relationship with Gelsa, wouldn't impact the relationship he shared with Robin. "Okay then, I'll see you both this evening," Eric said. Adam stepped back into the room, and Eric gave him a smile before he stood up and walked away.

Robin pulled at her restraints again. This time she pulled so hard it felt as if she would break something. It was no use, and ignoring the pain in her shoulder did nothing to increase her odds. The door opened and Victoria entered the room. "You won't free yourself," Victoria said. "Even without the stake in your shoulder, you still wouldn't be strong enough to break free. None of us are able to, not even Raven."

"Speaking of Raven," Robin said. "I assume that Ambrosha has already spoken with her, and that she refuses to handover Adam."

"You'll just worry yourself if I share the details with you. And why does it matter? You're going to be dead soon."

Robin wanted to scream out. She felt so helpless, but she refused to give Victoria the satisfaction. "I'm surprised Ambrosha has kept you alive for this long. She knows Raven will never give up that child. I wonder if I put in a good word would she kill you and be done with it." Robin melted into the mattress. What little hope she held was under attack again. Death was drawing near, but she rebuked it as a reality.

"Just leave, Victoria," Robin said, turning her eyes towards the ceiling.

Victoria giggled. "That's it, Robin. Let the realization grab hold of you. I'll see you in a few hours." Victoria turned to exit the room. Robin stared up at the ceiling for what seemed like an eternity. She blinked once, and the tears that had formed in the corners of her eyes gave way to the force of gravity.

They were like two siblings sharing the stage, but at different times with equal hours to perform on a designated section of the earth. And so it was with the moon who gave way to the sun. The two vampire houses teetered between sleep and insomnia in anticipation of the weighted task that lie ahead of them. Ambrosha's house felt confident, believing that they had the bargaining chips, thus giving them the upper hand. Raven's house on the other hand bore the burden of uncertainty. Exhausted as he was, sleep would have nothing to do with him. Thoughts of Robin and her uncertain fate, would not allow him proper rest. In another room just down the hall, Raven slept, but it had come to her only moments ago. The others were either asleep, or boarding on sleep, but however short their rest they would all have to sharp come sunset if they planned to succeed.

Eric leaned against one of the pillar supports, sipping on a cup of the coffee that he had purchased last night. His eyes felt weighted down. It was the price he was paying for only two hours of sleep. Everyone else seemed to be doing fine, which was a good thing, because Robin's life was totally dependent upon their ability to function at the highest level. He looked over at Adam who was sitting on a bar stool watching the women with an intense interest. Eric straightened himself and then headed over to where the boy sat.

"Do you understand what's going on?" Eric asked him.

Without a beat Adam nodded his head and said, "They're going to get Mommy."

"Who told you that?" Eric asked.

"Auntie Gelsa," he answered. Eric placed his hand on top of Adam's head and ruffled his hair. It suddenly dawned on him that his father used to do that exact thing to him.

"That's right," Eric said. "They're going to get Mommy." Both Gelsa and Thandie were busy helping the other women with zippers and what not. Eric shook his head. It looked like a scene straight out of a movie. Each of the women, for the exception of Gelsa and Thandie were dressed in black latex leather from the neck down. He'd never seen Robin dress in anything remotely close to what they were wearing, but he imaged at one time or another she had. Being a man of course, he tried to visualize what she might look like in the sexy attire. Raven walked over and stood before him. "We're heading out." Eric shook his head.

"Okay, but I'm not going to say good luck. What I will say is this. Bring her back, Raven." Guiliana called out from amongst the women who were standing next the door. "It's time."

Raven turned to Guiliana in acknowledgement. "We're going to do everything within our power, Eric."

"That's all I ask," he said. Raven turned and headed towards the door. He looked over at Thandie who was motioning for him and Adam to get up and follow. It only made sense to see them off.

The plan was simple. It was based on her ability to judge how predictable Raven would be. That was of course the easy part. Raven had only two choices; a rescue attempt on Robin in which she would have to divide her house for the sake of the child, or simply hand the child over in exchange for Robin. She never believed that the second was an option, so she had prepared for the first. Sabrina was the only one that she had ordered to stay behind. She had but one job, and that job was simple. Her job was to make the phone call if and when Raven showed up, and provide all the information she could so the operation would go smoothly. That information was vital, because it would tell her what she was up against. With nearly all her women with her, retrieving the child would be obtainable once she dispatched those that Raven had left behind. With the numbers in her favor, she would be able to move her hand against the others as she saw fit.

Robin shifted her weight slightly. Her comfort was threatened on so many levels. For starters, she still had the stake in her shoulder. Her hands were bound behind her back. Her ankles were secure, and they had placed a strip of tape over her mouth. Maxine sat in the second roll seat in front of her, chewing on a stick of gum. She turned around and smiled at Robin. *Why do I allow her to get under my skin?* Robin thought.

A ringtone erupted towards the front of the SUV. Ambrosha reached inside her vest pocket and removed a cell phone. "It's Raven." Ambrosha signaled for Vanessa to pull over along the shoulder of the highway. Vanessa slowed the vehicle down and brought it to a screeching halt. Robin lifted her head off the seat slightly, her senses on full alert to what was transpiring only a couple of seats in front of her. Ambrosha answered her phone. "Hello Raven."

"Ambrosha," Raven returned the greeting.

"Is Robin safe?"

"For the time being," Ambrosha answered. There was silence on Raven's end of the line.

"I have agreed to hand over the child in Robin's place," Raven said. "She will hate me for it, but I see no other avenue to take, besides, the child hasn't had enough time to plant deep enough roots in Robin's heart. The pain will be dealt with over time."

"I applaud you for seeing it as such," Ambrosha said.

"I only ask for another night since we are far into this one," Raven added.

"Fair enough, tomorrow then," Raven said before ended the phone call. Ambrosha turned around in her seat to look towards the back of the SUV. "You see what I mean, Robin. You're all weak. Your entire house is a disgrace to the nature of our being, and I am ashamed that I allowed myself to be a part of it for so long, but no more." Robin wanted to scream and curse, but how could she in her position. Ambrosha turned to face the front, and then signaled for Vanessa to get the vehicle on the road again.

Robin was almost certain that she knew what Ambrosha's plan was. If Raven was attempting to rescue her, then it would most certainly be tonight. While Ambrosha was busy moving against a helpless child, Raven was probably at this exact moment moving to try and save her. She couldn't blame Raven for trying; not when she had so little to work with. If she was attempting a rescue, who, and how many would she leave behind to protect Adam and Eric?

Robin shifted her weight again, hoping to find a brief moment of comfort. She had to do this every two minutes or so. She had made a plea to Ambrosha before they had taken off to loosen the restraints some, but that had gotten her nowhere. They weren't the only issue. The area around the stake was so tender, that it had become difficult for her to keep her mind off the pain. Robin forced herself to focus on possible ways that she might escape. A thought suddenly occurred to her. Unless Ambrosha's plan involved killing her on arrival, she would need to leave at least one person behind to keep watch over her. Perhaps there was hope after all. If she could get her hands out front of her then she might stand half a chance.

CHAPTER SIXTEEN

The room held a sort of bizarre silence, even over the high volume of the television set. "I'm going to make myself another cup of coffee," Eric said, rising to his feet. He glanced over at Adam as he was leaving the room. For the past half hour, he had become increasing interested in the various animals that the nature channel was presenting. It was obvious that he was still learning what he would have normally learned during his absent years.

Eric entered the kitchen where he headed straight for the pot of coffee that he had made several hours ago. His mind wandered to Robin and what she might be thinking at the precise moment. It was nerve wrecking to not have a single clue about what was going on beyond the walls of this house. All communication was cut off, and there would be no communication for a least a couple more hours.

Eric removed the coffee pot and then poured himself another cup. This would be the fourth cup this morning, and probably wouldn't be the last. He had turned down breakfast; well actually he had nibbled on a piece of toast. He just didn't have the stomach for food. Not while so much was going on. A question entered his mind. It was the question that he had been able to hold at bay up until now, which was, what if Raven failed? He was incapable of taking care of Adam on his own, and he couldn't very well continue living in a house full of vampires without Robin. Or could he? He shook his head roughly. It was a stark contrast of a person trying to scramble the thoughts inside his brain. "Robin is coming home," he told himself, so erase all doubt. This time tomorrow she was going to be safely in his arms, and back in Adam's life.

Beneath a tall redwood tree, stood five female vampires some forty yards away from what they referred to as the sister house. Getting on the grounds had been the easy part. An accomplished thief could have done so just as easily. Gaining access to the mansion's interior however, would require a bit more exertion; a very difficult task for an accomplished thief, but a pretty easy street for a vampire. "Shall we proceed? Guiliana asked.

"Not yet," Raven answered.

Guiliana walked over and stood next to Raven. "Getting a bad vibe?" she asked.

"Something of the sort," Raven answered. "Think it strange that all the shutters are buttoned down?"

Guiliana cocked her head. Why hadn't she noticed?

"You're right, it is strange," Leona said, walking up to stand beside the two women. "Something's off."

"I'm pretty certain that we avoided all the security cameras," Natalia said. "It appears as if they knew we were coming."

"But how could they have known?" Guiliana asked.

"Easy," Raven answered, "perhaps not in the way of certainty, but in the way of familiarity. I was afraid of this. To Ambrosha, I am not so hard to read. We have known one another forever."

"Do you think Robin is inside?"

"Judging by the way the place is buttoned down I would have to say yes," Raven answered, "but my judgments have cost us to some extent."

"Don't beat yourself up over this, Raven. The advantage has never been ours," Natalia added.

"So are we going in?" Savana asked.

"Yes, that hasn't changed, except...."

"Except what, Raven?"

Raven turned to the women and said, "Savana, I need you and Leona to race back to the mansion, but as soon as you reach the car I want you phone Gelsa and Thandie and tell them to get Eric and Adam out of there."

"You can't be thinking," Savana asked.

"It is exactly what I'm thinking," Raven said. "They're in real danger if Ambrosha is on her way there."

"What if you're wrong," Leona asked, "and they're all inside waiting? That leaves only you, Guiliana and Natalia. The three of you can't possibly go up against Ambrosha and the others by yourselves to rescue Robin."

"We don't have much of a choice," Raven said, "now go." Savana and Leona backed up a few steps and then turned to race back towards the vehicles, while Raven Guiliana and Natalia focused their attention once again on the mansion. There, Raven pointed to a window on the second floor of the mansions east wing. "We'll start with that room and work our way through the house. We stay alert and together. Let's go." The three vampires raced towards the mansion with stealthy speed, their weapons strapped to their backs.

Crouched low behind one of the grounds statues, Sabrina was privy not only to Raven's flock, but her intentions as well. She'd observed everything that had taken place between Raven, and those that she had brought with her in the attempt to free Robin, and just as Ambrosha had instructed, she had made the phone call immediately after their arrival. However something unexpected had taken place that had forced her to make a second phone call. From what she had gathered, Raven had ordered both Savana and Leona back to their mansion, which meant that the window that Ambrosha thought she had, had just been trimmed down.

The three vampires leaped effortlessly some fifteen feet from the ground, and onto the face of the mansion wall. They scurried along the brick surface like a startled lizard until finally coming to a stop at a second floor window. Raven grabbed hold of the bars on one side of the window, while Guiliana grabbed hold on the other side. With one powerful yank, they tore bars, nuts, and bolts free from the face of the brick wall, and then tossed it onto the lawn below.

Natalia entered the room first, with eyes and ears on full alert. Raven entered next, and then Guiliana. They stood frozen in place; their ears their most important survival tool for the moment. They glanced at one another for conformation and then moved cautiously towards the room's door. As much as this appeared to be a suicide mission, killing these three vampires would be an extremely difficult thing to do. The only person that was in any real danger was Robin.

Raven cracked the door and waited. She closed her eyes and listened for the sound of a heartbeat, any heartbeat other than the two that were already inside the room. Guiliana and Natalia kept a watchful eye on the open window. When Raven heard nothing she opened her eyes and stuck her head out into the hall. They moved from room to room as quietly as a mouse, always stopping just short of the doors to listen for any threatening sounds.

The three vampires had searched nearly half the rooms on the second floor, before their senses were bombarded by the scent of blood. They stopped just outside a door and stared at one another fearing the worst. There were a variety of blood types, but Robin's was the strongest.

"They took her with them," Guiliana said. "What do we do now?"

"Let's get out of here, although I fear we may be too late," Raven said. They returned to the room where they had entered and moved slowly towards the window. As they approached the window, Natalia thought she saw movement to the left of her out of the corner of her eye.

"I think we're being watched," Natalia said.

"How many?" Raven asked.

"I'm not sure, one maybe," Natalia answered.

"A spy no doubt," Guiliana said.

"What do we do about her?" Natalia asked.

"We need to know what she knows," Raven said, "therefore we need her alive."

"Roger that," Natalia said, springing from the window. Raven and Guiliana followed, unsheathing their weapons before they touch the ground.

Sabrina lowered herself behind the statue. *How could I have been so careless?* she thought. Seeking a better position, she had ultimately given her location away. She had to make a run for it. There was no way that she could face them. If she allowed herself to be captured,

Ambrosha would be livid. Sabrina turned towards the tree line and took off running at full speed.

All three women flanked in the direction that Sabrina had run. Unfortunately for Sabrina, her hesitation had cost her precious time. Sabrina entered the forest of dense trees cutting a path that only another vampire could follow. She blew past trees and tiny critters at speeds that stirred up the wind. The forest ended about two miles from her current position. There she would come upon a lake, and perhaps her only means of escape.

The three vampires were closing the distance. Raven out front, because she was by far the fastest of the three. Guiliana was trailing about five paces behind her, and then Natalia. Sabrina stole a quick glance over her shoulder that proved to be a mistake. She hadn't taken into account that Raven's speed was superior to her own. So on glancing over her shoulder, Raven's close proximity had actually startled her, causing her to stumble over her own footing. She could still make it. The lake was just thirty yards away, if that. *You're not getting away,* Raven thought, taking aim with her staff less than ten yards behind Sabrina. Sabrina didn't hear the canister shoot forth from Raven's staff, but she did feel more than half of the fifty or so one inch wooden shards in her back, and legs on the canisters explosion. Sabrina arched her back. At the same time her legs gave way, causing her to trip over her feet and tumble towards the ground. She might have tumbling across the surface of the forest ground close to fifteen yards before coming to a complete stop in a clearing. She had to lie still on her stomach and thighs. If she didn't, she risked pushing the wooden shards further into her skin.

The chase was over. Sabrina lifted her head. The lake was only yards away. Raven knelt down beside Sabrina and said, "You almost made it." Guiliana and Natalia rolled Sabrina onto her back and took pleasure in listening to her scream. "Now you're going to tell me what I need to know," Raven said.

Sabrina lowered her face onto the dirt surface and contemplated what might follow if she didn't comply with Raven's demand, but then again who was she kidding. Raven wasn't about to let her live, so fuck it. "I'm not telling you shit, Raven, and if you think that you can bargain with me you're mistaken. Ambrosha is dead set on killing the child as she should be. You're too late Raven. Ambrosha is well aware of who you left behind to protect the child. News flash, they're probably dead already."

Raven stared down at the vampire who had just framed herself a lost cause. "A shame," Raven said, rising to her feet and pulling her weapon apart.

"You wouldn't dare," Sabrina said. Raven raised one of the blades above her head and hesitated. The reflection from the moon glittered across the surface of the blade and blinded Sabrina for a brief moment. "You're so blind to understanding Ambrosha's purpose in what she is doing, Raven."

"No, I do understand," Raven answered. "I just don't think you're right." Raven brought the blade down, angling it towards Sabrina's neck. The wooden shards had served their purpose in preventing Sabrina from phasing; now her head lay next to her body, and the land was lapping up her blood. Raven wiped the bloody blade across Sabrina's clothing. "Now we can go," she said.

Robin's assumption had proven correct. Ambrosha had left one person behind to guard her, while she and the others moved to fulfill their twisted purpose. Now if she could only manage to free herself from these restraints, she might get an opportunity to settle a resent score.

Maxine was the one who had been instructed to guard her. The way she saw it, she owed the evil bitch big time after the way she had treated Eric. Robin listened with her highly tuned ears. From what she could gather, Maxine was somewhere towards the front of the vehicle. Her footsteps gave clue to an agitated and restless vampire who might have resented being left behind to babysit. With a little effort, she could probably sit up far enough to peer over the front seat, but that wasn't necessary, not when her ears could be relied upon.

There was a part of her that was actually surprised, that Maxine hadn't already resorted to torturing her in Ambrosha's absence, however the night was still young. *Here goes nothing,* she thought as she rolled from her side onto her back. When the pointed edge of the stake touched the floorboard, a burst of pain vibrated through her shoulder. She held her breath for a second or two waiting for the pain to subside. *Deal with it,* she told herself. Pulling her bound wrist from behind her back and up over her feet was going to be challenging. Before Ambrosha and the other's had left, they'd moved her to the very back of the SUV, which meant that the space for maneuvering was going to be a lot tighter. She would have to manage somehow.

Robin took a deep breath, raised her knees, and then brought her bound wrists up towards the heels of her feet which were also bound. The pain in her shoulder was excruciating but she pressed on. She struggled to get her wrists past her heels and toes, but she managed. Finally she had her hands in front of her.

Robin released the air that she had been holding within her lungs, and then contemplated her next move. Grabbing hold of the stake, she proceeded to pull it out, but hesitated after feeling the slightest sense of pain. She remembered what Ambrosha had said about the pain being worst coming out. She turned towards the vehicle's rear seat, and then sunk her teeth into wood and leather. When she was certain that the grip she had on the stake was tight, she pulled at it carefully. Ambrosha was right. Her eyes literally rolled towards the back of her head, but she couldn't afford to stop until it was out. Even after the tip was free, Robin still found herself biting down on wood and leather. She felt a streak of tears on her face, but at last she was free.

The wound would begin healing immediately, but unfortunate enough it would be a while before it healed completely. Then there was the rather large matter regarding her restraints. She would need a key for those. With any luck, Maxine would have one on her. Robin grabbed hold of the stake, and then called out like she was experiencing discomfort. Two seconds later she heard one of the vehicles side door opened. Now all she need do is wait for the right moment. The seat leather rustled under Maxine's weigh, and just as Robin had predicted, Maxine poked her head over the rear seat to check on her prisoner. Robin reacted immediately shoving the stake upwards through Maxine's mouth, and out through the crown of her head.

Maxine reached out blindly for the stake, missing every attempt made, perhaps a result of shock. Robin shoved Maxine over the seat, and with some difficulty she managed to pull herself up. She rolled herself over onto the seat in front and landed on her stomach. Meanwhile Maxine lay in between the seats on the floor, coughing up blood. It was going to take a lot more than what she had done to finish the bitch.

Robin reached down and grabbed Maxine by the hair and pulled her up onto the seat. She felt exhilarated for having been given the opportunity to stare into Maxine's eyes, and be the last person that she would see before she died. If given the opportunity, she would see all of them dead, from Ambrosha down. Robin stared into Maxine's pain filled eyes and spoke. "Where is it? Where's the key?" she asked. "If I have to ask you again, I'm going to start twisting that piece of wood around in your head."

Maxine lifted a shivering right hand, and placed it close to her front right pocket. Robin shoved Maxine's hand away, and began feeling around for the key to her restraints. Maxine had told the truth. The key was there inside her pocket. Robin tore at the leather material, until there was enough room to side her hand inside. "Got it!" With a little effort, she was able to maneuver the key into the slot of the lock using her teeth. Robin rotated her hands and wrist counter clockwise, while holding the key steady between her teeth. The lock clicked, and immediately she thanked God.

Robin removed the restraints and tossed them to the floor. She had no time to spare, but she would gladly make time for one last thing. She placed her face inches away from Maxine's, and stared once more into the vampire's pain-filled eyes. Maxine was barely conscious. "You deserve what is about to come next, Maxine. I've never done anything to warrant how you have treated me. I'm sorry, but I just can't say water under the bridge. I'm going to twist your head clean off your shoulders, and not lose an ounce of sleep for having done it." What happened next was exactly that.

Leona and Savana were still miles away from the mansion. Leona was pushing the vehicle at speeds of up to one hundred miles per hour, still they feared the worst. A phone call from Raven had only confirmed Ambrosha's intentions. As they blew past cars and trucks on the highway, they prayed that Gelsa and Thandie had been alert enough to either elude Ambrosha's assault, or at the least by themselves some time.

The alarm had alerted Gelsa and Thandie to at least two points of forced entry. The voice modulated security system had allowed Gelsa and Thandie to determine the direction of the treat, therefore providing an avenue of escape. They made time for a brief stop inside the weapons room, and from there towards the stairs where they would make their way to the second floor. Thandie led the way, with Eric and Adam following close behind. Gelsa took up the rear, glancing over her shoulder periodically as they hurried along. When they reached the stairs, Gelsa glanced back to see Tesa and Constance entering the hall further down. "Hurry!" she called out to Thandie. When Gelsa reached the top of the stairs she glanced around to see that Tesa had taken point, while Constance was yelling out to give away their location.

Tesa took the stairs three steps at a time, but veered towards caution when she reached the top. There was always the possibility for unexpected surprises. She immediately spotted her targets ten steps ahead running towards one end of the corridor. It was obviously clear to her that the child and the male, was to some extent slowing them all down. She would be on top of them in seconds.

Ambrosha and Victoria weren't far behind. When they finally reached the top of the stairs, Tesa and Constance was already engaged in combat with Gelsa. At the far end of the corridor she spotted Thandie leading Eric and the child into a room.

Once inside the room, Thandie led Eric and Adam straight to a window. She opened the shutters, gripped the bars with her small hands and pushed outward. She could feel the bolts give way from the foundation until finally there was complete separation between the two. Gelsa swung the bars outward, and seconds later they hit the grassy surface below with a thud. "Come to me Adam," Gelsa said. Adam obeyed without hesitation. Gelsa lifted Adam into her arms. "I'm going down first with Adam," she said to Eric. "When I tell you to jump, you jump." Before Eric could protest, Gelsa was out the window. He stuck his head out the window and stared down at the ground below; of course they were safe, she was a vampire. "Eric, jump," Gelsa yelled up. If he landed wrong, he would definitely break something.

"It's too far down," he yelled back at her.

"If you don't jump, you will die a different way. You choose," Gelsa told him.

Meanwhile Gelsa was holding her own against Tesa, and Constance, because she was more than there equal, but Ambrosha and Victoria were another matter. Tesa was experiencing a deep laceration on the left shoulder and Constance one across the collarbone. She had come close to decapitation.

Gelsa glanced beyond her two combatants to see Ambrosha and Victoria approach. Oddly enough they didn't seem to be in any rush. She was in deep shit and she knew it, but at this point it was all about buying Thandie and Eric time enough to escape. The blades sparked on contact within the dimly-lit corridor. Meanwhile, Ambrosha and Victoria rushed in seemingly headlong at first, but then veered off closer to the walls, Ambrosha on one side and Victoria on the other. Gelsa took notice, but if she had any chance at slowing the two vampire's pursuit, it would mean exposing herself to Tesa and Constance. Gelsa pressed on Tesa and Constance, forcing them to retreat backwards a few steps. She then peddled backwards, giving herself a brief cushion so that she could ready her two blades.

"Press," Ambrosha yelled, and as Tesa and Constance closed in, Ambrosha and Victoria leaped onto opposite sides of the walls, and attempted to run past the combatants at a near forty five degree angle. Gelsa slashed out with both blades, attempting to sever Ambrosha and

Victoria in two. All she got for her efforts was thin air, but it had been worth a try. Ambrosha and Victoria had phased through doing exactly what she would have done. The two vampires shifted back into their solid form once they were past.

In the meantime Gelsa would pay for the failed attempt by leaving herself exposed. She barely felt the tip of Tesa's staff when it entered her chest and heart, and then exit through her back. Gelsa dropped to the floor on both knees, gripping the handles of her blades so tight that her knuckles begin to turn white. The stake had only penetrated a small section of her heart, but it had been enough to cause her difficulty with breathing. She could ultimately survive such a wound of this magnitude; of course the stake would have to be removed. Unfortunately for her it would not happen this night. Gelsa released her grip on the blades, and then prepared herself for the worst. She stared up at Constance; watched the vampire raise the blade, and then bring it down on her.

Eric hit the ground hard, sending a jolt of pain through his feet and up both legs before he rolled onto his back. He needed a moment to allow the tingling sensation to pass in his feet and legs, but Thandie was already demanding that he get up. He wasn't on his feet for a complete second when he saw her. It was Vanessa bearing down on Thandie some fifteen yards behind her. It was either the expression on his face, her vampire spider senses, or her acute hearing, but Thandie turned to meet Vanessa and just in the nick of time. She brought her weapon up and parried what might have been a fatal blow. Vanessa's blade sank in the center of Thandie's wooden staff. Thandie quickly parted the weapon at its center and unsheathed both blades slashing outward. Vanessa bent her body like a reed, barely escaping decapitation.

"Eric, get Adam and get out of here now," Thandie yelled. Vanessa came at her much harder the second time, forcing her to focus solely on staying alive. Thandie could only hope that Eric was following her command, because Vanessa would be a difficult opponent to defeat, not to mention the others that were no doubt close behind.

Eric lifted Adam off the ground and into his arms. He glanced up at the window where he and Thandie had jumped, and then wondered what fate had befallen Gelsa. His eyes nearly popped out of their sockets when he turned around to see another vampire running towards him at high speed. *No place to run,* he thought. *No means of escape.* He glanced back at Thandie who was still engaged in combat with Vanessa, and then turned back towards his approaching assailant. Under the dark of light it was hard to make out which of the vampires was racing towards him. Eric braced himself angling Adam away from the approaching hostile, but as the vampire drew near, her features became clearer. He squinted focusing his eyes as best he could until he was certain that he could make her out. "Robin?" he said. Eric couldn't believe his eyes, but there she was standing right before his eyes.

She wrapped her arms around him, and then pulled away immediately. "We have to **go,**" she said.

"How did you get….."

Robin grabbed his arm before he could finish. "Never mind that, we have to get out of here," she reiterated, reaching for Adam. "I can run faster with him than you, just follow me." He handed Adam over to Robin and then waited to follow wherever she was planning to lead him. They both started running in the direction of the vehicles. Robin was ten yards ahead of Eric. She could have easily been further along, but she wasn't about to abandon her man. They were in this together. Robin was plenty thankful that she and Eric had decided to think old school where spare keys were a concern. It was only a month ago that he had purchased the set of key magnets; placed keys inside of each one, and then stuck them stuck them on the under carriage of both cars. Funny how such a small detail could be the key to saving your life. When they reached Eric's car, Robin handed Adam over to him. "Inside," she yelled, dropping to the ground to retrieve the hidden key magnet.

"Robin, I have my keys on me," Eric yelled. Robin got to her feet, and then ran around to the drive's side where she opened the door and jumped inside.

Victoria leaped from the second floor window, hitting the ground at Vanessa's back. Constance leaped next, followed by Ambrosha and then Tesa. "I'm fucked!" Thandie muttered beneath her breath. *I'm as good as dead now,* was her single thought.

Vanessa retreated backwards a few steps. "Robin got free," Vanessa said, glancing over at Ambrosha. "She led Eric and the child towards the vehicles."

"Finish her," Ambrosha ordered Vanessa. "Aid her, Tesa, in getting the job done. Victoria, Constance, follow me." Ambrosha started towards the vehicles with Constance and Victoria at her back, while Vanessa and Tesa circled Thandie as though she were a wounded dear.

Thandie settled into a defensive stance. Her odds had changed in favor of Ambrosha, but she mustn't give up yet, not when anything could happen. She tightened her grip on the handles of both blades, and then launched herself at Vanessa. Their blades rang for a moment in time before she was forced to make an adjustment to a double attack. The sound of metal and the glimmer of sparks produced a sound related to an ancient symphony of a battle between warriors.

Tesa's blade caught Thandie across the forearm and she was forced to take a few steps backwards. That was all the motivation the two vampires needed to press hard the attack. Thandie cursed her situation, but she would not be put down so easily. This was one kill they were going to have to earn.

Robin pushed the car into gear, and then pressed the accelerator to the floorboard. The tires spun in place for more time than they had to waste, before grabbing hold of the pavement and hurtling the car forward. She reached for her seatbelt, found it, and then strapped herself in for the ride. Adam was sitting in Eric's lap with only the lap belt to secure him. "Hold him close to you, Eric. I'm sure that I'll be driving fast enough to kill us all."

"Just remember that we're running away from death, not towards it," he said. Robin was holding the needle at fifty miles an hour, but they had only driven a quarter of a mile. She could probably get it up to sixty, but that was pushing it on the narrow stretch of road. Eric looked out of beyond his passenger side window and did a double take. "Robin," he called out. She didn't answer. She was probably too busy concentrating on the road ahead. "Robin," he said a little louder.

"Yes," she said in a slightly agitated tone of voice.

"They're fucking running head to head with the car," he said, his voice sounding more on the panic side.

"Fuck!" Robin cursed, glancing down at the speedometer gauge. Eric glanced over at it himself; curiosity being the driving force. Robin pushed the car up to sixty once she got past one of two of the slight bends that were on the long stretch of road. They were now more than half the distance to the main gate. Only a little further to go. Robin glanced out of the driver side window, and was startled to see Ambrosha only inches away from the window.

Meanwhile Eric's heart was racing faster than the speed of the car, and it didn't let up despite his realization that Victoria was giving up chase. "What the fuck?" he screamed, suddenly startled be the sound of shattered glass. He looked over to see Robin thwarting an attack from Ambrosha, but she was the least of their worries. The rear end of the car suddenly dropped like extra weight had been placed upon it. One of the vampires had managed to grab hold of the rear spoiler, and then proceeded to dig her heals into the ground. It served little purpose though. Eric glanced over his shoulder to see Constance slowing to a trot holding a piece of the broken spoiler in her one hand. He wanted to assault her with a triumphant grin, but thought better of it. They weren't out of the woods yet.

"I think they've given up," Robin said.

Eric swiveled back around towards the front. "I think you're right," he said in agreement. He looked down at Adam who seemed to be numb to what was happening all around him. He looked back up to see the main gate up ahead, only it was closing in on them fast. Actually it was Robin, who had made up in her mind not to slow down. "Robin!" he yelled, "I really don't think those iron gates are going to budge."

"Let's hope that you're wrong, Eric. I told you that I wasn't stopping for anything." Eric wrapped his arms tightly around Adam, and then braced for impact. Robin hit the iron gates dead center. The sound that the metal made on contact was terrifying at best. The car swerved right before turning in a complete circle. Robin pointed the car towards home and then sped off. Eric had but to look out towards the front of the car to see that most of the front end had been shredded like a piece of tin. "That was close," Eric said. "Are you okay?" he asked Robin.

"I will be once we put some distance between ourselves and them," she answered.

Eric took a deep breath, and then released the air from his lungs. He had to fight back asking a string of questions that were probably too heavy at the moment, so he asked just one. "Would you like me to drive? I'm thinking you two could use some catching up."

Robin looked over at Eric, and then Adam. Slowly the tension began to leave her body. Her facial muscles began to relaxed, as well as the firm grip that she had on the steering wheel. Tunnel vision, she thought. She barely had chance to just look at either of them, because she was too busy trying to save their lives.

"Sure," she answered. "I'll take the next exit, and then we can switch sides." Eric reached over and placed his hand on her thigh. They'd barely escaped with their lives. Gelsa and Thandie had not been so lucky, and what of Raven and the others. One thing was for sure, with Gelsa and Thandie dead, Ambrosha now had the numbers.

CHAPTER SEVENTEEN

The sound of blades clashing beneath the shroud of night had come to an end by the time Ambrosha and Victoria returned to the spot where they had left Vanessa and Tesa to deal with Thandie. Vanessa appeared to be unharmed for the most part. Tesa however, stood holding her gut, hands covered in blood. She would heal soon enough.

Ambrosha glanced down at Thandie who lay across the lawn with her severed head laying inches away from her body. "See how easily her house crumbles." A vehicle approached with its headlights off. It was only Constance. She had been given orders to fetch the vehicle after Robin and Eric had escaped. Constance brought the vehicle to a stop, and then stepped out of the driver's side seat. "Is Maxine dead?" Victoria asked. Constance glanced over at Thandie's beheaded body.

"Yes," Constance said, walking around to the back of the SUV. She lifted the hatch and stood there staring at what lay inside. By this time the other women had joined her, and they stood there utterly surprised by what they saw.

"I never would have thought she had it in her," Ambrosha said, making reference to Robin.

"She's going to pay for this," Vanessa said as she backed away from back of the vehicle to move towards the front passenger side door. Vanessa opened the door and removed her cell phone from the glove box. Under contacts she located Sabrina's name. After two failed attempts she turned to Ambrosha and said, "Sabrina's not picking up."

"It's probably nothing," Ambrosha said. "We need to get on the road. Leave the bodies where they lay. The visions will surely cause

Raven a great deal of pain." Vanessa didn't believe that it was nothing. Sabrina was her twin. A part of her knew that something was wrong.

Constance steered the vehicle onto the freeway where she sped towards home. If one truly assessed the situation, they would probably sum it up like this. The only thing that Ambrosha really accomplished this night was to weaken Raven's house by two, but she fell short of achieving her main goal in that Robin and the child managed to escape. *When you really tally up the damage, it was pretty even on both sides.* Ambrosha also lost two this night, and although she couldn't be certain of Sabrina's demise, common sense argued that Sabrina had probably suffered the same fate as Maxine.

Eric drove fifty miles before turning off the highway to look for a motel. The sun would be making its way over the horizon in another hour or so. It was imperative that they find something and get checked in, or everything, there escape, the senseless deaths. All would have been for nothing. Neither of them had their cell phones, so there had been no way to contact Raven or the others unless they stopped. Something they hadn't wanted to do until now. Eric drove most of the way, giving Robin an opportunity to make up for the lost hours away from Adam. Needless to say, they used the time wisely. They were genuinely happy to be together again.

They passed a shabby motel that looked like ninety percent of the clientele wondered in from the strip club next door. "I see a Holiday Inn sign up the road. How does that sound?" Eric asked.

"Has to be better than the crap we just passed," Robin answered. "God. I could use a shower. I stink, and I have forty-eight hours' worth of blood stains and grime all over me." Eric looked over at Robin and smiled. "My breath must be horrible," she added.

He couldn't help but chuckle. "We'll get you cleaned up in no time," he said as he turned into the parking lot of the Holiday Inn. Eric pulled up in front of the hotel office.

"Do you have money on you?" Robin asked. Eric unbuckled the seatbelt, and then reached into his back pocket to produce his wallet.

"That's a huge relief," Robin sighed, "because I'm not exactly sure where mine is. For all I know it could be lying on the floor in our house somewhere. I had it in my possession before Ambrosha kidnapped me."

"We should probably cancel the credit cards," he said.

"I agree. We can make the calls after we've settled into the room." Eric opened the door, and then stepped out of the car. "I'll be back shortly," he said slamming the door shut.

"Hurry," she said. Eric turned around and made his way towards the office. Robin watched him as he walked away thinking how fortunate they all were to be alive. She ran her fingers through Adam's hair. "Are you okay?" she asked him, stretching her head around to get a better look at his face. He turned his head slightly and said. "Yes." Robin saw something in his eyes though, that resembled a look of concern.

"Is Auntie Gelsa okay?" he asked. Robin hesitated. That was it. That was what she saw in his eyes. The last thing she wanted to do was lie to him.

"I can't say for sure," Robin answered, "but we should know something shortly, okay?"

"Okay." He had obviously grown particularly fond to Gelsa during her absence. How would he handle the devastation of her death? She owed Gelsa a debt of gratitude for keeping him safe. Hearing the sound of Adam's voice gave Robin a renewed sense of strength. Nothing had changed. She knew that she would protect him with her life. "I'm sorry about all the terrible things that you have witness Adam. Are you sure that you're alright?"

"Yes."

"Were you frightened?" Robin asked.

Adam shook his head. "No. Maybe a little," he said, changing his mind.

"Well I don't ever want you to have to be afraid of anything," she told him. "We're going to move someplace far away from all the trouble, okay?"

Adam looked up into her eyes. "But what about Auntie Gelsa, Auntie Raven, and everyone else?" he asked.

Robin had to force a smile. "Getting as far away as we can is best for now. Besides, we can always communicate by phone, and if Auntie Gelsa is okay, I'm sure that she will come visit us. They all will," Robin said to him.

The door opened and Eric slid into the driver's seat. "Our room is on the second floor", he said, starting the car up and shifting into gear.

"Perfect," Robin said. "We could all use a good day's rest." Only things weren't perfect. She and Adam were without their food supply. They would both feel the pains of hunger soon enough if she didn't think of something.

Raven stared down at Gelsa's lifeless body. *Senseless,* she thought, *all of it so unnecessary and senseless.* To make it worse, she didn't know if Robin, Eric, and Adam were dead or alive. "There will be no rest for any of us until Gelsa and Thandie's bodies are dealt with properly."

"What about Ambrosha?" Leona asked.

Raven looked away and stared off into space. "Not now, Leona," Raven said. "Let's just focus on our fallen." Leona nodded, and then reached down to assist Savana with Gelsa's body. Raven stood there until Leona and Savana disappeared out of sight, and then she headed towards the room where they had found Thandie's body lying below.

When she reached the room, she wandered towards the open window. Once there, she took a moment to visualize what had probably happened. After a few seconds had gone by she closed the shutters and stood there with her back against them. She could vastly recall the last time that she had felt so disappointed in herself. She had failed Thandie, she had failed Gelsa, and she had failed Robin, Eric and Adam. A little too late, but It was time that she shed every emotion except hate where Ambrosha is the concern. *She has made a fatal mistake calling out the pure vampire in me. Has she forgotten so quickly where we stand on the ladder of superiority? Obviously she has. I have for the most part behaved as though I we're a human. Ambrosha has clearly decided that to be the weakness of mine to play upon, but she will regret the night she chose to do so.*

Thirty-five miles west of the direction that they had come, five vampires had been forced to check in to a hotel also. They'd gotten two rooms. Ambrosha and Victoria were in one. Constance, Vanessa and Tesa were in the other. Ambrosha settled into the hotel bed, and then pulled the covers up to her waist. She had a lot to think about. In particularly what she planned to do after having failed to kill Robin and the child. Who was she kidding? It she didn't deal with Raven and her brood, she would never have opportunity at the child again. It had become liken unto a territory that two opposing forces were trying to conquer. It was true. Raven was superior to her in all the areas except one; beastly nature. It was serving her well thus far. Ambrosha had always known that she was a killer at heart. She had placed her pure vampire nature on a shelf, and had left it there up until the recent months. What can be said of Raven is that she embraces humanity as if there were some kind of reward to be received. Her mother Teresa outlook on life is her undying weakness, and because of that weakness, she will no doubt hesitate when it comes time to deliver the fatal blow. I on the other hand will not hesitate, and there lies my edge. She glanced over at the other bed where Victoria lay sound asleep. The do not disturb sign had been placed outside the door, and the bolt locks and chains set. It was time she got some rest herself.

"Thank God you're alive and safe, Robin. Thank God you all are. I didn't know what to think."

"We count ourselves lucky," Robin said.

"How in heavens did you manage to escape? You know what? Never mind that for now. The important thing is that the three of you are safe. We will get into more detail about the things that have happened at a later time."

"Of course," Robin said in agreement.

"Where are you?" Raven asked.

"We're holed up in a hotel for the night," Robin answered.

"Good," said Raven. "Words can't begin to express how happy I am to hear your voice."

"I am equally happy to hear your voice as well Raven, but what I need to know, is if everyone's okay." There was a brief moment of silence on Raven's end.

"Robin, I'm sorry, but we've lost Gelsa, and Thandie." Robin's heart plummeted within her chest. She knew that there was a chance they could be dead, but she was hopeful that they might have only suffered injury.

"I wish this was all a bad dream," Robin said. "Adam asked me earlier if Gelsa was okay. I honestly didn't know at the time, but I feel the news will devastate him, Raven."

"What you're feeling may be true, Robin, but you needn't withhold the truth from him. He will be fine. The important thing is that he still has you. Get some rest. I look forward to seeing the three of you tomorrow."

"Raven?"

"Yes Robin?"

"We don't plan on coming back. At least not while Ambrosha still lives and breathes. My plan is to put as much distance between her and Adam as I possibly can."

There was silence on Raven's end. "I understand your position, but have you thought about what you will do for food in the mean time?"

Robin sighed. "Some," she answered.

"Well I will offer you some advice. One of the reasons that I have cut you so much slack your entire existence as a vampire is because I know that I don't have to worry about your heart. You are capable of feeding on warm blood without succumbing to the darkness Robin. You do what you have to do to survive, and remember that whatever you need, whenever you need it, don't hesitate to make contact. As far as Ambrosha, she and I will settle our difference soon." Robin found comfort in Raven's words, like she had been given a warm coat in the dead of winter.

"Thanks, Raven, and I'll call again tomorrow. We can talk more then."

"Until then," said Raven. Robin ended the phone call. She sat there on the edge of the bathtub for a moment or so wondering, when would be the best time to share Gelsa and Thandie's fate with Adam. Then it dawned on her, that no time would be the best time for Adam. The real question was when would be the best time for her. Maybe Raven was wrong about her heart. She had killed Maxine and enjoyed it. Even now her thoughts towards Ambrosha and those who were intent on following her lead were as dark as black. Her heart was filled with rage, and her thoughts of death and revenge. These were the things that she hoped would find Ambrosha and her murderous household soon.

A brand new evening had arrived, but it was accompanied by yesterday's horrors. The pain and the sorrow was every bit as potent as the night before. Robin turned onto her side to check the time 6:18 p.m. She felt the emptiness within her stomach, and wondered from which direction her and Adams next meal would come. The subject of food would come up this even, and it would suddenly dawn on Eric that she and Adam were without. Adam stirred next to her, and she turned around to face him. *He's such a beautiful child*, she thought, *and he's going to be a very handsome man when he comes of age.*

Robin glanced over at Eric who had volunteered to sleep in the other bed, so that she could continue strengthening the bond between her and Adam. They may as well be fugitives on the run, because that is how their life will seem, at least for a while anyway. Once she and Eric figured on a place to settle, money wouldn't be an issue since Raven had control over the covenants wealth, something Ambrosha should have thought about before going over the deep end. She watched Adam stir again before opening his sleep-filled eyes. "Good morning?" she said to him.

Adam rubbed his eyes. "I had a bad dream," he said, turning onto his back to stare up at the hotel ceiling.

"What did you dream about?" Robin asked him, concerned.

Adam hesitated. "I dreamed about Auntie Gelsa and Thandie," he answered.

Robin suddenly felt sick in her stomach. She took a deep breath, and then said. "Adam, do you understand death?"

"I think so," he answered.

"Okay. Death is something that we all have to face. Sometimes it happens sooner than we would like, and sometimes it happens much, much later, but when it happens, it just means that we go to a better place. At least that's what we are taught."

"Taught by who?" he asked.

"By our parents, who were taught by their parents, going all the way back to the very first parents," she told him.

"Oh," he said, shaking his head.

"Adam, Auntie Gelsa and Auntie Thandie have gone to that place, never to be forgotten by us, because we will remember them always. Do you understand?"

"Yes," Adam said, nodding his head. Robin smiled at him. She had somehow gotten through the conversation that she feared so with flying colors, but food was going to have to be the next subject up for discussion with Eric first thing this morning. She wasn't comfortable with the idea of having to revert to a predator. It was not who she was, but she and Adam had to feed in order to survive. ? Would Eric fully support the sudden, but necessary change in life style? Would the images of her and Adam feeding on helpless human beings revolt him? Robin shook off the thought. *Stop*, she told herself. *You know this man, and he's not at all like that.* She leaned over and kisses Adam on the forehead. "Would you like to watch some television while I take a quick shower?" she asked.

"Yes," Adam nodded.

"*Okay*, but we'll keep the volume down low. We don't want to want to wake Eric." Robin walked Adam through the television remote, and then jumped in the shower.

Robin stepped out of the bathroom to find Eric making a fresh pot of coffee. "Good morning," he said kissing her once on the cheek.

"Um…Good morning babe, she smiled as she blotted her hair with one of the towels.

"I'm going to take a quick shower, and then we can talk about where we want to go from here, okay?"

"Okay," said Robin. Eric kissed her again, and then walked into the bathroom, closing the door behind him. Surprisingly, the coffee's aroma reminded her of food. Not human food, but blood. Robin walked over and hopped on the bed next to Adam. "I'm hungry," he said.

"I know, babe. I know. We'll eat something soon." she told him. Just as she had explained to him the nature of death, she was going to have to explain to him the importance of feeding on humans to survive. Robin turned and faced Adam. While Eric was in the shower, now was probably a better time than any to explain their situation to him. "Adam, I need to talk to you about something." Adam turned away from the television and faced her.

"Remember I explained to you the reason why we couldn't go back to Auntie Raven's house for a while," Robin said to him.

"Yes."

"Well I'm afraid there's more bad news." Adam stared up at Robin with sad eyes. Everything that had happened in the last seventy-two hours with the exception of Robin's return had been bad. "Since we are unable to go back to Auntie Raven's, we won't be able to eat the way that we used to, at least not until we are settled, which means that we are going to have to feed in a different way." Adam's eyebrow twitched. There are different ways that we can feed. We can feed the way that we are used to feeding, or we can get it straight from the source. Do you understand so far?" she asked. He nodded. "Okay. Have you learned how milk comes from a cow?" she was reaching, but it was worth a try. Adam nodded and smiled, obviously having knowledge of the subject thrilled him. "Well it's kind of the same way with humans, she explained. We can get food from them only we are not allowed to take too much because it would hurt them. Understand?"

"Yes, I think so," he answered.

"Awesome. Everything's going to be alright, okay? I'm going to need you to hang in there a little longer, and I promise you that our stomachs will be full before the night is over."

After Eric had showered and dressed, he and Robin stepped outside on the balcony to discuss their next move. "Nice night out, isn't it?" Eric asked, looking out past the lights, buildings, and moving cars.

"It is," she agreed.

"I want you to know Robin that I am fully aware of our situation. Are you starving?" He asked.

"Yes, she answered, but so is Adam."

"None of this is your fault, he told her, but you're going to have to feed, you both are if you're going to survive." Robin turned and faced him.

"I was a little nervous about having this conversation with you," she told him. "I don't know why."

"I prefer that it be difficult for you than easy, he said. I would be concerned if it were an easy conversation for you to have with me." Robin leaned in and kissed Eric on the cheek.

"Thank you," she said. "Thank you for being so understanding."

"You're welcome."

"I had a talk with Adam while you were in the shower," Robin said. "He's gotten so smart in such a short time, and he's taking Gelsa's and Thandie's deaths better than I had anticipated."

"He is incredibly bright for his age," Eric agreed.

"He is that. Come here. I'm in serious need of a hug." He wrapped his arms around her, and she nestled her head against his chest. "I've never had to do this before," she said closing her eyes. "The thought of feeding on people, strange people, discuss me."

"It's only temporary," Eric told her. "Things will get back to normal once we're settled."

"I hope normal is not too far away." Robin and Eric talked for about a half hour. They agreed that she should keep to the shadows, and if possible, choose loners. She honestly didn't know where to begin.

"Let's be clear on one thing, Ambrosha." Raven's tone was as sharp as knives. "I'm not going to rest until your blond head is severed from your shoulders, and the whole of you is made nothing more than ash."

"Your words are touching to say the least, Raven, but they lack the effect that you're hoping for. You lord over the covenant. You control our wealth. If I am to do things my way, and that includes snuffing the life out of that cursed child, I will need your seat. I challenge you for that right Raven. I look forward to nights filled with the freedom to live as vampires, true vampires."

"You speak as if you have already won the fight," Raven said.

"I have unfinished business, I simply will not be denied."

"Challenge accepted Ambrosha but mark my words. Neither Robin, nor Adam will suffer their fate at your hands. You can be sure of that. It's time we finished this."

"The old cemetery, say midnight sounds like the perfect place and time. Would you agree?"

"A wise choice, sister," said Raven.

"Until then."

"Until then."

Robin glanced over at Adam. He sat surprisingly calm staring out of the window from the passenger seat. This was not the kind of life that she dreamed for him or Eric. The very thought of Adam becoming dependent upon blood from the veins at his young age disturbed her deeply. But they were left without any real choice. She had barely escaped with her life. She doubted that she would be so lucky a next time.

Robin drove the car over a set of railroad tracks, and then continued along a road which led her into what appeared to be, one of the less kept parts of the city that they were in. There were people actually lying on the sidewalks in rolls, covering themselves with news paper and in some cases cardboard boxes. *So sad,* she thought, because across the tracks in the direction that she had come, life looked the opposite. There was money on the other side, not so much here. The people on this side of the tracks were at the center of hard times, and she hated the idea of contributing to their current hardships.

Robin lowered her speed as she passed by a group of men who were huddled around a big drum with flame tongues dancing beneath the palms of their hands. There were four men in all. Two of them had cigarettes between their lips, and one of the others was turning up a bottle.

One of them should do, she thought. Robin drove up a little ways before turning the car around. She glanced over at Adam, took a deep breath, and then breathed out. "We're going to stop for a second," she told him. "Whatever happens from this point on, there's no need to be afraid, okay?" Adam nodded.

Robin pulled the car up next to the sidewalk where the four men were huddled up, and then stepped outside of the car. The four men regarded her with curiosity as she approached them. *This is unusual,* they thought. This woman was obviously on the wrong side of the track, and she must not have good sense, otherwise she wouldn't have climbed out of the car.

Adam stared out of his window at the four men. He was hungry, and would have normally fed long before now, but he understood that food was the reason that they were here.

"Excuse me," Robin said to the men. "I need to get back to the interstate. I'm terrible with directions, but if one of you would be kind enough to show me the way, I will make it worth your while." She held up two twenty dollar bills; money that she had pulled out of Eric's bank account from one of those quick mart ATM machines. It was the only card that they had decided to keep.

"I got it one of the men rushed forward. I'll make sure you get to where you need to go," he said holding out his hand. Robin placed two twenty dollar bills in the palm of the man's hand, and then made her way back to the car. "Catch you bum's later," the guy said, looking back at his acquaintances.

Robin lifted the driver's side seat, so that the man could slide into the backseat behind her. He smelled absolutely wretched she thought, but his odor was something that they would have to look past if they wanted to satisfy their empty stomachs. Once he was inside, and she was back behind the wheel, he asked her if she could please move her seat up some to which she complied. "You're gonna want to go back the way you came," he told her. Robin shifted the car into gear, and drove off. "Nice car," the man said. "It's not every day that I get to sit inside a nice car. Is that your boy there?"

"He's my son," Robin answered.

"Well what's his name? What's your name, son?" the man asked, sticking his head between the two seats.

"Please sit back," Robin asked the man. "His name is Adam." The man reluctantly did as she asked, but with some attitude.

"So where you from," the man asked. Robin glanced at him through the rear view mirror.

"Florida," she answered.

"Geez you're a long way from home." Robin was starting to get annoyed. She was ready to get this over with, so she pulled the car over and stopped.

"How would you like to make more money?" she asked.

"Me? Hell yeah. Lady, I can always use more money. What do I have to do?"

Here we go, she thought. "Have sex with me," she answered.

The man practically jumped out his seat. He looked as though cold water had been poured over his face. "Are you shittin me lady? Are you fucking with me?"

"No, I'm not," Robin answered.

"Okay then, where we gonna do this?" he asked.

"Well I was hoping that you knew a place where we could go," she answered.

"Lady, I know just the place, but you're gonna have to turn the car back around."

"No problem," Robin said. She did just that. She whipped the car around and headed back in the other direction. They drove **past** the spot where she had picked him up. His acquaintances were still there huddled by the fire.

"Go up three blocks and take a left," the man instructed her.

Robin made the left turn. "How much further?" she asked.

He didn't answer right away. "See that house on the right, the one in not too good a shape. Pull up in front of that one," he told her. They all looked the same as far as she was concerned. Robin pulled over and stopped in front of a house. The right side corner of the house had been set ablaze and then extinguished. "What about the kid?" the man asked.

"I'm not about to leave him in the car," she said. "He's coming with us."

"Whatever floats your boat, lady." Robin stepped out of the car, and then raised the seat so the man could slide out. She then walked around to the passenger side to open the door for Adam.

"Follow me," the man said, walking towards the steps. Robin followed the man, guiding Adam by the hand. The man forced open the front door and they followed him inside.

The house reeked of moisture, piss, and shit. He led them up a set of stairs that were by no means safe. When they reached the top, the man stood there like he did before with his hand held out. Robin paused before reaching into her pocket to pull out another forty dollars. She placed it in the palm of his hand just as she had done before. "Right this way," he led them down a hall.

They entered a room that wasn't at all empty. Two men were lying on the floor against the far wall. One of the men lay asleep, the other wide awake. "What you got there, Herb?" the man asked, shaking his friend awake.

"Wouldn't you like to know?" he answered. "Okay, okay, the lady paid me to have sex with her."

"Bullshit," the man on the right responded. Herb held up the money that she had given him.

"Who's bullshitin, muther fuckers," Herb shot back. The two men stood there with their mouths agape.

"Don't worry, I'm willing to share," Herb told the two men. Herb reached inside his front pants pocket and pulled out a pocket knife. *He's making things easy for me,* she thought. She didn't want to hurt them, but they were forcing the issue.

Robin released Adam's hand. She was on top of Herb before he realized what was going on. She disarmed him, and then shoved him hard against the wall to her left. That should slow him down while she took care of the other two. Robin turned on the other two men. *Give me a break,* she thought. They had each pulled out knives, and they were waving them around at her. One of the knives was double in length of the one that she had taken from Herb. "Bitch, you gonna pay for roughing up Herb," the one on the right said.

"Yeah, you gonna pay," the other man chimed in. It should have been no surprise to her to find everyone on this side of the track caring a weapon of some kind, so she was thankful to have knives pointed at her instead of guns.

The two men charged at her with reckless abandonment. The one closest to her raised his knife high, and then angled it down towards her chest. Robin grabbed hold of the man's wrist and then swung him into his buddy. They both stumbled to the ground. One of the men got to his feet faster than the other, and charged at Robin again. She side stepped him, striking him to the back of the head with her fist. His legs gave out under him, and he hit the floor with a thump. The other man was already on his feet. He wasn't on them long. Robin lifted her right leg up, and then kicked him square in the center of his chest. He shot backwards hitting the wall with enough force to shake the room. In fact, a small amount of dust particles had settled on top of his head after having slump to the floor so graciously.

With the two men down, she returned her attention back to Herb, who at present was on his knees attempting to shake away the cobwebs that were clinging to his brain. Robin glanced back at Adam, who was standing in the frame of the door. She hated the fact that he had to see her this way. When she was certain that the other two men were unconscious, she walked over and stood before Herb. He stared up at her with hazed eyes. Robin pushed him back to the floor. "Don't kill me," he begged.

"I'm not going to kill you," Robin told him. "You have something that me, and my son need. We will take it from you, and then be on our way." Robin knelt down beside the man and grabbed hold of his wrist. "Come Adam," she called. "You need to see this." Adam came around and stood next to Robin. "Pay attention," she told him. Robin placed her other hand on the man's forearm and then sank her teeth into one of the veins. The warm blood passed from her mouth to her throat, and she had to admit that it was intoxicating. She had only fed from one other human in her life, and that was Eric during their lovemaking, but she had always made certain that she was full from the packaged blood first. She was staring now, and that was the difference.

Robin fed insatiably, but she knew at some point that she would have to stop. She was hungrier than she had realized, so she would probably have to feed Adam from one of the other men. After a minute or so she released her grip on Herb. She dare not show the full extent of her satisfaction, from fear that it would carry over to Adam. "Come Adam," she motioned to him. Adam walked over and placed his hand in hers. Robin rose to her feet, and then led Adam over to the closest body. "It's safe, she told him. Just do as I did." Reluctantly, Adam grabbed hold of the man's wrist and began to feed. Robin was felt a sense of relief. The night had been a total success so far, but despair quickly followed triumph as she was reminded that she and Adam would have to live this every single night until they were finally settled.

Robin watched Adam closely while he fed. There were moments when she felt concern, because his body would twitch and shake in the most peculiar way. Still he fed on, and she allowed it thinking that his excitement was in part due to his hunger, and his first taste of blood from the veins. Adam released the man's wrist, and then fell over onto his side. "Adam!" she screamed, but he didn't respond. "Adam!" She called out his name again shaking him as she did so. She turned him onto his back. His eyes fluttered, never completely closing, never completely opening. Suddenly his body stiffened, and then she realized that they were reliving the nightmare that they had suffered short of a week ago. Adam screamed out just as he had the first time, and like the first time, she was helpless to do anything that would comfort him.

The attack went on for seemed to be about a dozen minutes or so. She had sat there the whole time with her knees pulled to her chest. When it was over, she couldn't believe her eyes. She was relieved, but she was also angry; angry because Adam's life was passing before her eyes. *When will it stop?* she thought. Adam lay on the floor next to her, barely conscious. She lifted him off the floor and carried him back the way they had come. He was exhausted. Another four, maybe five years, had again been added to his life.

CHAPTER EIGHTEEN

It was ten minutes to midnight according to her watch, and there was no sign of Ambrosha as of yet. Raven, Guiliana, Natalia, Savana, and Leona stood restlessly at the center of the cemetery. They had a shroud of moonlight and darkness over them. They were surrounded by decades of death beneath their feet, and there were trees filled with life around them.

Finally, she heard a vehicle approaching. Ambrosha was making good on her challenge it would seem. The SUV came to a halt just short of a grave stone. The lights went out, the engine went dead, and five vampires emerged from the cabin. Those that were still alive from Ambrosha's house were Victoria, Tesa, Vanessa, and Constance. The numbers were even, but the experience and skill level were off-set favoring Raven and those of her house. For the most part they were immortals. It was a half truth given all the facts, because although they were capable of living well beyond the years of a normal human being, they were still subject to death, however difficult dying might be. Ambrosha and the four other vampires approached with caution.

"Death all around us, death yet to come," Ambrosha said, glancing around. Raven grinned.

"You're hilarious Ambrosha, and fake. You try to hide behind your fear with words and sarcasm, but you're right about one thing. Our audience is indiscriminate; making reference to the dead, and this place forever welcoming." She was making reference to the cemetery.

"Enough pre-battle conversation, Raven. I will see you dead this night, and that goes for the rest of you." She pointed to the women at Raven's side.

"Are you planning to kill us with words?" Raven shot back. Angered, Ambrosha parted her staff to expose the blades therein. Vampires from both sides reacted on reflex. Raven commanded her women to spread out, just seconds before Ambrosha and her women charged in. Ambrosha must have instructed her women in whom they were to match up with Raven gathered; judging by the way they crossed over one another to get their opponent.

Ambrosha believed the matches to be even. What her women lacked in skill, they more than made up for in their ruthlessness.

Victoria squared off against Guiliana, Constance against Natalia, Vanessa against Leona, and Tesa against Savana, leaving the two titans, Raven and Ambrosha. It was as if the stars were in direct alignment for this very night.

The battle was fully engaged. Before a single vampire fell, there was sure to be plenty of cuts, slashes, and maybe an arm or two. This battle would stream well into the morning for some, for others?

Some warriors relied solely upon skill. Concentration and focus, was key to surviving a battle. Others relied on skill coupled with the art of distraction. Words used in the right context, could be as good a weapon as any sword. Ambrosha was one such person. She was cable of running her mouth while she fought. In other words, she could get under the skin if her opponent allowed it. Raven pushed the attack, but no matter what move she tried, she could find no weakness in Ambrosha's defense. This could go on for hours. She let up and allowed Ambrosha to go on the offense. Ambrosha pressed hard, but it came as no surprise to her how easily Raven fended off her attacks. They were probably the two vampires who could easily carry their disagreement well into the next night if the sun allowed for it.

A full hour and a half of fighting, and each death match pressed on. It was just a matter of time, but one, or more vampires would certainly to fall victim to impatience. It was the way of the warrior who was solely focused on the knock-out punch.

Savana and Tesa were already suffering from minor cuts and gashes. The less significant ones had begun to heal, but it was more difficult for the others because they were constantly flexing their bodies.

They were two of the youngest and less skillful of all the vampires, and perhaps the less patient.

Another hour gone by, met with the fall of the first vampire. Savana was the first to die. Her mistake was over reaching. She was looking for the knock-out punch while attempting to perform an un-mastered move. She had shifted from solid to mist form dodging near decapitation. Her momentum had carried her too far downward. Part of the move required her to relinquish control of her blades to gravity, so when she had shifted back into solid form, her blades weren't where they should have been, so instead of steel, she grasped at thin air. In a panic, she had sought the location of her blades, giving Tesa another opportunity at her head which she gladly took. Tesa could now aid one of the other sisters from her house, advantage goes to Ambrosha.

Leona and Vanessa were suffering from a few minor cuts and gashes as well. They were fighting like a couple of enraged lionesses. Tesa took a moment to observe the battles that were taking place around her. She dared not interfere with Raven and Ambrosha, because theirs was a private matter, nor was she comfortable aiding Victoria against Guiliana, but Vanessa might welcome her help. It was an opportunity to take out another one of Raven's fighters.

Tesa circled around the two combatants so that Vanessa would see her coming, and to surprise Leona from the vantage point. She chose an angle, and was about to execute it when she caught movement from the corner of her left eye. She barely had time to raise her blade to thwart off the attack. Tesa rolled to the ground, and then back to her feet blade out in front of her at the ready. "Natalia," Tesa barked through gritted teeth.

"You look surprised, and sneaky like a rat," Natalia said.

"Fuck you, Natalia. As a matter of fact I was just on my way over to remove Leona's head from her shoulders before you so rudely interrupted. Her head would have been the second tonight for me, the first being Savana's." Natalia laughed.

"You're mistaken, Tesa. Constance is standing on the other side wondering what the fuck happened. You can explain it all to her in a few seconds."

"Bitch," Tesa screamed, lunging at Natalia with blind fury in her eyes.

"That's it Tesa, give in to your rage," Natalia whispered. The two women fought each other as if there were a hatred centuries-old between them. They fought relentlessly for a steady fifteen minutes, each trying to overpower the other. A full half hour of intense fighting and they were both feeding the ground with blood from deeply opened wounds.

"You don't look so good," Natalia said.

"And you do?" was Tesa's response. The two women had inadvertently taken the battle some distance from where they had started. Guiliana and Victoria were just fifteen yards away. Tesa eased towards their direction while keeping a watchful eye on Natalia. For every step Tesa took, Natalia took one as well.

"Where do you think you're going?" Natalia asked.

"I'm not running away, if that's what you're wondering," Tesa answered. They had moved a total of ten yards before Natalia, Tesa, Victoria, and Guiliana were all in the same proximity of one another. The vampires stopped swinging swords long enough to analyze the situation. "Are you okay?" Guiliana asked Natalia.

"I'm fine," Natalia answered, "but I believe Tesa looks a lot more-worse for wear than I do. Let's finish this."

"Yeah, let's," Guiliana said, trading a glance with Natalia. They charged at their opponents. Guiliana had Victoria completely on the defensive, while Tesa held her own against Natalia. Natalia was amazed by Tesa's endurance. She was a solid two hundred years younger, but you could hardly tell. Her will to press on was incredibly strong. I was time I ended this, Natalia thought, purposely giving Tesa an opportunity to in flick the death dealing blow. Tesa took the bait. Her eyes beamed at the opportunity that Natalia had afforded her. She took it, swinging her blade towards Natalia's open midsection. Natalia phased to her mist form seconds before Tesa's blade touched flesh. Slicing nothing but air threw Tesa off balance leaving her open to injury or and perhaps death. Natalia phased back to solid form catching her blades before gravity could move them from her reach. She grabbed both blades swinging one of them up and towards Tesa's throat, but the blade merely nicked her chin. "Fuck!" Natalia grunted. Tesa simply refused to enter into the next world.

Tesa saw Natalia's next move a mile away, and yet her only chance to avoid it would be to do as Natalia had done and phase out. She did so with a single thought and Natalia's blades sailed right through her. She willed her molecular structure to take its solid form again, but realized a little too late her mistake. Natalia's first move had been a prelude to a second one. She felt the wooden end of Natalia's staff as it penetrated her chest. Tesa's eyes were threatening to pop right out of their sockets. She dropped to her knees gasping for air while Natalia stood over her.

"You fought well Tesa, far better than I would have expected from you. Give my regards to our fallen sisters." With that, Natalia took her head. Natalia glanced around to see Guiliana and Victoria fighting about twenty yards away. She dropped to her knees. She hadn't realized it, but she was in pretty bad shape herself. She forced herself to her feet and started towards the two combatants.

Natalia was less than ten yards away from the two combatants when she witnessed it. Guiliana had taken one of Victoria's blades clean through the chest. The wooden stake end of her staff followed leaving Guiliana helpless to whatever came next. Guiliana dropped to the ground on her side.

"Turn over," Victoria yelled. "I want to see your dying face." Guiliana rolled over onto her back. Victoria raised her blade, but she was robbed of any opportunity to finish the final stroke. Guiliana glared up at a stunned Victoria. She couldn't miss the blade that was protruding from Victoria's forehead. She got to her feet just as Victoria was falling to the ground. Guiliana looked up to see Natalia making her way towards her, and she appeared to be in pretty bad shape.

"Thanks, I owe you one," Guiliana told her. Natalia had done the only thing that she was capable of doing in her condition to aid Guiliana, which was to throw one of her blades from where she stood, and pray that she struck her target.

"Come on, I'm sure one of the others could use some help," Natalia said.

"There's not many of us left I'm afraid."

"Well let's salvage who we can," Natalia said.

They followed the sound that metal made when it was being put to the test. Less than twenty yards away from them, Raven and Ambrosha fought as if their battle had just begun. Neither seemed at all fatigued, still sooner or later, one would fall.

Guiliana and Natalia watched in amazement as the two titans fought with nearly flawless fighting skills. Both vampires suffered from minor cuts and slashes across the arms, but Ambrosha had taken injuries elsewhere. She had a deep gash across her midsection and another across her left thigh. The speed at which they fought was mindboggling, and almost impossible to the watchful eye. When the two combatants realized they had an audience. They stopped swinging their blades and backed away from one another. Only then did one realize that they breathing heavily.

"Where are the others?" Raven asked.

"Everyone else has fallen," Guiliana answered. "Ambrosha, you stand alone in this."

Ambrosha raised her blade in Guiliana's direction. "You think this is over, don't you? Well if you haven't noticed, I'm still standing, and I will be the only one standing in the end."

"Listen to me, Natalia," Raven said, "and do not question the order that I am about to give you. Get Guiliana back to the mansion and wait for me there."

"Are you serious?" Natalia asked.

"Do as I ask," Raven screamed. Natalia glanced over at Ambrosha, and then back at Raven.

"Okay, Raven. I trust that you know exactly what you're doing. Get home in one piece." The two vampires did as Raven commanded and headed back to the vehicles.

"I'll be coming for you both," Ambrosha yell behind them.

"You'll be dead soon, Ambrosha. You won't be able to tie your shoe from the grave, let alone make empty threats.

"You still haven't given me reason to be afraid," Ambrosha grinned. "The truth is you have under estimated me. Did you think defeating me would be so easy?"

"You're dead already, Ambrosha. You just don't know it yet."

Ambrosha charged at Raven. After hours of going toe to toe with her old friend, made new enemy, her confidence was exactly where she needed it to be. The two vampires continued their deathly brawl while another hour rolled past. Fatigue had only just begun to settle in for the both of them, presently seen in just about every one of their moves. But at last dawn was approaching, which raises the question. Were they too caught up in battle to notice? Both vampires had sustained deep cuts and lacerations; many of them over the past hour. The two women circled one another, their blades pointed towards the ground.

Ambrosha was fully aware of the approaching danger. "Face it, Raven, I have proven myself as your equal. How do you feel about that?"

"You will never be equal to me in anything, Ambrosha. Given enough time you would have surely died by my hand. Perhaps we should have started this earlier."

"Perhaps? Tonight's outcome is unfortunate. As much as I wanted to see you dead and gone, the sun is now the issue. I guess we'll have to pick up where we left off tomorrow." Ambrosha glanced around. There were tombs in every direction. She couldn't care less about Raven at this point. It was time for her to take shelter. "Stalemate," Ambrosha said as she began to back away.

"Where do you think you're going?" Raven asked.

Ambrosha raised her blades and pointed them towards Raven. "Look around you. Our options are limited where shelter is a concern. I'm going to find myself a nice tomb to hold up in; allow the injuries that you in flicked on me however minor to heal. You can do whatever the fuck you want. Just don't follow me."

Raven grinned.

"You're not going anywhere, Ambrosha. This is where it all ends."

Ambrosha studied Raven's face. "You conniving bitch!" Ambrosha screamed. "You're fucking insane if you think you can keep me out here with that ball of death threatening to come up over the horizon. Oh no. I will not be dying with you today, Raven." Ambrosha turned, and then took off running towards the nearest tomb. Raven ran after her. The hard truth was that they this was the only way to defeat Ambrosha short of being able to fight uninterrupted; take for instance the sun. It was all that she could do to protect Robin, Adam, and those who had survived.

Ambrosha was a mere ten steps away from the tomb that she chosen when she felt the sharp pain at her back. She stumbled, but managed to stay on her feet long enough to reach the tomb door. She stared down at her breast and noticed that two inches of blade was sticking out between them. "Fuck!" she groaned through gritted teeth, reaching around with her hand to try and pull it out. It was no use. It would have to stay in. All that mattered now was gaining entrance to the tomb. She pushed against the door, but was yanked backwards before she could even open it.

Ambrosha stumbled to her feet. "Get out of my way, Raven," she screamed.

"I can't do that."

Ambrosha glanced over her shoulder towards the horizon. "This is it? This is how chose to defeat me? Where is the honor in that?"

"This isn't about honor. It's about saving lives."

"Okay, you win," Ambrosha said. "I submit. Now allow me entrance to the tomb."

"I'm sorry but I can't," Raven said," and even if I wanted to. I'm afraid it's too late." Raven raised her hand up to shield her eyes as the sun began to bring forth a new day. The harbinger of heat was upon their skin now. What quickly followed was a blistering pain that would be unbearable in seconds, ultimately resulting in their deaths. "Raven please," Ambrosha begged. Raven dropped to her knees beside Ambrosha. Ambrosha screamed first, and then Raven, as the blood within their veins reached boiling hot temperatures. Within seconds their bodies were set aflame, and what followed was the natural reaction that a body experienced under the torture of flame; death.

EPILOGUE

Robin opened the door to the hotel room to find Eric at the sink near the bathroom washing his hands. He nearly jumped out of his skin when he turned around, and saw Robin carrying who obviously had to be Adam in her arms. She laid Adam across the bed. He was unconscious, but breathing normal.

"Oh my God," Eric said, rushing over to shut the door behind her.

"What happened to him?" Eric asked. Robin sat on the edge of the bed and broke down in tears.

"It happened again. It was right after he fed, she explained. Eric, I'm so afraid for him." Eric ran his hand through his hair. He didn't know what to say or do. He leaned across the bed to inspect Adam. "He seems to be doing okay. Has he been asleep the whole time?"

"Yes," Robin answered. Eric sat down on the bed next to her. "He's going to be okay, Robin. This has to stop at some point."

"I'm not so sure that it will, she said through tears. I'm not so sure that it will. Eric felt completely helpless. There was nothing that he could say, or do for that matter. That was his harsh reality, but there was another reality, the reality that the three of them shared together, and that was the unknown.

Other titles in this series by Cedric R. Curry

Bloodlines: The Reckoning

Following the destruction of his mother's covenant, and the death of his father. Adam is left with his mother Robin, and the two surviving vampires Leona and Savana. Adam has reached maturity now and in a very short period of time. Although he is competent in his nature as a vampire, that power which is true to his birthright has yet to surface until now. It didn't take the demon Entu long to discover the whereabouts of the male warlock child that with the aid of its true mother managed its escape. Now the demon has set his sights on Adam once again, and Adam will have to enlist the aid of a light elf from a completely different realm, that just so happens to have a vendetta against the eater of hearts of her own to best the demon. Lives will be lost in this battle but only one side will feel the tragedy the most.

BLOODLINES:
THE RECKONING

CHAPTER ONE

Anaheim California, This was not the kind of life that he had envisioned for himself, twenty years ago today. He blames Afghanistan for much of his misfortune, government psychologist and Veteran Affairs for the rest. The system wasn't worth a damn back then and he doubted that it was any different today. The truth of the matter was that when he had returned home from the War all those years ago, he had come back a few parked cars short of a full parking lot and unable to sustain employment for any length of time.

It had taken him less than a year to fuck up his marriage, and any hopes of a relationship with his two kids of which he hasn't seen in over fifteen years. Life is a bitch, and there wasn't a day that went by that she didn't have her dildo up his ass at some point to remind him.

Excuse me he said stepping over just one of a hundred or so people, who were no better off than he was. This was his community, and it was just one of many, that had been forced to find a stake in this vast and brutal world wherever money wasn't required. He shook his head as he made his way past the familiar shapes that had formed pallets on the cold cement along the south wall of the park.

Sleep was a welcomed companion for the homeless bum. She was just about the only thing that hugged back with a smile, regardless of whether or not you brushed your teeth or hadn't taken a shower in weeks. You had to be worthy of her company though. Some of her ways were like that of a woman. She required your full attention if you were expecting her to meet that one need in particular; which was a good night's sleep. You had to leave your everyday problems at the door before coming to bed. Well maybe not quite like a woman. A woman could literally talk your head off in the sack. Sleep offered rest and a promise to those who would succumb to her a transition from this realm into the next.

He picked up the pace a little. Thoughts of sleep and the next realm were stimulating. It had been an antagonizing day, so he was quite anxious to get there. For the most part you took up wherever you could lay your head, but not him. He had been sleeping in the same spot for two years now.

Of course there have been nights when he has had to confront a person or two for trying to take up residence in the location where he has slept, cried, and had his fair share of dreams and nightmares; an innocent mistake, and usually by someone who was fairly new to the community.

There was one thing in this world that he had little problem with. It was letting the next one know that like the wolf or the dog, he had chosen that spot; mark it with his own piss, and claimed it for his own. "Hey there Jim," the voice was but a whisper to the left of him.

He turned his head to see who had spoken, and at a closer glance he recognized the man beneath dirty skull cap. It was Thomas.

"I haven't seen you going on close to two months. Where you been?"

"Westside of town, Thomas answered. "Don't know what I was thinking. This is paradise considering if you know what I mean."

"Well it took you long enough to find your way back."

"I'm of the same mind Jim. Take my advice for what it's worth. It is far from greener on the other side of town."

"You don't have to concern yourself with me, Jim said. I've made peace with the fact that I will probably die here."

"Good for you Jim. I guess I should be thinking the same."

"Well...I'll see you tomorrow if there is one Thomas." The man grunted, and then went back to doing whatever it was he had been doing before their conversation erupted. "Not much further," he spoke to his tired bones." He was fifty one years old, but his body felt a decade or so older. "Hard goddamn life," he cursed.

When he had finally reached his self-proclaimed bed area, he was relieved to find that he wouldn't have to chase anyone off tonight. He was just too damn tired for that. He slid the straps of his back sack over his shoulders and then set it near the spot where he usually laid out his bed. He hated toting the thing around, but if he was intent on keeping the possessions that really mattered to him, he would do well to keep it in his sight at all times. It contained his bedding, an extra pair of pants, a flannel shirt, a pair of shoe strings, a bottle of water, a toothbrush that he hasn't used since he ran out of toothpaste over a month ago, small odds and ends, and an old worn out photo of his two children. Oh…and a half eaten sandwich.

He knelt down on one knee and loosened the draw strings on the back sack. Before he did anything else he needed to deal with his hunger. He removed the sandwich that Gail had slipped him earlier today, when he had made his usual round to the dinner that she and her husband owned. Gail was probably one of the kindest persons that he had met during his long miserable existence.

Gail began slipping him food a little over a year ago, after she had caught him rummaging through the dumpster at the back of her establishment. Since that day, there hasn't been a day that has gone by that he didn't have a promising meal. He could always count on a sandwich of some sort. Sometimes, though not as often as he would have liked, she would add a slice of apple or cherry pie. *Damn,* he thought, salivating at the mere thought of the desert that he hadn't had in weeks.

He gently pulled the Saran Wrap away from the roast beef sandwich. He had taken two bites from it earlier, but it had hardly been enough to pry his stomach away from his back. Still, something was better than nothing at all.

He finished the sandwich in what might have been record timing. He licked his fingers and thumbs thoroughly, and when he could extract no more flavor from them, he reached for his bottled water to wash the food down. Sleep should come quick tonight. He was tired and decently fed. "Now let's get you rolled out," he said removing the bedding from the back sack.

The area where he slept was one of the more secluded areas in the park. The large tree provided an ample amount of cover from the elements that could be especially unpleasant during the rainy season.

The down side was, if someone had in their mind to slit his throat while he slept, it might take days before anyone discovered his body, not that it mattered, he was after all alone in this world for the most part. He rolled his bed out at the base of the tree, and then settled into it like it was his mother's arms.

Jim rolled over on his back and opened his eyes. Something was off, and not like someone suddenly startled by the sound of a hooting owl off, but an eerie or uncanny off. He sat upright and squinted until the familiar objects around him came into focus. *Nothing looked out of the ordinary*, he thought glancing around. "Maybe it was that sandwich I ate," he tried to reason with himself.

He stretched out a yawn and was just about to settle back onto the pallet when the feeling returned. He jumped at the strange sound that was suddenly at his left in the small clearing ten to fifteen yards away from his tree. He scrambled to his knees; his instincts now in fight or flight.

The sound was completely alien to anything that he had ever heard before. What was troubling to him was the fact that there was nothing physically visual in view to support the sound that if he absolutely had to describe it, might resemble the sound of a pot of boiling water accompanied by short burst of gushing winds.

He rose to his feet and wrestled with the thought of taking a few steps forward to investigate. "Wait a minute," he asked himself. "Why am I even contemplating something that has stupid written all over it?"

Anyone who was in their right mind would have already taken off in the opposite direction. Whatever this is, it will probably be a lot healthier for him to hear about it in tomorrow's news and yet he stayed put, letting curiosity get the best of him. Curiosity was going to get his ass killed.

He took a few steps backwards thinking the calculation might mean the difference between life and death. *He was still being foolish,* he thought.

What happened next pushed the envelope on the subjects that he often found himself standing in the middle of the road on, those being God, and life on other planets to name a few.

Suddenly, an enormous flash of light burst forth. The light assaulted his retinas forcing him to seal his eyes and shield them with both his hands.

He steadied himself waiting for his eyes to regain focus. *I'm fucked,* he thought. Not only was he completely helpless, and temporarily void of vision; he was also scared shitless with no longer the option to run.

Jesus! he thought standing there fearing that when he finally did open his eyes, a hideous monster would be standing before him salivating at the mouth waiting to lap up his blood right after it ripped open his throat.

He opened his eyes slowly and glanced around. His vision was returning and faster than he had expected, because the emission from the light had been frightfully painful.

When he was finally able to make out the forms around him, there was only one that stood out as unfamiliar. Fifteen feet away from him hovering at least a foot above ground was a sphere. It was at least ten feet in diameter, and looked to be made of a silvery liquid substance of some sort. His entire being was screaming run for your life, instead, he just stood there, gazing at something that he could not make sense of.

He leaned his head to one side, a jester that dogs made when they were either curious or confused. He eased forward a bit, but then stopped himself to look around on the ground for a weapon of some sort.

The closest thing that he could find was a dead branch, which was about two feet in length, and maybe two inch in diameter. He walked towards the sphere slowly, stopping eight to ten feet short of it. "What in the hell?" he said beneath his breath. He rubbed his chin while he studied the freakish object.

The urge to circle the damn thing tugged at him something fierce. He held the tree branch out towards it and moved in closer thinking, *I'll just give it a gentle poke,* but before he could play out his intentions the strange object dropped suddenly to the ground and burst like a water balloon. He jumped back to insure that none of the liquid substance would get on his shoes and pants.

The fluid washed over the ground leaving in its wake what appeared to be a person, though he couldn't make out whether it was male or female. Jim stood in place mesmerized.

The figure on the ground laid motionless in the fetal position facing away from him. It was fully clothed and drenched in the liquid stuff that at present was slowly seeping into the ground. He took a couple steps forward.

The closer he got, the more it began to look like a female. It was a female he decided. He kept the tree branch out front of him. "Hey! Are you alright? He asked. Do you need help?" A few seconds went by. "Holy shit!" he yelled, when she or rather it turned to face him. Too afraid to take his eyes off her he began walking backwards slowly.

Syi rolled onto her knees and stood up slowly. She surveyed the area around her. *Beautiful,* she thought.

Jim stopped backing up once he decided that he had put enough distance between them. He figured that he could get to safety before she could get to him if it came to that.

What he could make out from his position was that she was strange looking and small in frame. She had black coffee colored skin, but her hair was as white as snow and long, stopping just short of her butt.

He jumped a little when she knelt down towards the ground to pick up something that he was unable to see from his position. She straightened up bringing the object into plain view. Hell he knew exactly what it was; a fucking sword. "Ok, I'm done," he uttered.

He turned around and ran in the direction where he knew there would be lots of people. It frightened him to have to turn his back on her, but he couldn't run as fast as he hoped to run and keep his eyes on her at the same time. While he ran, he sounded the alarm yelling Alien in his wake.

Syi placed the thin sword in the sheath at her back and began walking in the opposite direction that the human had run off. She had never wondered beyond her realm until now, but she had listened intently to stories told to her by her father, describing more than a dozen or so of the different realms that he himself has visited, all in some way different than her own.

Though she has never seen one with her own eyes before tonight, she possessed an extensive amount of knowledge on most of them. So far, this place called earth resembled much of what had been described in her father's stories, but her time here was still young.

Syi wondered deeper into the brush. If she was going to pass for a human, she would have to involve magic, and magic was something of a private matter. The human that she had encountered, would no doubt be back with others. Putting some distance between the area where she had arrived, and a mob of humans is what she sought now.

Syi pushed deeper into the wooded area. She paused for a second to examine a leaf that caught her eye. It was unidentifiable to anything in her home realm. Not surprising, she thought. There will be a great many things that she would come across in this realm; things that she will experience for the first time.

She looked up towards the ball of light that stared back at her far above the leaves and branches, and stood in awe by another noticeable difference between this realm and her own. Her father hadn't exaggerated at all when he had told her about the two great lights that governed this realm.

The expanse where her home lies is governed by a total of seven, and each of them considerably smaller in size than the two lights of this realm combined. Another distinction between earth and her world is how it rotates on an axis.

The seven suns that governed her planet were position in such a way that the surface never experiences darkness, but there is an inner-world within her planet, home to another race of elves, a dark and sinister race. It is how we come by our names, light and dark elves.

She has only seen one dark elf in her time, and that was on an occasion during a meet between the two kings, her father Nauwgie the light elf king of the over-world, and the inner-worlds dark elf king Peinthal.

Our races have always been at peace with one another. The inability of the dark elves to live in the presence of light, even the light as dim as this world's moon, has been the stanchion between any potential meddling, or serious disagreements between the two realms. Every meeting that has ever taken place between the two realms has been conducted deep within the caverns of inner-world because of the dark elves light sensitive eyes.

Syi stepped into a small clearing that was no more than ten feet in diameter. The area provided an excessive amount of cover that was both necessary and perfect for her intentions. *This will do just fine,* she thought kneeling on one knee.

She reached around her waist and removed a small pouch from her belt. The pouch was made from a material frequently used by her people to protect against the surface elements of her world. The outer surface of the pouch still bore evidence of the liquid substance from the portal bubble, so she gently wiped it away with the back of her hand.

Her knowledge of this realms planet, included knowledge of its earthquakes, storms, winter and summer seasons. These types of events were absent on her home world. However, her world did possess its own way of distributing water and moisture for the planets survival since it is a necessary substance for the survival of any life form.

On exactly the same hour during the early parts of the morning, heavy dew covered entire surface of her planet. If not for this event, life on over-world and inner-world could not survive.

The dew provided moisture and enriched vitamins, and minerals that were essential to the planet's needs. What can be said of any world is that their children share in there likeness. If this planet's makeup is 70 percent water, then so are her children. There are no oceans, lakes, or rivers on her home world. Bulga, the name of her planet, provides all that her children need in the vegetation including water.

Syi opened the pouch and removed a tiny round metal object. There were a number of these items within, but each one of them contained a different marking inscribed on the lid signifying a different purpose. These markings identified the spells there-in.

The canister that she removed from the pouch would prove vital to her if she planned to move about freely among the people of this world. She reached inside the pouch again and removed a ring containing several measuring spoons. After identifying the one that she would need, she carefully unscrewed the top on the canister. She had to be extremely carefully as she dared not waste any of the contents.

This particular spell would last give or take seventy two hours. She probably had just enough to last a little over a week. Hopefully that was more than enough to complete her task.

She stuck the measuring spoon inside the canister and scooped out an ample amount of the finely grained power. Using the edge of the lid she leveled the spoon returning the excess to canister. She tilted her head back, opened her mouth, and then sprinkled the substance beneath her tongue. She was by no means a witch, nor was she a sorcerer. Her people were alchemist, some greater than others. It was expected, it was not a choice that she practice and learn the craft of alchemy at an early age. She was a student to perhaps the most powerful alchemist in over-world. By all means she was a master at the craft.

The ingredients of the spell that was slowly working its way into her system, was designed to give her the appearance of a human. Syi screwed the lid on tight and placed the small metal container back inside the pouch. She was already beginning to feel the spells effects.

She settled on to both knees and closed her eyes while she waited. She had performed this type of spell a dozen times over before finally owning the pain that was accompanied by it.

Her skin began to tingle. It was a sign that the spell was in its adolescents. A moment later, the tingling was followed by the stretching and contorting of bone and flesh.

Syi dug the fingers on both hands deep into the soft padded grass and dirt to steady her body, while the transformation completed its final stage. One of the ingredients in the spell was taken from a rare worm tree found on her world.

According to her teacher, it acted as a numbing agent on the neurotransmitters of the brain to stifle the pain while the process was taking place.

She stopped believing that somewhere around her third transformation, reasoning that the ingredient was nothing more than the added production of a placebo effect.

When the spell was finally complete, Syi traced her new features with the tips of her fingers to verify what she already knew to be a success. There was really no need to glance back at her reflection, because her appearance was always the same with each transformation, and the same with her hair. It always remained as white as the Dregen; the large hairy creature that made its home on the cliffs of her world.

Syi reached inside the small pouch and pulled out an octagon shaped object. She prided it open and stared back at herself through a mirror. Better safe than sorry, she thought.

Under the cover of darkness surrounded by brush, Syi studied her surrounds once more. She had extraordinary vision. For instance, she could just make out what she understood to be a beetle on this planet.

Over to her right, a cricket rubbed its legs together continuously, and although the sound that it made traveled across the night, the tiny creature was unhidden from her sight. So far everything was going according to how she had planned, but even the most well thought out plans had a way of coming unraveled at the seams at some point or juncture along the way.

She settled onto the ground legs crossed, and then removed the sword from its sheath. She would rest here for a while. It was as good a place as any, for an alien life form having just arrived to a place where tales were all that she knew. Tomorrow she would begin seeking out one of the most valuable instruments that she would need in her quest. Once that piece was obtained, she would have what she needed to orchestrate an end game. Syi stretched out on her back and stared up into a vast sky. Beautiful she thought, and then she closed her eyes.

High on the corners edge of a long forgotten industrial building stood a figure, whose attention at the moment remained transfixed like the sight on the barrel of a rifle. These were dangerous times, but the scum, the degenerates, the child molesters, and the abusers of family, were the factions relating to his survival. Down below, gathered this side of a parked car, stood four men and a small child, a little girl. Even from this distance, which was over three stories up, he could clearly make out the handle of the 9mm handgun that protruded from the fat man's trousers. His vision was unique, rivaling that of ordinary men.

What he was witnessing here was a travesty of actions being played out by men who were without conscious. They are nothing more than debased organisms, whose paths have chosen them to become that which they prey upon, prey themselves. How did he know this? The answer lied within justice and balance. In order for him to survive, he had to feed. Blood banks were no longer an option these days due to the strict mandate that had put in place six months ago.

The authorization called for stricter guidelines in monitoring and distribution, and if that weren't enough, government officials had the feds looking over their shoulders twenty four seven. So what were a vampire's choices? First of all there weren't many. However, he would go on to make a choice based on the principles of morality.

He never fed on the innocent, helpless or weak. Not when the world provided him with a food source that would never leave him riddled with guilt. As long as there was scum there would be food. The issue here was not about some fat man carrying a handgun, or the currency that was inside the tall slim man's briefcase. The issue here was the child. She was the victim, a commodity for the sex slave trade market; one of the wealthiest illegal enterprises of this dark and unremorseful age. Unfortunately, he was but a single vampire. Perhaps if more existed, more innocents would be saved.

The fat man placed a hand on the little girl's back and nudged her forward. The tall slim man took hold of the child's wrist and then handed the briefcase over to the fat man. You would have thought that such a transaction would have been made in a less public place and not in the open, like in the belly of the alley at the side of the building. Adam traced the length of the alley to where it stopped at a dead end. "Criminals would rather operate in plain sight than trust each other in private," he muttered.

The tall slim man opened the rear passenger side door to the car that they were standing next to, and bid the little girl to step inside. She did so willingly, for there was nothing else that she could do. She was all alone, and the worst part might have been, that the one person she may have once trusted with her life was the very same person offering her up to a situation that was worse than hell.

Adam stepped away from the corner's edge and hurried headlong towards the roof's exit. From the upper platform overlooking the empty plant, he leaped over a guard rail that was some three stories high and then allowed gravity to do the rest.

The distance was hardly his limit, having leaped from higher distances before. He landed gracefully, and then raced towards the exit that was located at the southeast end of the plant. The exit led to the alley where he had parked his bike after becoming suspicious of the two characters posing with the little girl.

He pushed the door open, and then stepped out into the night. The black and silver Hayabusa was parked near a pile of debris practically hidden in the darkness from anyone passing by on the streets.

Adam mounted the bike making haste. The car which held the little girl was probably pulling off by now. He started the bike, and then rev-up the engine. The rear tire jumped twice before grabbing hold of the pavement.

He pointed the bike towards the alley's exit where it rocketed forward. When he turned onto the street the car was some thirty yards away. He had no idea the distance the vehicle had to travel before it would reached its destination, nor was it a concern. He need only wait for the right moment, the right time, which was bound to present itself at some point with hope very soon.

The slim man took a right turn at the intersection and drove the car three blocks before guiding it onto a less traveled route. Adam grinned once he realized that he wouldn't have to wait too long.

He tailed the vehicle three car lengths. This was a stretch of highway that catered to a minimum number of vehicles. He couldn't have asked for a more opportune development in light of the situation.

He followed the vehicle a little over a quarter mile, and not once did a vehicle pass him on the opposite side of the two lane road. Adam glanced in the rearview mirror and saw that there were no vehicles tailing behind, and then increased his speed closing the gap to within two cars lengths. He reached into the black leather saddle bag that was attached to the right side of the bike and came away with a single handed crossbow. Holding the bow out in front of him, he carefully took aim. Hitting his target from this distance was going to be extremely difficult, even for someone endowed with his abilities.

Adam released the air from his lungs, and then squeezed gently on the bow's trigger. The arrow shot forward from its housing, and planted itself into the rear right passenger side tire of the vehicle. The rear end slumped slightly as the air rushed from the torn rubber. The car swerved a bit before finally slowing down and coming to a complete stop along the shoulder of the road.

Adam shoved the bow back inside the saddle bag seconds before passing the impaired vehicle. A quick glance inside the interior of the vehicle revealed the tall slim man behind the wheel, and a safe but alert little girl sitting in the back seat.

Adam drove the bike up the road a bit and then reduced his speed. He turned the bike around, and then headed back towards the parked car. It would go over well if it looked like he was just out to help a man and a little girl having a stroke of bad luck.

He pulled the bike up next to the car just as the tall slim man was stepping out. Adam was without a helmet, so the man could identify who was coming to his assistance right off.

"Problem," Adam asked.

"A flat tire," the man answered sizing Adam up.

"I'm pretty good with my hands, said Adam. Let me take a look." The man hesitated a second.

"Sure, I could use a hand." Adam nodded, and then pulled the bike around to the rear of the vehicle. He killed the bike's engine, and then hoped off.

"I'll just remove the spare from the trunk," the man said as he was making his way towards the back of the vehicle. The slim man stuck a key inside the lock of the trunk, and then turned it gently to the right. When he felt the lock release he lifted the trunk.

Adam glanced over his shoulder to see if there were any approaching cars at his back. When he saw that there was nothing in the distance, neither in front, nor at the back of the stranded vehicle, he didn't hesitate. He pounced on the tall slim man like a leopard would on a poor defenseless rabbit. Adam grabbed the man by the throat and lifted him clear off the ground.

The look across the man's face was obviously one of surprise. "Tell me, Adam asked. Who is the little girl to you?" A burst of spittle accompanied by a lie erupted from the man's mouth.

"She's…my niece, he answered with difficultly, a result of the pressure that Adam had on his throat.

"I think not," Adam said.

Adam bared his fangs in the face of the tall slim man before sinking them deep into the left artery of the man's throat. The tall slim man dug his fingers futilely into the sleeves of Adam's thin leather jacket.

As the blood rushed down Adam's throat, his eyes turned to a deeper color violet than what was normal for them. It had everything to do with the blood. Adam drank until his thirst was quenched, and the hunger was no more.

The tall slim man still had life left in him; an observation that bore no merit on his sealed fate. Before the man's feet could touch the ground Adam snapped his neck. It was a death far too merciful for his kind Adam felt.

Adam tossed the dead husk inside the trunk of the car, and then closed it shut. Curiosity had obviously gotten the best of the little girl, because she was completely turned around in her seat and staring out of the back window with her eyes transfixed on Adam.

Adam lifted his right hand and ran the back of it across his lips. What he didn't need was for her to see something closely resembling an animal. He did however need her to trust him. He walked around to the right passenger side rear door and pulled at the handle. "Locked?" He should have known as much.

He contemplated walking around to the driver's side door thinking the slim man may have left it unlock, but quickly dismissed the thought. He was done wasting time. Instead he gave the door a solid tug, nothing too dramatic, like say ripping it from its hinges.

The metal resisted his will at first. It was only after he challenged it further did it finally give way. He may as well have left the blood on his mouth and lips. Surely the little girl was intelligent enough to know what a normal man was capable of, and by forcing the door open he had caused the metal to scream as if being tortured. Surely the sound had been enough to cause her fear. After all, she was without mother, father, and home.

Adam stood in the archway of the vehicle's door staring into the eyes of an expressionless child. "Don't be afraid, he said. I made the bad man to go away." Motionless, she never took her eyes off him. In fact, the child's dark brown eyes resisted what was the natural tendency to blink.

The child began moving backwards until finally she was pressed against the rear driver's side door. "Come, I won't harm you, nor will I allow anyone else to. I'm going to take you to a safe place. I promise," he said with a soft tone to his voice, but she continued to shy away. "I promise," he said a second time. The little girl took her eyes off him just long enough to glance out the rear window of the car. When she turned her head to face him again he met her with a smile.

It must have been the smile. The girl placed her hands on the seat and slowly, she began to crawl towards him. Adam held out his arms and she grabbed hold of them once she realized that they were her life lines. Adam pulled her out of the back seat that was symbolic of a mobile prison cell. "Let's get you to safety," he said. If he had to guess, he would probably say that the child was somewhere between eight and nine years of age.

As he walked towards his bike guiding the little girl by the hand, he suddenly realized that he was faced with yet another challenge; two wheel transportation. The child was extremely small in stature. It was probably safe to say that she had never ridden on the back of a motorcycle before. "Have you ever been on one of these before?" he asked. She looked up at him and shook her head indicating that she hadn't.

Adam lifted his right leg and through it across seat. He then motioned for her to come. She hesitated. "Its ok he assured her. Remember I promised not to let anything happen to you."

Adam held out his arms, and again she indicated her trust in him as she reached out and grabbed his hand.

Adam lifted the little girl from the ground and swung her onto the back of the bike. He leaned over, reached into the leather saddle bag, and came away with another pair of dark sunglasses. "Here, he said reaching back to hand her the shades. These will keep the bugs out of your eyes." She took the shades from his hand, and then placed them over her eyes. "Wrap your arms around my waist and hang on understand?" I don't want you to fall off accidently. She rested her head against Adam's back and then wrapped her arms around his waist. Adam started up the bike and then rev the engine. "Hang on," he told her.

Adam kept the bike at 45 mph for the first 100 yards. When he was confident that the girl could hold on, he bumped the speed up to 65. He was about 2 miles away from the car that he and the girl abandoned when he saw the first vehicle on the road since he had first stopped.

He drove past the vehicle without so much as a thought for what its occupants would find should they decide to pull over and give the vehicle a closer inspection. He felt the girls grip tighten around his waist. It felt good to know that he had a part in her safety, and that her future though uncertain, was now much better off because he had intervened.

He would have to stop along the way. His home wasn't equipped to meet the nutritional needs for a normal human being. Strange he thought. Assuming that he had gotten it right and the girl was somewhere around eight years of age; that would make her older than him by an estimated seven years since he was only a year into his total existence. He looked every bit a 25 year old man, though he was probably closer to 20.

The enigma surrounding his growth was something of a mystery. He and his mother's best guess was that he had sprouted towards adulthood in 5 year increments. He had reached an estimated 20 years of age in a span of weeks. He stopped worrying about the aging months ago believing that the vampire properties in his blood would guarantee him much like his mother, immortal life.

Adam turned the bike into one of those quick-mart gas stations. Hopefully it would serve purpose for the idea quick-fix items that the little girl could eat without having to cook over a stovetop. He steered the bike up to the front of the mart in between a new model car, and an old rusted out pickup truck. He turned the bike off, and then reached around his back to help the girl off. "You hungry?" he asked. She shook her head indicating a positive yes. "Well that's why we're here, he said swinging his leg over the seat. We're going see about getting you something to eat."

Adam walked up to the Marts entrance with the little girl practically hugging the side of his right leg. Of course there were the basic questions that he wanted to ask the girl, like where are your parents, and if she could answer that, then the next obvious question would be, how long have you been separated from them. He would wait to ask his questions later when she felt more comfortable, but first thing first. He needed to get her fed and into a nice warm bed. She didn't know it yet, but her time with him was brief; two to three nights at the most. There were places for children like her. Places equipped to help.

Once inside he bid her to take her time and grab whatever she wanted, but because she was unable to fully grasp her situation, twice he had to insist that she make another pass through the Mart. He needed to make sure that she had more than enough to get her through a two to three night's stay. It was during the little girls' fifth trip of gathering snacks and treats that he had a revelation. How did he expect to transport the girl and the groceries on his bike?

Adam scanned the Mart for a suitable solution. Near the door where he had entered the Mart was a section filled with memorabilia of the States College. The top shelf was lined with coffee cups and shot glasses plastered with the schools emblem, colors, and mascot. Folded neatly on the second shelf were T-shirts and sweat-shirts, likewise they we're designed to represent the school in the same fashion.

What interested him more was the school backpacks hanging along hooks on the side of the wooden shelf. As he was reaching to grab one, the little girl returned to his side with two small bags of treats. The label on one of them read Jelly Beans, the label on the other Gummy Worms.

Without thinking he removed his shades and said. "Don't you think you should grab a couple of those frozen meat meals? I'm sure they provide more substance than those sweets."

"You said that I could get what I wanted." She must have read his mind. Adam fixed his lips into a tight grin and said,

"I did say that, didn't I?" He removed the backpack from the hook, and then instructed her to take the treats up to the counter where the rest of her things sat in a small mountain of a pile while he followed.

The senior age Hispanic woman standing behind the counter smiled at him. "You have very unusual color eyes," she said with a smile. Adam smiled back at the woman and quickly donned his shades.

The woman shifted her focus from Adam to the little girl. "Well aren't you adorable the lady said staring down at the child. Will that be all?" The child looked up at the woman and shook her head with a positive yes. "The total is $37.28," the lady said to Adam.

Adam reached into his back pocket and came away with his wallet. He generally kept around two hundred dollars or so inside the leather bill folder, as money was still a necessary commodity even for him.

This would be a first for him, purchasing items he had no use for. Adam handed the lady a hundred dollar bill. She held it up to the light for a second or two before placing it inside the drawer of the register and counting out his change.

He waved off the bag that the lady was preparing to place his purchases in, and unzipped the backpack. He was halfway through shoving the purchased items inside the backpack when the little girl reached over the counter and snatched up a bag of treats. Adam glanced down at her. He wasn't about to object, because he was no stranger to hunger. "Children," Adam said to the lady behind the counter.

"Don't apologize was the ladies response, we do love our sweets, and besides, she's adorable. How can you possible say no to a face like that?"

"Thank you," Adam said zipping up the backpack and motioning the little girl to head for the exit.

Once they were outside though Adam held his hand out for the bag of treats that she had already opened. "Take a few more out of the bag, he said to her. You can't hold on to me and eat those at the same time." She gave him a disapproving look, and then reached inside the bag to grab a handful of the gummies before handing the bag to Adam. He placed the bag of treats inside the backpack with the other items and walked over to his bike.

He looked around and noticed that there were only three cars in the stores little parking lot. Two of them were at the pumps. The third was pulling up to a parking space one space over to the left of him. "Come on, he beckoned to the little girl. We only have a couple hours left before the sun comes up."

"What happens then?" the little girl asked scurrying over to the bike.

"Let's just say I get an allergic reaction when it touches my skin."

"How come?" she asked him. Adam avoided the question, and asked one of his own.

"What's your name anyway?" The girl stared up at him, and then said.

"Nyianna. Nyianna Le Washington."

"Pretty cool name, he told her. Now hop on."

Nyianna shoved the rest of the gummies into her mouth and climbed onto the bike with Adam's help.